THE DICTOGRAPH CASE

Their families paid the price.
Now it's time someone paid attention.

Diane Wahn Shotton

To the citizens of my hometown
who were forced to reject their German heritage—
so they could belong.

Patriotism is the last refuge of the scoundrel.
—Samuel Johnson - 1775

Chapter One

Michael Schumann studies his assignment slips for a bridge tournament and a Lindy Hop contest, wondering if he's forever relegated to page four of the Ellington Journal, when his editor's voice cuts through the hum of the newsroom.

"Schumann! Get in here."

Michael stands and stubs out his cigarette, his chair squealing in protest as it rolls away.

"Sit," Baxter orders.

Michael flops into the chair, stretches his long legs, and flips open his notebook. "What am I chasing now, Chief? An old lady who swears her husband's spirit took over her dog?" He's sick and tired of getting stuck with assignments that produce print barely worth lining a birdcage.

"Shut it," Baxter mutters, eyes fixed on the storyboard propped against the wall. "Old man got beat up last night. Eleventh Street underpass."

Michael sits upright. He hasn't had a story like this in months. "Robbery?"

"Nah. Left a few bucks and a nice watch."

With other guys on staff, he wonders why now. Why him?

Baxter answers his unasked question. "Pritchett's out and the guy's German. You know some, right?"

With the Depression in its eighth year, the *Journal's* staff is thin. Michael's survived by agreeing to cover local events in exchange for staying employed.

"I can get by." The last time he heard German was two years ago at his grandfather's funeral.

"Guy's name is Wilhelm Haber. Took him to St. Boniface, unconscious. Kellerman took the report."

Abe Kellerman. *Journal* reporters trade whiskey for tips. Good cop. Lousy breath.

Baxter speaks out of the side of his mouth, cigar clenched between his teeth. "Witness said the attackers muttered warnings we haven't heard since the Great War."

Michael raises an eyebrow. "Warnings?"

"Schumann, I got no details. That's your job. Now get over to the hospital and dig."

Michael pauses at his desk to slip a pack of Lucky Strikes into his shirt pocket. He grabs his hat, shrugs on his threadbare coat, and heads for the door, pounding down the stairs into the bright bustle of Ellington's streets—a stark contrast to the hazy newsroom. He doesn't know if this is a real story or just another column filler.

But "speaks German" and "warnings" in the same breath needle at a distant memory, like a splinter working its way to the surface. Maybe it's nothing. By the time he's a block closer to the hospital, he doesn't mind the bridge tournaments so much. Real muckraking takes time, and this might be a start.

* * *

Taking a streetcar would have him at the hospital in a few minutes, but a bakery truck with a flat tire blocks everything going his way. He doesn't need to hurry, but a sense of urgency propels him along the six blocks on a humid morning under full sun.

Darting up the stairs, he enters the cool lobby, where an attendant directs him to the third floor. A nurse is seated behind the counter, engrossed in paperwork.

Without looking up, she asks, "How can I help you?"

"I'd like to see Wilhelm Haber."

She sighs, flipping a page on her clipboard. "Are you family?"

"No, I'm a reporter with the *Journal*." Shit! He probably shouldn't have told her that.

Her gaze snaps up, expression firm. "Then I can't tell you anything."

"I just need to know if he's all right." He lowers his voice, careful to sound concerned rather than nosy.

"All I can tell you is that he is here." The response is clipped, automatic—she's said it a hundred times before.

Michael leans in, making eye contact. "Do you know why he's here?"

She shakes her head.

"Assaulted by three men last night. So was his son. What room is he in?"

"Three men?" Her voice drops. "Against an old man?"

Checking her clipboard again, she says, "Wilhelm Haber is listed as a patient."

"Maybe I can take a look. See if any family are with him."

She hesitates, tapping the clipboard with her pencil. She doesn't say yes, but she also doesn't say no.

"If I could just speak with someone in the family," he says.

She tilts her head down the hallway. "Room 307."

He slides his business card across the counter. "Can you let me know when he wakes up?"

She studies the card—Michael Schumann, *Ellington Journal*. After a beat, she opens a drawer and tucks it away. "Just in case."

Michael tips his hat and pivots toward Room 307.

* * *

A quiet busyness pervades the halls, marked by hushed conversations, staff bustling from room to room, equipment carts rolling past. A sudden cry punctuates the stillness, a stark reminder of the human frailty this place attends to.

Two voices drift from 307—one male, one female. Michael sticks his head past the doorjamb and stops short. The scene inside gives him pause—it would be rude and insensitive to intrude. He lingers, choosing to eavesdrop before making his presence known.

A woman with tired eyes and a lined face sits by the bed, her hand covering that of a motionless man whose head is wrapped in white bandages, tufts of silver hair protruding in uneven wisps.

A man sits on the opposite side of the bed, his back to Michael. Low sobs wrack his narrow shoulders, his cries muffled by hands covering his face.

Michael waits until a shuddering sigh signals the man may have regained control. Clearing his throat, he taps his knuckles on the doorframe.

The woman's head snaps up with sudden alertness, her eyes wide before narrowing in suspicion. The man turns toward the door, unabashedly wiping his tear-streaked face.

"Verzeihen Sie," Michael says, trying on a simple German phrase. "I'm sorry to disturb you. How is Mr. Haber?"

The woman drops her husband's hand and moves between Michael and the man in the bed. "Wer sind Sie?"

"I'm Michael Schumann. Are you Mrs. Haber?"

A slight nod confirms her identity and that she understands English.

The woman is tall, shoulders pulled back, chin lifted—a defensive posture. But Michael catches the slight furrow of her brow, fleeting glances toward her husband—revealing her uncertainty beneath her stern facade.

Michael will need to win her over to gain her trust. He hands her his business card. "I'm with the *Ellington Journal* and I understand your husband was attacked last night."

Mrs. Haber stiffens.

The young man, still teary-eyed, offers his hand. "I'm Fredrick Haber. What business is my father's attack to the newspaper?"

Michael starts to answer, but Mrs. Haber's authority asserts itself, cuts him off.

A firm wave of her hands shoos him away. "Leave," she demands, her heavy accent sharp with anger. "We have nothing to say."

He's had rejections before, but her dismissal is swift, a shield against intrusion, her husband's first line of defense.

"A report in the paper can help identify who did this to him." He motions toward the bed and Mrs. Haber follows his glance.

"The police will help," Mrs. Haber says, her voice taut. "We don't want snoops."

"Fredrick, I'd like to help." Michael shifts his attention to the son.

Fredrick looks to his mother for approval. But her pinched mouth and sharp gaze flick from her son to Michael then back again.

"Five minutes. Three questions." Michael offers a compromise.

Fredrick hesitates, his jaw tightening, then nods. "Three questions. Then you go."

"Fair enough," Michael says. "Do you know why someone would harm your father?"

Fredrick answers instantly. "No." He glances at his mother. "Mama?"

Michael waits for Mrs. Haber's response, deferring to her. She shrugs, lips tight, a forlorn sigh punctuating her lack of a reason.

"What happened?" Michael asks, his pencil hovering over his notebook.

Fredrick hesitates, casting another wary glance at his mother before taking a breath. "Papa and I were walking home from the store after buying cigarettes."

"What time was this?" Michael presses. The question slips out before he can stop it.

"Around eight, I think. The sky was pink."

"We live on Tenth and when a freight train blocked our way home, we took the underpass. Halfway through, when we heard footsteps approaching from the other end of the tunnel, so we moved to the side to let them pass."

Fredrick rakes a hand through his hair, expression tightening. "It happened so fast. Three men. One grabbed Papa by the throat. Another punched me in the stomach, shoved me down, and pinned me with his knee. I couldn't move."

A scrape on Fredrick Haber's cheek runs from the corner of his eye to his jaw, raw and swelling.

"Called us dirty Huns."

Michael freezes. Those words stir up an old fear he thought he'd outgrown.

"I couldn't see what they did to Papa," Fredrick says. "He screamed, asking what he'd done. The third man stood over me—brown leather shoes aimed at my face. He lit a cigarette, dropped the match—I smelled the sulfur. I heard nothing from Papa after that. Just low groans. Then the man said, 'We got rid of your kind before, and we'll do it again.'"

The slur claws at something long buried—a phrase spat during the Great War. One Michael thought had faded when the war ended. His blood runs cold, but he pushes the reaction down, focusing on Fredrick's account.

"Can you describe the men?"

Fredrick lets out a shaky breath, his voice hollow. "Shapes in the dark."

Mrs. Haber, wary as a cornered cat, interrupts. "You ask more than three questions. Now go."

"Yes, Mrs. Haber. I'm going." Michael dips his head toward the sleeping man. "That's how he ended up like this?"

A tear slips down Fredrick's face. "The men fled, and before I could reach him, Papa stumbled and struck his head against the underpass column. He's been unconscious since." His voice catches. "If only I'd been quicker."

The gravity of the situation settles on Michael. Who would do this to an old man? What if Haber doesn't regain consciousness? What if, God forbid, he dies?

Michael glances at Mrs. Haber, aware he has mere seconds before she ends this conversation. "I'm sorry this happened to your family. I'll talk to the police, then run the story. If it makes the front page, hopefully someone will come forward with information."

In deference to Mrs. Haber, he makes eye contact and says, "I hope your husband recovers quickly. Guten Tag, Frau Haber."

Stepping out into the mid-morning sunshine, Michael lights a cigarette and considers his next step. This story promises to break him out of journalistic purgatory, but there's only one man's word and an old woman's fear. He needs more or his report will read like a police blotter.

He glances left toward Eleventh Street, deciding if it's worth taking a look. Having traversed the underpass many times, Michael knows every crack in the concrete, every stain on the walls. He pictures the scene. Dusk. Deserted. The paper mill on one side of the tracks, a warehouse on the other. He'd learn nothing new in broad daylight. But the anti-German taunts get under his skin, and he can't shake a prickling sense of déjà vu.

* * *

McCabe, the front desk cop at Ellington Police Headquarters says Kellerman's at lunch.

A block later, his stomach growling, Michael pushes into Dixie's, a mix of diner and greasy spoon. He spies the stocky cop at the counter and signals Mabel for the special and black coffee.

Michael slides onto the cracked red vinyl stool beside the cop, nudging him with his elbow. "Hey."

A forkful of mashed potatoes halts midway to Kellerman's mouth. "Mike! How's it going?"

The cop's breath is bad as usual, a mix of unbrushed teeth and old coffee. "Not too bad."

There's another cop on Kellerman's left; one he's never met, but they exchange nods.

Kellerman uses his fork to punctuate garbled words Michael can hardly understand. "Baxter got you on the Haber case?"

He sips his coffee. "Yeah. He needed someone who spoke German."

"Poor guy. Got it bad." Kellerman shakes his head, his expression one of genuine sympathy.

"That's what I heard. What's your take on it?"

Kellerman sighs, glancing at the clock. "Hoodlums, most likely. Making my life hell."

This doesn't track with Fredrick Haber's description. He flips open his notebook. "Can you confirm what I have so far?"

Kellerman tosses his napkin on his plate and fishes in his pocket for change.

"Three men attacked the elderly man and held his son on the ground. Wilhelm Haber is unconscious at St. Boniface. The son was unable to do more than give vague descriptions."

"That's it for now. I'll go back later for the father's statement." Kellerman slides off the stool and heads toward the door, the other cop in tow.

"Motive?" asks Michael.

Straightening his cap on his head, Kellerman shrugs.

As the two men in blue exit Dixie's, the other cop says, "He's German. That's reason enough."

"True," Kellerman answers as the door opens and the street sounds swallow their voices.

The words and Kellerman's agreement sting.

Michael reviews the scrawny bits of information he's gathered and jots down the basics of his report in his notebook. He taps his pencil against the counter, frowning at his draft. Should he say the man was German? Mention what the attackers said?

The German angle might fly, but what the men said—that's hearsay. Baxter wants facts.

We got rid of your kind before, and we'll do it again. The challenge in those words is unmistakable. Is it a personal warning or something bigger? Is Hitler's rise provoking anti-German hysteria? Again?

He turned fifteen and joined the Boy Scouts when America entered the war in 1917. He did his part, selling stamps and bonds to raise money. When his troop leader told them to report anyone who refused to buy, the spirit of raising money dimmed. Most folks he collected from had pennies to spare for the war effort, but most gave something. When the troop leader told the boys to name people who didn't buy stamps, especially Germans, he quit the Scouts.

In school, everything German was outlawed. The language class disappeared. The librarian purged the shelves of German language books and lit a match to the pile in the schoolyard for all to see.

It's been years since he dared remember what happened during the war. When being German carried an invisible mark on your back. When having a conversation with friends got you arrested on charges of disloyalty.

"Anything else?" Mabel asks, startling him from his reverie.

Michael pays his bill, downs the last of his frigid coffee, and bursts through the door, in search of reasons for Haber's attack.

At the *Journal*, he takes the stairs two at a time and types up his story along with the rest of his assignments. It's too small. Too insignificant. One paragraph on the front page, placed so low and small it might as well be invisible.

How many others in Ellington think like that cop? That being German is reason enough?

Chapter Two

Olivia Kendall presses the light switch. The bulbs flicker awake as she sets her briefcase on the desk and unpacks her materials in tidy stacks.

The desks stand at attention, perfectly spaced, awaiting their occupants. On the chalkboard, yesterday's lesson on German propaganda lingers like a ghost. The discussion had felt timely—necessary even—with reports of Hitler's activity on the front page almost daily.

But it's not the lesson plan that occupies her thoughts this morning.

"Father says people here don't like Germans."

Hans Haber's quiet confession still echoes in her mind. The fear in his voice hadn't been loud, but it had been real—and hits unmistakably close to home.

Trying to shake the memory, she opens the *Ellington Journal* in search of something to spark today's current events discussion. Local headlines take up three-quarters of the front page—factory layoffs, a ribbon-cutting at the post office—until a small article near the bottom corner gets her attention.

Underpass Assault

She reads. "Three men attacked Wilhelm Haber, an elderly man, and held his son on the ground. Haber was taken to St. Boniface, where he remains unconscious. The son, Fredrick Haber, was unable to identify the attackers."

Her mind catches on one detail: 'Wilhelm Haber.' Her eyes shoot immediately to Hans's empty desk. Haber. The same name. Her chest tightens as yesterday's conversation echoes.

The door opens, and students flood in for first period. Olivia tucks the article into her planner, unsure if she's relieved or heartsick to see

Hans slip quietly into his seat, head down, his lank form hunched over the desktop.

She addresses the class. "Did anyone read the world news this morning?"

A few heads shake. Then Frannie raises her hand, tentative.

"My dad said that Jewish-owned shops are being taken away. Is that true?"

Olivia pauses, grateful for the opening. "That's the process the Nazis call Aryanization. It's when Jewish businesses are forcibly transferred to non-Jewish, so-called 'Aryan' owners. Sometimes they're paid a fraction of the value. Most times, nothing at all."

The room quiets under the weight of what she's described.

She holds the newspaper just below eye level, watching the class as she reads. "A family-owned bakery in Berlin, run for three generations, was handed over to new owners. No charges. No crimes. Just a change in who's considered 'acceptable.'"

She goes to the board and picks up a piece of chalk.

"I want us to think about what this means—not just in Germany, but anywhere this kind of thinking takes hold."

She writes two questions:

What does it mean to lose your place in society because of your name? Your ancestry? Or your language?

What happens when a community decides a neighbor is an enemy—because someone in power tells them so?

The silence that follows hangs thick in the air. No shuffling papers, no whispered jokes. Her student's faces turn serious, shoulders straighten as the gravity of her questions settles over them.

Sam's hand shoots up. "It makes me think about fairness. Like, how unfair it is to judge someone by their name. You have no control over that."

Olivia nods. "Good, Sam."

Ann adds, "It's scary. Because that kind of thinking spreads and if people go along with it, it becomes normal."

Phil raises his hand slowly. "My dad said that during the war, his family almost changed our last name—just to fit in. They didn't want people to know they were German."

A few students turn toward him, surprised.

Olivia meets his gaze. "That's an important detail, Phil. That kind of pressure—to change your name, to hide who you are—can be just as damaging as open hostility. It's the quiet kind of fear that seeps in and stays. I knew someone, once, who faced that kind of scrutiny. It leaves scars."

The words slip out before she can stop them—*I knew someone, once*—and immediately wants to take them back. Her rule is to guide, not confess. But Phil's story has cracked something open, memories she thought she'd buried deep enough.

She draws a breath, grounding herself, then taps the second question on the board to refocus the class. "So, what if a neighbor becomes the enemy because someone powerful says they are?"

A hand goes up in the second row. Nora rarely volunteers, but today she's thoughtful, almost worried. "Is it like...when people believe a rumor just because someone important says it?"

"Exactly. When we accept something as truth, without questioning it, just because it comes from someone in power, that's where the danger lies. How fear is spread, how lies get accepted. It's not just a rumor anymore; it becomes the story they want you to believe."

She lets the words settle before adding, "Think about what Hitler is doing right now. He's built his message on fear—fear that Jews control the banks, the newspapers, the government. That Jews caused Germany's defeat in the last war. He wrote *Mein Kampf*, repeating it, until people believe it."

She pauses, her gaze sweeping the room.

"When a lie is told often enough, it starts to feel like truth. Fear isn't just spreading—it's being organized and aimed at a goal. Hitler wants to force all Jews out of Germany—to make it a country with only what he considers 'pure' Germans".

A few students shift in their seats. The room stills—the kind of stillness that means something important has landed.

Olivia gestures to the board. "What if the school principal told you a fellow student was your enemy?"

The tension in the room spikes. Some students glance nervously at each other; others study their desktops like they're bracing for an exam.

Olivia's eyes search for Hans. He sits rigid, staring straight ahead.

"I think I'd trust the principal," Frannie says. "And maybe... try not to be seen with that student."

"I wouldn't want to be seen with you either!" Dorothy blurts, breaking her silence.

"Then we'll be enemies forever." Frannie sticks out her tongue.

Dorothy stiffens and pointedly turns away.

If a mouse ran across the room, Olivia would have heard its tiny feet on the tile. She lets the silence stretch, then says quietly, "Because we trust leaders, our fate is in their hands, isn't it?"

She lets the question linger.

Doors opening and voices spilling into the corridor signal the end of class.

"Class dismissed."

As students file out, Olivia approaches Hans, waiting while he stuffs books into his bag.

She slips the folded newspaper onto his desk. "The name caught my eye. Is this your family?"

Hans glances at the article. His lips press into a tight line. "Wilhelm is my grandfather. My father was the one they held down."

Olivia's throat tightens. "Hans, I'm so sorry."

He sniffs and buckles the straps.

Olivia sits in the desk across the aisle. "How are they?"

"Grandfather is unconscious. Father's face is scraped up, but mostly he's feeling guilty for not being able to help Grandfather."

"That's difficult. I hope he recovers quickly."

Hans turns toward her, and for the first time all year, she sees real anger in his face. "Father said they just kept hitting him. Said they'd get rid of our kind, like they were proud of it." He's trembling—fighting to keep control.

Olivia inhales sharply. *Get rid of our kind.* The words lodge in her chest—sharp, suffocating. She draws back as if slapped. Sour memories surface—the accusations, the boycotts, the whispers that scarred her high school years.

"I bet you're scared. I would be." Olivia wants to share her experience with him, give him some solace that others have gone through this and survived. "Let me know if I can help."

He slings his bag over his shoulder. "I'm late," he says, his voice tight, struggling to be strong.

As Hans leaves the classroom, Olivia exhales slowly. The conversation stirs buried memories that still sting, despite the distance between then and now—nearly twenty years.

She wants to tell him it gets better. But, she's not sure it does.

Chapter Three

The phrase nags at Michael—pricks the back of his neck like a premonition. He's heard it before, but where, and why? His mind searches for avenues to expand on "we got rid of your kind," but it comes up blank.

He grabs his notebook, stubs out his cigarette, and removes the key ring from the pegboard by the door. A round tag labels it "Morgue," the room in the basement where archived newspapers are stored dating back to the mid-1800s when the *Journal* was established.

The door groans in protest as Michael pushes it open and steps into the dim room. A wave of stale, earthy air hits him, thick with dust and something older—like the past itself has been sealed in and left to rot.

He finds the volume marked *1918,* pulls it from the shelf, and places it on the table. A plume of dust billows up, forcing a sneeze that reverberates through the stillness.

He thumbs through the brittle pages until he locates what he's looking for. July 4, 1918. The bold headline screams, "SEVEN ARE ACCUSED BY LEAGUE". Michael swallows. His grandfather was one of the seven.

The memory of that morning bubbles up to the surface.

A police officer at their front door, shouting. "Bernard Warner, you're under arrest."

"Whatever for, Jack?" the naïve sixty-six-year-old asked the man who'd been under his command when he served as police chief of South Ellington back in the nineties.

"For making remarks that violate the Sedition Act." Jack shifted his weight from one foot to the other, glancing around as if searching for an escape route. He wouldn't meet his grandfather's eyes, instead fixing his gaze on the scuffed floorboards of the entryway.

A loyal citizen and proud business owner, his grandfather protested the charge. "The Sedition Act? I would never disobey the law."

"Come with me, Barney. I'm sure we'll have this cleared up in no time. I'm just doing my job."

Another officer gripped his forearm and marched him to an open-air truck idling in front of their house, in full view of their neighbors gathering for the Independence Day parade.

Michael followed the men outside, desperate to stop them from taking his grandfather away. Even now, he recalls his helplessness, his grandfather's silent composure, and the sound of his own screams—begging the men to stop the truck—running behind until his legs gave out.

Today at the hospital, Fredrick Haber's face, bruised and guilt-ridden, mirrored the helplessness he'd felt then.

Michael scans the article beneath the headline, murmuring the subheading aloud: "Dictograph Used By League To Effect Arrests". The "League" in the headline refers to the Citizens Patriotic League of Ellington—the CPLE.

He's not sure what happened in court. He was at home with his sister, frightened beyond measure, waiting for his parents and grandparents to return.

Michael reads the article with journalistic eyes. The boy he was, could wait.

The court of inquiry assembled within hours of the arrests—an unusual speed that suggested prior planning. County attorney William Hawthorne, massive legal briefs in hand, spent an hour relaying the charges to the judge, the accused, and an eager audience.

He suspects the arrests were orchestrated for maximum spectacle—respected men paraded before the public on a holiday. The Dictograph, installed under the guise of an electric meter, transmitted conversations to detectives—conversations later deemed prosecutable under the Sedition Act, passed in May 1918 to root out wartime disloyalty.

More than four hundred spectators packed the courtroom. The *Ellington Journal* splashed the story across page one in the evening edition.

As Michael flips through the rest of July, he can almost hear his grandfather's voice—those worried dinner conversations, the forced optimism that it would all blow over.

In late August, Michael finds the damning headline. **Warner Is Found Guilty**

The *Journal* screamed his grandfather's guilt, branding the family pro-German—and therefore anti-American. The stigma followed them like a shadow for years.

Nineteen years later, it's just him, his sister, and his mother. He and Clara survived, but his mother never recovered. Those months took a heavy toll, and to this day, she never speaks of that time. What happened to Haber isn't the same as what his grandfather endured, but the anti-German sentiment behind both is unmistakable.

Michael checks his watch, surprised to find he's been down here for hours. He replaces *1918* on the shelf, locks the door, and climbs the stairs to the exit. If he's lucky, he can catch Kellerman at the bar.

* * *

Late afternoon shadows stretch Michael's lanky frame on the sidewalk as he heads to Nick's. Inside, the dim light from a row of bulbs casts a weak amber glow across the mahogany bar.

The air reeks with cigarette smoke, whiskey, and this morning's Aqua Velva—the aftershave every man slaps on before heading out the door. At this hour, the place is quiet but steady, a retreat for men in loosened ties and rolled-up sleeves, unwinding after a long day.

At the far end of the bar, Abe Kellerman's bulk teeters precariously on a stool, his round face half-lit by the overhead glow, fingers tapping on an empty shot glass.

Michael throws a dollar bill on the bar, removes his hat and jacket. "A cold one, Nick. And whatever Abe wants."

Abe's face splits with a grin. "Thanks kid."

"There's more where that came from." The price of information usually costs a few drinks.

Michael takes a long pull on his beer, the frosty brew cooling his parched throat.

Abe orders a shot of Old Forester.

"Did you make it to the hospital?"

Abe downs his shot, drops the glass on the bar, and gives Michael a sidelong look. "Yeah. Guy's still out, but I got a few more details from the son."

Michael finishes his beer and contemplates another. He thinks better of it; he needs to stay sharp.

"He caught shapes, shadows. Two tall, one short."

Michael hesitates, then drops the question casually, like it's no big deal. "Did he tell you what they said?"

Abe studies the amber liquid in his glass like it holds the answer. "Feels like anti-German stuff. Again."

Michael plays dumb. "What do you mean, again?"

Abe exhales cheap whiskey and sour milk. Michael pinches his thigh to keep his lips from curling in distaste.

"You were just a kid, but we dealt with the same kind of thing back in '18."

Michael keeps his tone casual, masking the tension coiling in his chest. "What kind of thing?"

Abe's voice drops in volume and tone. "Beatings. Ridicule. Stalking. All in the name of one hundred percent American."

His beady eyes dart around the bar. "That's what the CPLE preached. Got so I couldn't stand hearing it anymore."

The mention of the organization behind his grandfather's arrest jolts Michael, souring his stomach. He clenches his fist in his lap, forcing himself to stay composed.

"CPLE? What did they do?"

"Patriot police. If you didn't show enough loyalty, bad things happened."

The free drinks are working. "You were a cop back then?"

Abe swipes his hands over his face as if he's erasing the memory. "I'm second generation. Kept my head down and did what I was told. Went to every damn rally, bought every bond they sold, cheered when they told me to cheer. Not because I hated Germans—but because not showing up meant being next. My parents came over in 1880. Hell, half this town is German. But the Patriotic League," he spits the words, "they wiped out everything. Newspapers, the language, even changed street names."

"I remember some of it. My grandfather was from Germany," Michael says carefully, watching Abe's reflection in the mirror behind the bar.

"Terrible time. Most folks believed the League helped win the war by going after anyone they saw as unpatriotic. But plenty of others went along because they were scared. Sign the petition or have your neighbors wonder why your name wasn't on it."

Abe glances over his shoulder. "They even harassed a priest. Can you imagine?"

The revelation twists something in Michael's chest. A priest. The accusation strikes him as both absurd and painfully personal. As a Catholic, the thought of a man of God getting caught up in the hysteria shakes him.

He opens his mouth, on the brink of revealing his grandfather's story, but thinks better of it. Kellerman appears to be on his side, but the cop's sly glances and nervous energy give him pause.

"Who was the Patriotic League?"

Abe shifts in his seat and nearly tips off the stool. The drinks are starting to show. "A bunch of city officials, businessmen, and citizens. Started with a few who held rallies for the war effort. By the end of the war, I bet there were hundreds, maybe thousands in it. A mob of deputized citizens."

"Who led them?"

Abe hesitates, then shakes his head. "Can't remember."

Michael doesn't buy it. Whoever led the CPLE back then might still hold power or be pulling strings behind the scenes. And Kellerman won't stick his neck out.

"Was it Hawthorne?" He takes a calculated guess based on what he read about his grandfather's case.

Abe sips and eyes him from under lowered lids. "Him and some others."

He finishes the shot and bangs the glass on the counter.

"You gotta be careful, Mike."

"Why's that?" Michael asks, afraid of the answer.

Abe shoves his peaked service cap onto his salt and pepper hair, the visor tipped low over his eyes.

"Just... leave it."

After Abe ambles out the door, Michael orders a shot of whiskey and flips open his notebook, jotting down what he's learned. Too many connections to ignore. No way in hell he's leaving this alone.

There must be records, stories, someone willing to talk. Plenty of ways to find out who's behind Haber's attack.

Snapping the notebook shut, Michael's jaw tightens. Tomorrow, he'll dig deeper. Talk to Baxter. See if anyone at the *Journal* remembers that time.

He has one other source. One much closer to home—his mother—who has never spoken to him about the trial or its aftermath.

The thought of asking her to relive those years—of confronting the truth he suspects still simmers beneath Ellington's surface—unsettles him more than the League itself.

* * *

Michael steps into Schmitty's Corner—a five-way intersection in the heart of South Ellington, the end of the southbound streetcar line.

A fountain in the center commemorates twenty South Ellington soldiers who perished during the Great War. He digs in his pocket for a penny, a tradition that helps the town raise funds, but the best he has is a nickel. He pitches it in. Maybe it will bring him five times the luck he'll need confronting his mother.

Strolling toward home, he studies the house his grandfather built in 1885. A simple, two-story structure, it marked the moment Bernard Warner moved his family south from Ellington proper to open a shoe shop. As the business gained a foothold, so did his influence. Over the years, he served as police chief, city councilman, and a member of several societies and church clubs. A respected citizen.

Until that fateful morning.

Michael's stomach twists at the memory. Instead of attending the parade, his parents and grandmother spent the day trying to find out what had happened. His father, desperate to help, went downtown and didn't return until later that evening. Thanks to a wealthy friend, also caught in the snare, his grandfather posted bail.

Michael and Clara were sent to bed, but they hovered at the top of the stairs, straining to hear. They caught fragments: his mother asking, "Who gave them access?" His father saying, "We need a lawyer." His grandfather muttering, "I didn't say those things." Then his grandmother crying, "It's not fair. How could this happen to reputable men who have done so much for this county?"

The screen door slaps shut behind him. The smell of something frying—ordinary, familiar—fills the same house where in the course of one extraordinary day everything changed.

"I'm home, Mama." He ducks into the tiny kitchen and plants a kiss on her cheek.

"You're late." She half-smiles, her tone more observation than accusation.

"Sorry. I'll clean up."

He climbs the narrow stairs to his room, trades his work clothes for dungarees, and splashes water on his face. When he returns, he finds his sister in the front room, her nose buried in McCall's.

Clara, a book worm two years his senior, looks up when he plucks the magazine from her hands and flips it around. "What're you reading?"

"Hey!" Clara snatches it back, mock outrage in her tone.

He smirks, glimpsing a two-page spread of dresses. "I like the green one."

Clara holds up the page and taps a white dress with red polka dots and a matching belt. "This one's more my style."

"Dinner!" Mama's call from the kitchen breaks their banter.

Michael offers Clara his hand, helping her up from the chair.

On the dining room table, there's half a fried chicken, mashed potatoes, and green beans drowned in gravy, a means of adding flavor and heft to Depression-sized meals.

In between bites, they catch up on local events and weekend plans.

Michael stays quiet for most of the meal, reluctant to confront his mother about the past. He waits for a lull in the conversation. "I spent the day chasing a story."

"Something better than a flower show, I hope," his mother says.

He sets down his fork, laces his fingers together, and props his elbows on the table.

"An elderly German man was assaulted under the Eleventh Street underpass last night." He rushes on so his mother won't interrupt before he's finished. "I don't think it was random. They may have targeted him for being German, using the same tactics as 1918."

Mama's face goes pale. Her knife and fork clatter against the plate as she sets them down with trembling hands.

"The signs point to Hawthorne and friends of the Patriotic League."

"Hawthorne?" Clara whispers the name like it's holy.

Mama slams both palms on the table. The plates rattle. Silverware jumps. Even the gravy quivers. "We are not discussing this!"

Clara flinches, her fork slips from her hand, landing with a soft thud on the tablecloth.

Michael peers at his mother over his hands. He hasn't heard this tone, this kind of demand since he'd tried to pin a broken window on Clara and got caught.

"I forbid it!" Mama rises, grabs her plate and silverware, pauses next to Michael. "You hear me, Michael?"

He meets her fiery gaze and holds it. "I hear you, Mama, but..."

"No buts!" Mama yells over her shoulder as she exits, leaving Clara at the table staring open mouthed.

Michael follows his mother into the kitchen.

"Mama, I need your help." His gaze and his body hold her in place. "The man is unconscious and has a family."

Mama's lips press into a thin line, her narrowed blue eyes like ice. "Let sleeping dogs lie."

"What if that dog is awake and biting people again? It's my job, and after what the CPLE did nineteen years ago, it's my duty to investigate. Maybe it's a random act. But what if it's not?"

She leans forward until her forehead rests against his chest, her words muffled in his shirt. "Leave it alone, Michael."

He should obey his mother, make the promise, and stick to it, but there's a nagging doubt in his gut saying her resistance is significant.

He pecks a kiss on her gray hair and surrounds her with his arms.

Usually, he can cajole her into relenting, to listen to his point of view. But she's frightened. A bone-deep fear he hasn't seen since his father died of a heart attack in 1924.

Before releasing her, he apologizes. "I'm sorry I upset you."

She expects him to say he'll leave it alone, but he can't. There's more to this than meets the eye.

* * *

The mood is somber as Michael and Clara put the dining room in order while Mama handles the kitchen. He expected her reluctance, but the sharpness of her response unsettles him.

"Take a walk, Sis?" He pops a cigarette from his pack. Maybe she could shed light on Mama's reaction.

"I could use some air. Let me get a sweater."

Outside, Michael lights the cigarette. "I didn't expect such a fierce reaction from Mama."

"You saw her. I thought she was going to faint when you mentioned Hawthorne."

"Why would his name turn her into a crazy person?"

"Isn't it obvious? He put Grandfather in jail."

"But that's ancient history." Michael exhales a long stream of smoke.

Clara shrugs.

"Can I ask you a question?"

"I don't know why she won't talk about it." Clara assumes his intent.

"Not my question. Why do you think Grandfather and his friends were arrested?"

"You know why! That damned Dictograph thing. Those detectives listening."

"Yes, I'm aware how they got the evidence. But I can't figure out why. Why target that shop? Out of all the places in town, why there?"

Clara shrugs. "Being German."

"Too obvious."

"They talked a lot about the war. I never understood most of what they said because they spoke in German. Also, I didn't care. Just a bunch of old men gabbing about things they could do nothing to change. Reminded me of Mama and Oma gossiping with our neighbors over the back fence."

Michael sums it up. "German. Old. Respected members of the community. Makes no sense."

They walk half a block, then musing aloud, he says, "Unless you wanted to teach the town a lesson. Send a message."

Clara grabs his arm, halting his forward progress. "Wait. What kind of message?"

Michael faces her. "One that says, 'you will not be German.'"

Clara's face pales in the moonlight. "I never thought of it that way."

"I bet Mama did. Still does."

At the corner, Clara turns on her heel, heading back toward home. "Bringing it up again is too much."

"Yeah." Michael agrees.

They stroll in uneasy silence; each lost in their own thoughts.

"I still feel guilty. I was the one who let them install that damned machine."

Michael slows his pace. "Clara. I can't imagine. I was just..."

"A boy." She places a hand on his cheek. "We protected you as much as we could. Maybe Mama still is."

"You have your own demons, don't you?"

"We all have demons," Clara says, her voice husky.

At the back door, she kisses his cheek and goes inside. Michael lights another cigarette and sits on the steps, his mind replaying his mother's terror. He inhales and the gloom of the yard brightens momentarily.

Now what? He empathizes with his mother and sister, what they've been through, what they want to avoid. Yet, the case is more compelling than ever, with his mother's outburst revealing a deep fear he never knew existed.

Chapter Four

A week later, Olivia fills in fourth quarter grades for the 1936-37 school year. She jots a B in the column next to Hans Haber and wonders how his grandfather is doing. Yesterday, he shared that he was still unconscious. The boy's dark shadows under his eyes and the tension in his voice tell her he's worried.

The end of the school year always leaves Olivia feeling unmoored. The structure of schedules, lesson plans, and deadlines give her purpose, keep her tethered. Without them, summer stretches ahead like an open sea, untamed and daunting.

But this summer, she has a goal to steady herself—preparing Aunt Becky's house for sale. It had been her aunt and father's childhood home and with no children of her own, Becky left it to her when she died six months ago. She can't continue to avoid the memories or painful decisions.

The streetcar drops her in Sterling Woods, a neighborhood of hundred-year-old oaks and stately homes built before the turn of the century. On Lincoln Avenue, she recalls evening strolls with her parents, walking and talking until darkness chased them inside.

Olivia turns onto the paved path that approaches the modest brick house. She hates the thought of selling it, but practicality outweighs sentimentality. Her studio apartment two blocks from school fits her modest needs.

She unlocks the front door and pushes in, spreading accumulated mail across the foyer. A wave of stale air assaults her nostrils as displaced dust motes dance in late afternoon sunbeams.

She drops the groceries on the kitchen table and anxious for fresh air, she draws the curtains and opens the first-floor windows, then does the same upstairs. A gentle breeze carrying the faint scent of jasmine

27

from the trellised vines below, accompanies her as she unpacks her overnight bag in what had always been 'her' room.

Covering the short distance to Aunt Becky's room across the hall, Olivia eyes it, unchanged since she was admitted to the hospital with a stroke in January. An ivory comb and brush set rests on the dresser beside a mirrored tray adorned with elaborate perfume bottles. On the bedside table, books are stacked next to a pair of glasses and a pill bottle.

Opening the closet, her eyes widen. It's stuffed with clothing, shoes, hats, and God knows what else. Aunt Becky's housecoat, brown and yellow paisley hangs on the back of the closet door and she remembers the afternoons spent baking and fixing meals. Thanks to her aunt, she's a good cook, though she seldom has the opportunity to practice.

Since Aunt Becky didn't leave instructions on how to handle her possessions, Olivia will salvage what she can and see if Saint Catherine's Society can take care of the rest. With money tight for everyone, leaving anything to waste is irresponsible.

She makes a sandwich while she jots a few notes about what needs to be done. Feeling more in control, she pops the cap on a Coca-Cola and sips it as she wanders through the first floor assessing the daunting task before her.

The furniture can stay with the house. Maybe keep a few pieces of art and sell the rest. She'll box up personal items and family photographs.

Examining the framed images on the mantle, she's drawn to a studio portrait of her parents, hand-tinted with lifelike colors, taken around 1900 when they got engaged. Her father wears a dark suit and tie and is clean shaven—his wife never could stand him with whiskers. Her mother is in a simple light-colored dress, a string of pearls lay across her chest, her auburn hair cascading in waves to her shoulders. Olivia's fingers touch the glass as if she can caress them. So young. So full of life. A bright future cut short.

Turning to the dining room, she eyes the Chippendale table with six side chairs and two captains. Pulling the lace tablecloth aside, she palms the cherry mahogany where her aunt entertained, and she and her parents came for lunch every Sunday after church. Chucking away a tear, she twirls around and examines the breakfront, an enormous cabinet, matching the dining set.

A full set of Haviland China is on display—cobalt with gold accents, a wedding gift from her father's parents. She'd eaten more meals than she could count on those dishes and dried the fine porcelain with a soft towel and only with permission. Giving them away is unthinkable. Storage is the only option for now.

After a few tugs, the doors at the bottom swing open, revealing a shelf lined with matching serving dishes. On the bottom is a box, tall and wide. Curious, she tilts it this way and that, until finally she gets it positioned just so and with one final pull, it lands on the floor with a thud.

Lifting the lid, Olivia extracts a book bound in thick red cardboard. It is labeled Olivia. She's seen this before and flips through it, stopping briefly to examine her favorite photos.

On the last page is one taken at her sixteenth birthday party. Father is on one side, his smile contagious and proud. On the other, one arm slung across her shoulders, is Uncle John whose face is blurry for having moved. John Simpson was dubbed her uncle, not for blood kinship, but to honor the friendship he had with her father. She remembers his gift; the leather satchel she used in college and now ports her teaching supplies to and from Ellington High. The brass clasp bears her initials. OAK. Olivia Adams Kendall.

Sniffing and drawing the back of her hand under her nose, she closes the album and lifts another book from the box. This one is labeled *Victor* and was compiled by her mother and Aunt Becky. This book is not new to her either, but she spends a few minutes skimming through important events in her father's youth, his law career, and as a loving husband and father.

A chilly breeze raises goosebumps on Olivia's bare arms. The sun has gone behind clouds that threaten rain. Tucking the book under her arm, she lays it on the coffee table in the parlor and scurries from room to room, upstairs and down, closing and locking the windows.

As she returns to the dining room, something white catches her eye on the floor by the China cabinet. Stooping to pick it up, a chill runs through her as she examines the details.

The handwriting is bold. Slanted. Unmistakably her mother's. Addressed to Becky Kendall. The postmark reads April 7, 1920.

The day her mother died.

A sharp rapping startles her. A woodpecker, its cadence matching her heartbeat.

She isn't sure she wants to know what's inside.

The tapping continues, chipping away at her composure.

Turning her back on the envelope, she retreats into the parlor, removes the stopper on a half-full decanter of brandy, sloshes some into a glass, and swallows before she even realizes what she's done.

There can be nothing good in that envelope. She pours another drink and takes it with her into the hall where she contemplates what to do with the letter, its contents destined to upset her equilibrium.

The late afternoon light reminds her of another day just like this one.

"I'm home, Aunt Becky!" Olivia called sending her voice up the stairs. Listening for a reply, she heard soft moans and raced up to her aunt's room, where she found her face down in a pillow.

"Oh Auntie!" Olivia sat beside her and laid a comforting hand on her shoulder. "What is it?"

Her aunt, salt of the earth, rarely got upset or cried. Something was terribly wrong.

"Are you hurt? In pain? Can I get you some water?" Olivia mentally flipped through a list of things that would make her aunt cry, like...like she did when her father died.

Olivia sprang up from the bed putting distance between her and the awful news she knew would come.

Her aunt threw her legs over the side of the bed with a loud sniff. Eyes red and puffy, her meticulously coiffed hair in turmoil, she wiped a handkerchief under her nose and patted the bed beside her.

"Tell me." Olivia refused the offered seat. "Mother?"

Aunt Becky didn't look at her. Just nodded.

It was her final moment as someone's child.

"Oh, Olivia... She's gone."

The words slammed into her chest. Paralyzed, until her aunt reached for her hand, and she flung herself into her arms.

"I—I'm an orphan." As soon as she said it, heat rose to her face. Her mother had died—and she made it all about herself. She clenched her fists, ashamed. But the grief felt too big, the words, too true.

After she'd cried herself out, Olivia slid from her aunt's arms to the floor.

"What happened? She wasn't sick, was she?"

Aunt Becky shook her head.

Fresh tears flooded Olivia's eyes, barely able to read the slip of paper bearing the Western Union logo. Ten words said all she needed to know.

"Jane died today from a fall into the cistern. Jim."

Uncle Jim didn't say suicide. He didn't have to.

Aunt Becky hesitated, struggling to speak. "Her grief ran deep, Olivia. Your father meant the world to her."

"And I suppose I meant nothing!" Olivia shoved the telegram at her aunt. "I lost him too."

She understood, a little, why her mother chose to die rather than live without her beloved husband. She left no note, and all Uncle Jim said was that she went into the yard and didn't return.

After her father's death, Jane Kendall, once a vibrant pillar of the community, wasted away, refusing to go out or entertain. Olivia cared for her mother during her final year of high school. She often found her crying in a corner or staring into space. When Uncle Jim offered his sister a getaway to his home in the country, Olivia pressed her to go. And she's never forgiven herself for pushing her.

Maybe the letter held her mother's explanation, the key to letting Olivia rest, know what she thought. Maybe it held words of love, despite actions to the contrary.

Downing the brandy, Olivia slams the glass on the dining table, and stoops to pick up the envelope. She tugs out a single sheet of paper. Her mother's handwriting is slightly slanted and sloppy, as if she's written it in haste. There's no date.

Becky,

That so-called accident took my husband. I tried to find out what really happened, but every path led nowhere. Take care of Olivia. Keep her safe. I fear my questions may have consequences.

Jane

Her mother's words couldn't be further from what she expected. She rereads slowly, studying each sentence independent of the others.

So-called accident.

Olivia's stomach churns. Is her mother implying her father was murdered? Had she tried to uncover what really happened? What had her mother discovered—or failed to discover?

And then, keep her safe. What does she need to be protected from?

Questions with consequences?

A chill runs through her. Why had Aunt Becky never mentioned this letter? For seventeen years, she'd kept this explosive suspicion hidden. Why?

Olivia would have preferred a typical suicide note explaining why she left her daughter, why it was more important to die than live.

But this. This is far more disturbing: her mother searching for the truth when all Olivia remembers is a woman sobbing in her bathrobe day after day.

Yet, the handwriting is hers. The warning raises goosebumps on her arms.

Raking her fingers through her hair, seeking distraction, Olivia goes into the parlor and places the scrapbook on her lap. She flips quickly through the pages of her father's life, skimming the headlines, the photographs, the notes in the margin. Searching for something she can't name.

Tucked in the back between the last page and the cover, is a bulky manila envelope. "Dictograph Case" is scrawled on the front.

"What's this?" she says aloud and pinches the clasp. She peeks inside and spies yellowed news clippings of assorted sizes and shapes. Tilting the envelope, old newsprint cascades onto the coffee table. The one on top has a bold headline: "Seven Are Accused By League". The subheading reads, "Dictograph Used by Patriotic League to Affect Arrests".

The case her father defended, right in their hometown, where anything German was subject to elimination.

The taunts from classmates come rushing back. "German lover. Traitor"—fresh and sharp as if no time has passed. Her father's words, dismissive yet firm, always taking the high road, echo in her mind: "Imagine how they feel. They are German."

But Olivia only remembers how she felt—ostracized, humiliated, alone.

The pile is devoted entirely to the case. Most are front-page stories about this or that defendant, their testimony, the verdicts, and near the bottom of the stack, a two-paragraph blurb announcing the date for the appeal hearing.

April 5, 1919.

Two days later, her father was dead.

Olivia gathers the scattered clippings, sliding them back into the envelope with trembling fingers.

She rereads her mother's letter, sighs, and lets it rest in her lap—as heavy as one of Father's law books.

Olivia bites a thumbnail, eyes narrowed, forehead scrunched, like when she's working a crossword puzzle.

Maybe she could test the waters—do a little digging. After all this time, she's likely to end up with dead ends, but it gives her something to do besides clearing Aunt Becky's house.

Tomorrow she'll examine the scrapbooks and clippings and let things flow naturally. It might be all for naught, but if her mother thought something was awry, it's her duty to check a few details.

What harm can it do?

Chapter Five

Effie Winslow, office secretary and assistant editor, shouts across the aisle, "Michael, phone call."

He picks up the receiver. "Michael Schumann."

"This is Charlotte Franklin."

Franklin? The name doesn't click at first.

"St. Boniface Hospital," she says—just as it hits him. The nurse.

"Hello, Nurse Franklin."

He braces for the worst—that Haber has died.

"He's awake," she says with clinical detachment.

Michael exhales. "That's great news. When can I see him? I can be there in an hour."

"My, you are anxious," she says. "His wife is here now."

Damn. He didn't want to interview Haber with his wife there. She'd shut him down quicker than a church lady spotting sin.

"Any chance I can speak with him alone?"

"Mm. Let me think."

Tamping a cigarette on the desk, he waits.

"How about this? I can arrange his morning bath at ten. That should chase his wife away for a little while."

Interviewing a man mid-bath would be a first. "Well, that might be a bit uncomfortable..."

Nurse Franklin chuckles. "I'll pretend his bath is at ten. You get in, get out, and no one's the wiser."

Michael smirks. The woman can make her way around difficult situations. "Perfect. I'll be there at ten."

"Meet me at the nurse's station."

The line goes dead. Michael sets the receiver down and flips open his notebook, his mind already ticking through the questions he needs to ask.

* * *

Nurse Franklin sits at her station.

Michael removes his hat. "Morning."

"Hello, Mr. Schumann." A pair of hunter green eyes flash a brief smile. She's a pretty woman, around his age, and if not for his urgent need to see Haber and return to the newsroom, he'd ask her on a date.

"You can go on back. I'll come by in a bit."

"Mrs. Haber?"

"Left the hospital a few minutes ago."

Michael nods his thanks.

In 307, Wilhelm Haber is sitting up, pillows propped behind his back. The old man's face has hints of color in his cheeks, a stark contrast from a few days ago. He's staring straight ahead, hands resting loosely atop the blanket.

Something about Haber's posture—the way he holds his chin up despite everything—reminds Michael of his grandfather. The same defiant dignity he'd worn even in handcuffs. Michael's chest tightens unexpectedly.

He taps quietly on the open door. "Entschuldigen Sie, Herr Haber—I'm sorry to disturb you. May I have a moment?"

Haber's head swivels toward the sound. His eyes narrow. He doesn't answer right away, studying Michael like he's trying to decide if he can be trusted.

"If you're giving me a bath, you should change out of that suit." He looks Michael up and down.

"I'm not here for the bath."

"Then what do you want?"

"Michael Schumann." Striding up to the bed, he extends his hand. "I'm with the *Ellington Journal.*"

Haber shakes his hand, sizing him up. "I heard you spoke with my son. You already know what happened."

"I did and I'm grateful for his side of the story. However, I'd like to hear yours. Are you willing?" Michael pulls his notebook from his inside pocket and holds it up. "All right?"

The man gestures to the chair beside the bed.

Haber tells the same story as Fredrick. Dusk, the dark underpass, three men, punches to the stomach, falling, then waking up in the hospital.

"How did they know you were German?"

Haber's cloudy blue eyes fix on the ceiling, speaking as if describing a picture or photograph. "Besides my accent, you mean?" He chuckles. "There's a saloon where I meet some friends."

"What do you talk about?" Michael asks, although the question is intrusive.

"Our wives, children, jobs, politics, and home."

"Home?"

"Bavaria. This town reminds me of that area, rolling hills, cobblestone streets, and houses of similar construction. While my friends are not all from the same area in Germany, we have much in common."

Michael nods. His grandfather used to say Ellington looked like the old country.

"Last week, we were talking of Hitler's antics. And stupidly, I raised my hand and said, Heil Hitler." Haber mimics the action.

Michael winces at the idiocy. That salute got lots of press during the Olympics. None of it good. Taken out of context, it could easily be seen as pro-German.

"Why in the world would you do that?"

"I was telling my friends we left Germany in 1933 because our country fell under the control of a man who acts like a king, demanding clicking heels and raised arms. He's a madman with too much power. It was meant to be a joke. My folly is most likely the reason the men attacked us."

Then his eyes lock with Michael's, a question hovering in his gaze. "Am I safe? My family? Will those men want to finish the job?"

Michael wonders this himself. "They didn't do much harm to your son and if you hadn't hit your head on the pillar, you would have gotten away with just bruises and a sore stomach."

"I should've kept my mouth shut. But this is America. This isn't supposed to happen." He taps his bandaged head gently.

"I'll let you rest," Michael says. He stands and shoves his notebook into his coat pocket. "May I visit again if I have questions?"

"Yes, Mr. Schumann." The old man's grin is small and tight. "I hope to be going home in a day or two."

"That's good news. It was nice meeting you."

* * *

Haber's mock salute must have touched a nerve with someone. It was everywhere—in the newsreels, headlines on every corner. America hated it. Hated what it stood for. Undivided loyalty to a short man with a toothbrush mustache.

But that didn't justify attacking an old man. In the dark. From behind.

After the interview, it boiled down to two things—either anti-German sentiment was rearing its ugly head again, or a few men didn't like Haber's idea of a joke. The connection to 1918 is as delicate as a spider's web.

Effie hails Michael when he enters the newsroom. "Chief wants you."

Michael settles into the chair opposite his boss.

"What d'ya got?" Baxter plucks the cigar butt from the corner of his mouth and leans back in his office chair.

"You'll call it a hunch and guesswork," Michael says. "But I say it's got legs."

"Lay it on me."

"Haber's awake. Only reason he's got for the attack is that he made the Nazi salute in a saloon he frequents."

"Pretty dumb. Sounds like he deserved it."

"I agree he did something stupid. But he also spoke German in the bar. Kellerman said it felt a lot like 18 when all the anti-German stuff went on in Ellington."

Michael glances up from his notes, sees he has Baxter's attention, and plows on.

"I went through back issues of the *Journal* from 1918 and found lots of stories about a county-wide anti-German push led by a group organized as the Citizens Patriotic League of Ellington."

Baxter stiffens. The slight movement alerts Michael. The League means something.

"That all you got?"

Michael nods.

Baxter leans forward, elbows on his desk. "We got other fish to fry, Schumann. Get something on my desk by tomorrow morning or I'm killing the story."

"But Chief," Michael presses, "I need more time."

"Effie!" Baxter roars.

Michael flinches.

The petite middle-aged woman sticks her head in the office. "What?"

Neither his boss nor the office secretary stand on ceremony.

"Who was on the news desk in 18?" Baxter sinks back into his chair, smoke swirling with his arm movement.

"Well, Jameson died in 30 and Smith left in 28."

"I don't care who's not here."

Effie sighs. "Well, I'm doing it by process of elimination."

"Eliminate faster. I ain't got time. And Schumann needs his story by tomorrow."

She scans the newsroom. "Pritchett."

"Get with Pritchett." Baxter stabs the air with his cigar.

Effie stares at Michael. "If you don't mind me asking, what are you working on? I was here in 18."

"An old man..."

Baxter interrupts. "Never you mind. It's not a story yet so let's get moving and find one. All right with you two?"

Not waiting for a reply, he turns his attention to the galley proofs.

Effie slips away and Michael follows.

At Effie's desk, he pauses. "What do you know about the CPLE? You saw that story about the old German guy beat up under the underpass. Were there any similar acts of violence back in 18?"

Effie nods imperceptibly, scribbles something on her pink telephone pad, and hands it to Michael.

Michael frowns at the pink slip. Why write it down instead of just telling him? He reads: '1919. German sued the CPLE.'

Stuffing the paper into his pocket, he grabs his coat, notebook, and a pack of Lucky Strikes and heads to the morgue where he's becoming all too familiar with the dank, dark space.

He doesn't know exactly what he's looking for, but he hopes he'll know it when he sees it.

* * *

He scans the shelves until he finds *1919*. If there was a lawsuit, it would be front-page news.

In the middle of January, a headline stretches across the page: "Judge Is Named In $50,000 Suit", followed by "Attorney Declares He Was Called A German Spy".

A headline of that size is usually reserved for major events of national or international significance. After scanning the article, Michael summarizes it in his notebook: George Landwehr, an Ellington attorney and former city solicitor, sued a police court judge for calling him a German spy at a CPLE meeting. He was represented by Victor Kendall, John Simpson, and DJ Matthews—the same defense attorneys in the Dictograph Case. The judge's attorneys were William Hawthorne, Howard Pitts, and Harry Evans.

After searching February and March, a headline in early April catches his eye.

Lawyer Is Killed By Auto. Victor D. Kendall. Victim of Speeding Machine.

Michael's pulse ticks up a few notches. Kendall. He recalls his grandfather's dismay at the lawyer's death—not just for his valiant defense, but because the tragedy stalled his appeal. He makes a note to look into Kendall's death later.

He pages through May. He's exhausted, thirsty, and needs a smoke. But then a headline is sprawled across the *Journal* on June 5, 1919.

CPLE MEMBERS SUED BY GOETZ. ELLINGTON MAN ASKS FOR $50,000

A voice from behind pierces the quiet. "Did you find it?"

Reflexively, Michael covers the paper with his arm and turns. "Effie! You scared the hell out of me."

She stands next to him, brushing his arm aside to see the paper. "Ah, yes. June 1919."

Michael reads aloud. "Herman Goetz alleged that on June 5, 1918, William Hawthorne, Howard Pitts, and others, banded, confederated, and conspired to terrify, humiliate, disgrace, injure and assault him."

"Is this it? The link to Haber's attack?" he whispers, looking to Effie for confirmation.

Effie shrugs. "I think the trial lasted over a year, exposing the dirty deeds of the CPLE. But don't get too excited. Goetz won, sure enough. But the jury's award? One cent. One lousy cent."

Shock registers on Michael's face.

Effie's smug smile tugs at her mouth, deepening the creases above her lip, betraying a long affair with cigarettes. "Quite the insult, isn't it?"

Michael sets down his pencil and looks at her directly. "Not sure you knew it, but my grandfather was one of the convicted men in the Dictograph case. It's personal for me. What's in it for you?"

"In addition to seeing you get a story with teeth, I have a connection to what happened back then, as well"

"What's that?"

Her eyes narrow slightly, and for a moment she appears older, harder. "I want to ferret out the people that nearly destroyed my marriage."

Michael waits, sensing there's more.

"My late husband ate up everything the CPLE fed him. Proud member, true believer. But me? I kept my mouth shut and went along because that's what wives do. To go any other way wasn't to spite the CPLE, but to put a wedge in my marriage."

She paces the tiny space, meets the wall, and turns back. "I watched him worship men who turned neighbors against each other, who made this town sick with suspicion. And I smiled and nodded because the alternative was losing him."

Michael absorbs this, her confession explaining her willingness to help. "I'm sorry, Effie."

"Don't be. He's dead now. Can't hold me hostage any longer. You just get the truth out there. Maybe then people will see what those 'patriots' really were."

Michael stares at the newspaper, wanting that cigarette more than he's wanted anything in his life.

"I've got to go. Write enough for Baxter and go home. This place is creepy."

He escorts her to the street exit. "Let me buy you lunch one day next week."

"That'd be fine. But Michael, Pritchett was a CPLE guy, and he still talks to them."

Michael frowns. "The CPLE still exists?"

"No, not like before. But Hawthorne is on the city council and the board of the Chamber of Commerce. You think what you do in this newsroom doesn't get back to him? Think again."

"Baxter?"

Effie shakes her head. "Baxter wasn't here back then. But Pritchett? He was. And he still knows who to keep happy. You say the wrong thing around him, Hawthorne will know before you stub out your cigarette."

With a swirl of her skirts and a "Ta!" Effie leaves Michael to his research.

He should go home. He's exhausted. But fifty grand? For a beating? That's no small deal.

He flips through *1919*, jotting down key information from numerous articles describing witnesses retelling violent attacks on defenseless citizens at home, at work, and in saloons. One witness said he was dragged from his shop and beaten while customers looked on. No charges were ever filed. The Goetz case stems from Hawthorne striking and humiliating him in front of patrons in a bar. While Haber wasn't attacked in the bar, the similarity is too remarkable to ignore.

After reading until his eyes water, the tiny type on yellowed paper taking its toll, he pushes the volume aside and creates an outline for the story.

Michael stares at Victor Kendall's name in his notes. Was his untimely death bad luck or something else entirely? A pit forms in his stomach. The CPLE hadn't just ruined lives, had they silenced people, too?

The parallels to the Goetz case are too sharp to ignore. Haber's attack felt like a warning. Was this just a few angry men acting on old prejudices—or was the CPLE back in everything but name?

He can't prove it yet. But the past isn't done with Ellington.

Chapter Six

She hasn't slept this poorly since her mother's funeral. Snippets of her childhood flickered through her dreams like scenes at the picture show. Her father twirling her on the tire swing in the backyard. Her mother dotting her nose with a powder puff before snapping her silver compact closed. Distorted faces of friends sticking out their tongues.

She lies in bed longer than usual avoiding the scrapbook and Mother's letter.

"Coffee," she mutters under her breath. While the pot perks, she opens the scrapbook dedicated to her father.

The front page details her father's family tree—the Kendalls immigrated from England in the early 1800s. She drifts through mementos of Becky and Victor's childhood, his marriage to her mother, Jane Adams, a pretty, young socialite. There are glimpses of their early years together followed by his accomplishments as a lawyer and statesman.

The newspaper headline announcing her father's death, pasted on the last page sends her hurtling back in time.

A dog barks somewhere down the block.

A car rumbles past.

In the distance, sounds drift toward her—the click-clack of trolley car wheels, the screech of tires, the sickening thud of the impact.

Rundell Road.

Father tugged the bell rope, and as it jerked to a stop, he stepped down from the car. She rushed to catch up, but he'd already rounded the end of the trolley. An automobile sped by on the wrong side of the road, then a sickening thump and her mother's scream.

Her mother pushed her aside and rounded the rear of the car. "Victor! Victor!"

Olivia edged toward her mother's shouts, dreading what was on the other side of the trolley car. Standing over her father's prone body, blood pooling behind his head, she fell beside him, heedless of scraped knees and torn stockings.

At the hospital, the doctors said his skull was fractured. He regained consciousness for a few moments, his eyes seeking his wife and daughter, finding them, then minutes later, he lapsed into unconsciousness and died within the hour.

In the days that followed, James Mellon, the driver, was arrested on manslaughter charges. Tried three times. Three hung juries.

Her mother's letter, the unresolved verdict, and the Dictograph clippings only sharpen her need to know what really happened.

A knock interrupts her reverie. A man clutching a bundle of fresh flowers stands on the stoop.

Appearance matters. She pauses at the mirror, adjusts her hair, pinches color into her cheeks, bites her lips, and moves to the door.

"Uncle John? What are you doing here?"

"I'm visiting my favorite person. Can't an uncle check in from time to time?"

"Yes, of course," she says, and accepts the flowers from his outstretched hands. "How did you know I was here?"

"I went to your place yesterday. A neighbor said you were at your aunt's."

Taller than her by a foot, he removes his hat, and stands in the hall, taking stock of his former partner's daughter. His bright blue eyes narrow as he nods approvingly. "It's good to see you."

"And you," Olivia replies. "Have a seat while I put these in water. Something to drink?"

"Coffee would be nice."

She returns to the parlor with the flowers in a crystal vase. "Coffee's on."

Her uncle gazes at the photographs on the mantle. "This was your graduation, wasn't it?"

" Yes, from college."

Twelve years had passed since Uncle John and Aunt Becky—the only family she had left—watched her accept her diploma.

She leaves him staring at the other photographs and returns with the coffee service.

Uncle John sips and studies her over the rim. "You seem a little out of sorts. Are you all right?"

She forces a small smile and blames it on the house. "Coming here is difficult. I've put off selling it too long."

John nods, glancing around. "Hard to come back to a place full of ghosts."

She studies her coffee, his assessment hitting close to home.

John's eyes convey his sorrow at her loss. "Becky's been gone, what, six months?"

Olivia nods. A mere half year since her aunt, her unofficial guardian, died. Six months, and she's done nothing but exist. Tears threaten.

"I'm sorry. I didn't mean—"

Sniffing, Olivia says, "No, it's fine. I suppose I'm a little on edge. But enough about me."

She turns to him, feigns a look of interest and a tone to match. She's not feeling as chipper as she sounds, but her inner voice, her mother's prompt, says to ignore her emotions and pay attention to others.

"How's Aunt Mary and the children?"

"All doing well, thank you. Sam's working at the Ellington National Bank and Delia's two boys keep her busy. Mary sends her love."

She hasn't seen him since Aunt Becky's funeral. "It's funny. I was thinking of you just yesterday."

His bushy brown eyebrows shoot up. "You were? Good timing."

Olivia makes a snap decision. She moves the coffee tray to the side table and reveals the scrapbook underneath.

John reads the inscription, smoothing a hand over the cover. "Victor."

"I found that and another with my history. Yesterday was full of trips down memory lane."

"Mind if I look?"

Over the next half hour, they exchange memories prompted by the contents. From the envelope of clippings, she extracts the headline about the seven men accused by the League and straightens it on the coffee table.

"Kids in school turned on me when Father defended these men."

"No! They did?" John's head jerks around to her, his mouth open in astonishment. "I'm sorry."

"Not your fault." Olivia empties the envelope onto the table.

Uncle John's stare is fixed. His body is still except for a jiggling knee.

She spreads the clippings over the table, inviting him to look with her at the headlines and plucks one from the pile.

"This Dictograph," she points to the newspaper. "was a big deal."

John pauses. "Yes, it was."

"Father said using this machine should have been illegal, for listening in on private conversations."

John stiffens visibly. A hand presses his knee, halting its tremor while he stares at the headline. "Victor tried to get the evidence thrown out, but the judge declared its use instrumental in ferreting out pro-German activists."

She taps the headline, "This League. Who were they?"

John rises unexpectedly from his seat, his cheeks flushed. "What's all this about, Olivia? It was a long time ago."

His reaction startles her. It's an innocent question.

"I guess I'm interested in the work Father did before he died."

He sits down beside her and pulls her into his arms. It's an awkward embrace—her head squished against his shoulder. She resists pulling away but is uncomfortable this close to him, and with no apparent reason to hug her.

The clock on the mantle chimes. John releases her.

"I have a meeting. Thank you for the coffee."

Puzzled by his sudden, urgent need to leave, she says, "Before you go, I'd like your help with something."

His eyes squint under a furrowed brow. Checking the time again, he says, "I can't stay long."

Steeling herself, she pulls the letter from her skirt pocket and holds the envelope in both hands, like an offering. "I found this."

John's eyebrows lift with interest. "What's this?" He reaches for the envelope, examining the postmark. "That's when Jane..." His voice trails off as recognition dawns.

"Read it," Olivia says and swallows.

He unfolds the letter and reads slowly, his lips moving slightly, mouthing her mother's words of warning.

"My God, Olivia." He stops reading, meets her eyes, then returns to the page. Folding the letter, he hands it to her.

"Well," Olivia asks, searching his face.

John sighs. "Oh sweetheart." His tone is gentle, almost pitying. "Your mother was...she was so broken after Victor died. This shows how much pain she was in."

"What if she was right?"

His head shakes. His features soften. "Olivia, no. I was there. I knew your father's work better than anyone. If there had been any danger, any threat, I would have known. An accident, pure and simple. A man and his family out for a Sunday drive who stupidly chose to pass the trolley instead of waiting for it to move along."

"This mattered to Mother. I know she wasn't always in her right mind, but this is different. Can you help me find the truth? Was his death more than an accident?"

John clutches his keys tight, whitening his knuckles. He edges toward the door.

"That's foolishness, Olivia." His tone sharpens—not in shock, but in warning. "What do you hope to gain? It won't bring your father back or your mother, for that matter."

Olivia fixes an intense gaze on her father's partner, conveying the seriousness of her proposal.

"I wish I could, but I have a heavy case load. An associate quit, and I'm stretched to the gills."

He leans in and Olivia offers her cheek to say good-bye.

The clock chimes again, and Uncle John slides his hat on.

"Don't take that letter too seriously." He steps out the door. "Nothing good comes of digging up the past."

She forces a wan smile watching him get in his car and wave merrily, as if they'd had coffee and a nice chat, not the edgy conversation questioning her mother's sanity and dismissing Olivia's concerns.

She holds the letter against her heart, its words echoing in her mind. Maybe Uncle John is right. Maybe she should let it go.

In the parlor, she straightens the clippings. As she slides the letter back into its envelope, her fingers linger. Not all messes can be tidied up and put away. Some demand to be dealt with.

She's been frozen too long. Being here, in this house, is stirring up something she can't ignore. Maybe it's not about letting go, but about figuring out what still matters. Maybe this—this search for answers—is its own kind of cleaning, not of things, but of the cobwebs that have kept her from moving forward.

She reads the news article again. There's a faint pencil line underneath William Hawthorne's name.

A chill prickles at the base of her spine. There's something here. The county attorney is the leader of the League. Isn't that a conflict of interest?

Olivia exhales, steadies herself. "I will take it seriously, Uncle John," she says aloud.

She doesn't know what she'll find—but she knows she can't pretend her mother's letter doesn't matter.

Chapter Seven

Michael sits in Baxter's office, rubbing a clammy palm along his thigh. Across the desk, the chief reads Michael's article aloud, his usual method of deciding what goes to print and what hits the trash.

"Elderly Man Recovering from Attack. Wilhelm Haber, of East Tenth Street, remains hospitalized after an assault Tuesday night..."

Michael has it memorized after three revisions, the details still fresh: the underpass, the slurs, the faceless men who ran. He holds his breath when Baxter gets to the second half—the part that ties the present to the past.

Baxter continues, "In 1918..." Then he trails off, going silent, skimming the lines.

Here it comes. Michael waits as Baxter goes silent, eyes skimming the lines about the Citizen's Patriotic League. The raids. The beatings. The name: Hawthorne.

Baxter grunts. "Interesting."

Michael sits up straighter, a fragile flicker of hope catching.

"I get the parallels," Baxter says, setting the paper down, "but you're drawing conclusions. Cut the name of the group. Leave Hawthorne out. You'll stir up a hornet's nest."

Anger and heat crawl up his neck. "You're asking me to print half a story."

"No," Baxter says, pencil already marking up the page, "I'm asking you to print one that keeps this paper running. Fix it and have it back to me by five."

Frustration knots in his chest. He snatches the paper off the desk.

Baxter leans back, arms crossed over his middle. "You want to take a swing at a city man like Hawthorne? Fine. Bring me proof."

Not what he wants. But it's all he gets.

* * *

An hour later, the story skewered and approved, he digs through his notes and sketches an outline of who he should interview. Hawthorne tops the list, followed by Albert Stone, the state's district attorney, and John Simpson, co-defense attorney with Victor Kendall.

As he drains his umpteenth cup of coffee, Tom Pritchett, a balding, wiry guy with a pencil-thin mustache, drops himself unceremoniously on Michael's desk—right on top of his notebook.

He makes a mental note to tear out that page. And the next two.

Pritchett takes a long pull from his mug, then sets it on the edge of Michael's desk. Rumor has it he likes his coffee with a splash of something stronger.

"Chief said you wanted to talk to me."

"Yeah, since you were here during that period, I was hoping you'd have a few ideas on how the attack on an elderly German man last week might be connected to what happened in 1918. Witness said anti-German slurs were used."

"None I can think of." Pritchett sips, eyeing him over the rim. "That was a long time ago."

He thinks Pritchett would at least ask what it had to do with now, but he's already shutting him down.

Michael hands him the paper with the Haber attack story. "See this?"

Pritchett takes it, skims it, and tosses it back onto Michael's desk. "So?"

"No connection?"

"Nope," Pritchett says, peering down his nose.

"I guess the Chief was mistaken."

When Pritchett finally stands, Michael lifts the notebook between thumb and forefinger. Without ceremony, he tears out the poor, abused pages—and a few more for good measure—as Pritchett watches, oblivious.

The senior reporter's voice is low, deliberate. "You're digging in places better left untouched, Schumann. Your curiosity will get you the wrong kind of attention. I'll let the Chief know I advised restraint."

Michael snorts. "You don't get to disapprove."

"I've been here longer than you've been alive," Pritchett says. "My opinion carries weight."

Pritchett lays his hands flat on the desk—a man preparing to deliver unwelcome news. "If you were smart, you'd know that in this business, men like Hawthorne can be your friend just as easy as your enemy."

"Oh? And why's that?"

"He's got ties to everyone who matters. Built a career on keeping order—with a firm hand and a long memory. If you had half a brain, you'd make sure you were on his good side."

The fact that Pritchett is rattled enough to defend Hawthorne means something. Michael lets the old man's words settle, then offers a slow, easy grin. He leans over the mug and sniffs. The rumors are true.

"Do you take your orders from Hawthorne, or does he just send you a note with your morning brew?"

Michael's thoughts shift between the Haber assault and the Dictograph Case, looking for a connection. His instinct says the CPLE's at the center of it—but he still has to prove it.

Before he'd graduated to junior reporter, his mentor, a grizzled journalist who'd seen it all, told him this. "If you want to uncover the truth, go straight to the source. But keep your intentions under wraps—don't let them see you coming."

The source is Hawthorne. That's his next move. Before he can change his mind, he approaches Effie, who keeps a list of frequently called numbers.

"City Hall," he says under his breath.

Effie scribbles the number and hands it to Michael. "I hope you know what you're doing."

"I don't." His lopsided grin is returned with a *cool gaze and a slight shake of her head.*

He dials the number. Posing as a reporter doing an exposé on prominent citizens, the secretary offers an appointment for tomorrow morning at nine. Michael drops the phone receiver into the cradle, the secretary's polite confirmation still ringing in his ears.

Interviewing William Hawthorne is equal parts thrilling and unnerving. His goal is simple: catch him at his own game and hope he admits the CPLE is behind the anti-German violence.

It's a long shot. But if Hawthorne talks—even just a little—it might be enough to get Baxter to listen.

Chapter Eight

Uncle John's visit unsettles her.

After Father's death, it was John her mother turned to—for legal advice, for comfort, for a port in the storm. If her mother had shared her suspicions about the accident with him, then he'd just lied. And if she hadn't? Perhaps she wasn't sure he could be trusted.

Either way, Olivia is wary.

Her mother didn't have the means to investigate what happened—not alone. She had to have had help. Olivia remembers DJ Matthews, one of her father's closest friends. He may have insight into why her mother thought something was wrong.

She finds his number in Aunt Becky's address book. On the third ring, a woman picks up.

"Matthews' residence."

"I'm looking for DJ Matthews."

"May I ask who's calling?"

"This is Olivia Kendall."

"Olivia! Of course. This is Cynthia—DJ's wife. Do you remember me?"

Olivia searches the corners of her memory and finds a woman in a tailored dress with a loud laugh and a flower pinned to her shoulder. "Yes, I remember. Nice to hear your voice, Mrs. Matthews."

"It's been so long. I was sorry to hear about Becky."

"I'm staying at her house for the summer while I prepare to sell it."

"Well, take care of yourself, dear. Let me get DJ."

The line goes quiet, and Olivia is left with the tick of the kitchen clock and the hum of the telephone line. A minute later, DJ's voice comes through, deep and familiar.

"Olivia! I can't believe it's you."

"Hello, Mr. Matthews. It's been a while."

"DJ, please. How are you?"

They trade pleasantries, the kind that fill time and mean little.

"So, what brings you to me after all these years?" he asks.

She hesitates, then says, "I'm looking into my father's death."

Silence. Then a single word, carefully measured. "Oh."

"I wanted to ask you about—"

He cuts her off. "It was an accident, Olivia."

The words are flat. Controlled. No room for questions.

"A sad one. I'm sure you still miss him."

She does. And her mother too. But that's not why she called.

"I'm not sure what you want from me," DJ says, the warmth draining from his voice.

She pushes past her nerves. The words rush out like a creek after a thunderstorm. "I have reason to believe his death wasn't an accident."

Another pause. Then muffled voices, the faint click of a closing door, and a breath drawn slow and sharp, comes over the line.

"Did you hear me?"

"I heard you," he says. "And you need to stop."

There it was. The chill. The warning. The same quiet threat she heard from John.

But she's not stupid. "Don't you think it's convenient he was hit during the Dictograph appeal? I'd bet anything his death derailed the defense."

He laughs, but there's no humor in it. "That's your theory? Don't be ridiculous. You're chasing ghosts. There was a trial. A confession. Witnesses. The man admitted to reckless driving. That's it. There's nothing left to find."

But his insistence only sharpens her doubt.

"I see," she says, though she doesn't.

"One more question," she adds.

He exhales, long and slow.

"If everyone believed it was an accident, why didn't my mother?"

This time, the pause is longer. Longer than it should've been. When he speaks, each word is deliberate.

"Olivia. Let. It. Go."

She doesn't respond. Just lowers the receiver back into the cradle.

This wasn't the DJ she remembered—the man who used to stay too late at card games, laughing at Father's jokes. This DJ clearly doesn't want her digging.

Her eyes sting. Is she chasing shadows? Was it only grief that drove her mother to believe anything but the truth?

Olivia can't shake her doubt. Her gut tells her something is off.

She spills the envelope of clippings onto the table—blaring headlines and trial summaries dressed up for the spectators who couldn't get inside the courtroom. The victims' families are never mentioned. But they existed. They must have been devastated.

She'll find them and see if they'll talk to her. Maybe someone has answers to the questions circling in her mind.

Still, Olivia won't rush. She's methodical. Careful. She jots down names—lawyers, defendants, witnesses—anyone who might hold a piece of the truth.

In the phone directory, she finds about half of them. She circles one.

William Hawthorne. City attorney. Leader of the CPLE.

If there's a thread to pull, it likely runs through him. She doesn't know him, but she has a strong sense that trusting him would be risky.

She drafts a plan—an excuse to see him. Something legal and plausible. Settling Aunt Becky's estate will work.

Her finger hovers over the rotary dial before she begins to turn it.

She tells herself it's just a conversation, but she's fooling herself.

The only way forward is going around the people who want her to stop.

Chapter Nine

Michael reads the Haber story on the front page. Exactly as he'd written it. Just the facts. No mention of Hawthorne or the League.

He needs to turn his meeting with the City Solicitor from the fake prominent citizen profile angle into drawing out Hawthorne's attitude about Germans in present-day Ellington. If he buys it, he might let something slip. If not, the door slams shut.

Waiting at Effie's desk as she prepares his assignments for the day, Michael shifts his weight, foot to foot, and fidgets with his tie. She hands over five stories—routine beats, nothing he can't cover after he meets Hawthorne.

Her gaze sweeps the newsroom, left and right. "You know he's got a reputation for being anti-everything. Takes an opposite stance just to cause a stir. Voted down the bus rate increase that really ticked off the commissioner."

Michael nods. "I've heard him called the stormy petrel."

A sly smile crosses her face. "Ruffle his feathers. See if he squawks."

* * *

Michael follows the secretary into Hawthorne's office. The ancient, stern, and unreadable woman leaves him no opening for even a complimentary lie. You never know when a disgruntled office worker is willing to spill the beans on their boss.

The office is paneled in dark wood, floor to ceiling—the kind that swallows light. A spartan desk sits angled in a corner, like a judge's bench more than a work area.

The attorney rises and extends a hand.

"William Hawthorne."

"Michael Schumann."

Michael grips the hand, expecting the usual formality, but Hawthorne's pressure tightens—a display of dominance. Mid-fifties, average height and stout, the man stands proud and ramrod straight, gesturing to the chair in front of the desk.

Bookshelves line one wall, windows on another, and behind Hawthorne, a large portrait of the room's inhabitant hangs in a gilt frame. It portrays a younger version: dark hair, gray at the temples, square jaw, and a Roman nose above lips pressed into a diplomatic line. The artist portrayed a man who stood for justice, likely around the time he was County Attorney and leader of the Citizen's Patriotic League.

Michael sits, legs crossed at the knee, his standard position for interviewing so his target can tell he's genuinely interested in what he has to say.

"So, how's Baxter these days?" Hawthorne leans back in his chair. "Haven't seen him in a while."

Michael keeps his face neutral, but inside, a thread of unease spools. How well did his boss know Hawthorne? And more importantly, how much of this interview would make it back to his editor before he was ready?

"Doing well. He put you first on the list for this series of articles."

The lie is smooth. But if Hawthorne says anything to Baxter...

"I have a series of questions prepared so I can maintain consistency between your interview and the others."

"Who else do you have in mind?" Hawthorne wants to know what kind of company he'll be keeping in the *Journal*.

"Mayor Cushing and a few others. As we haven't contacted him yet, I hope you'll keep that in confidence."

Hawthorne's smile is radiant. "My lips are sealed."

"Ready?" Michael asks, his throat dry, tapping his pencil on his notebook, hoping Hawthorne doesn't detect his nervousness.

"Could you walk me through your early years—how you became an attorney and which offices you've held?"

Hawthorne is all too happy to describe his climb up the ladder, naming men who supported him along the way.

"And you've been Ellington City Solicitor twice?"

"Yes, but the terms were not sequential as I was this district's State Attorney from 1914 to 1922."

He's arrived at the period he's most interested in. "Must have been quite exciting during the war years."

Hawthorne pops forward, lays his forearms on the desk, and his face lights up like he's been given an award.

"You know, I've been fighting German influence in this state since I was a young man. Back when I was starting my career, Otto Mueller, a German politician nearly destroyed this state. Corruption, back-door deals, even violence. Got away with murder—literally. That's when I learned what happens when you let the wrong people gain political power. As county attorney under the Sedition Act, I had real authority, and I wasn't about to let Ellington make the same mistakes. Did you know it was because of me that we could claim Ellington 100% American?"

Pride swells in the man—a memory treated like a medal. Tension coils in Michael's gut. He needs to keep the ruse alive. "What's 100% American?"

Hawthorne leans back in his chair, tents his hands, and speaks over his fingertips. "When we did what was necessary to rid this town of everything German and ensure everyone supported the war. This county was number one in the state for raising money through Liberty Bonds and Stamps."

"I was in the Boy Scouts. Sold thrift stamps." Michael hadn't meant to reveal any of his own personal background.

Hawthorne slaps an open palm on the desk. "There you go! Well done."

Michael lets the silence stretch just long enough to see if Hawthorne will offer more. When he doesn't, he moves in with the next question.

"You mentioned a thousand citizens. That's quite a large group. I think I read that you were one of its leaders."

Hawthorne nods. "Naturally, other respected citizens joined me—we held rallies, invited important men to speak, raised money, and I personally paid visits to pro-Germans. Ah! Those were the days when the law helped fight the war here at home."

Michael's pen stills on the page. Hawthorne is congratulating himself—for threats, intimidation, maybe worse. Michael needs a moment to recover from the man's self-aggrandizement.

"May I have a glass of water?"

"Yes of course." Hawthorne pushes a button on a box on his desk and speaks into it. "Grace, can you bring us some water?"

The secretary responds promptly.

Hawthorne taps the box.

"This is how we caught a bunch of seditionists back in Eighteen. A Dictograph. Much sleeker now, but same principle. Transmits sound from room to room. Wonderful invention."

Michael eyes the device.

His pulse ticks up. Clara had described the one from the shoe shop—small enough to hide in a grandfather clock.

This one is the size of a bread box. Modern. Efficient.

Dangerous all the same.

He swallows, shifting his focus back to Hawthorne. "Baxter just yells."

Grace enters the room and places water glasses on the desk. "Is that all, Mr. Hawthorne?"

"Yes, thank you."

Michael sips the water, checks his notes, and dives into the deep end—the real reason he's here.

"Tell me about the Goetz case," Michael says, baiting Hawthorne into a potential parallel with the attack on Wilhelm Haber. "You assaulted him in a saloon, he sued for fifty thousand dollars, but the judge awarded him a penny."

Hawthorne is all smiles. "The jury gave him the win—I did strike him. But once it came out he was tied to pro-German activity, the judge reduced the damages to a single cent. A just reward for a dirty Hun, don't you think?"

Michael stiffens, the words hitting him like a slap—the same slur hurled at Wilhelm Haber. Leaning back, as if the insult means nothing at all, he schools his face into a mask.

He'd come here to bait Hawthorne into a mistake. Now, with one rhetorical question, Hawthorne turns the tables. Or is he just full of himself?

The attorney's hands rest on his stomach, as if he's just finished a satisfying meal.

Michael slips his notebook into his pocket. Doesn't need it for his parting shot.

"Last question."

"Fire away." Hawthorne loves talking about himself.

"Is the Citizens Patriotic League of Ellington still in existence, and are you still their leader?" Michael locks eyes with the man.

Hawthorne's jovial smile fades. "So, what if it is?"

Michael breathes in and delivers his response on the exhale. "Because beating up men for being German or saying something considered un-American is against the law now—unlike **when** you and your henchmen used the Sedition Act as a cover for fear tactics to achieve your 100% agenda. Or did you assault people because you liked it?"

Hawthorne peers down at Michael. "You do read the news, don't you? Being a newspaper man and all. With Hitler rearming Germany and stirring up trouble, anyone who doesn't stand with America is against it. The tactics used in 18 should work again."

"So, you're admitting the CPLE is behind the attack on an elderly man for no other crime than being German?"

"Ah. Now, I see. That report in the *Journal* this morning. Before you get too judgmental, I'll remind you that pro-German sentiment, especially with Hitler's rise and an increase in German immigration, is detrimental to this town. We must remain vigilant."

Michael knows that's a lie—immigration from Germany plummeted since the Depression—but he keeps his expression neutral.

"So, the League is alive and well."

Hawthorne shrugs, a slow, indifferent movement, as if the answer doesn't matter.

Michael stands. "Thank you for your time."

Hawthorne's eyebrows shoot up. "That's all? Don't you want to hear about the railroad case, or the new businesses bringing jobs I've supported?"

Michael tilts his head. "Wouldn't that contradict your reputation?"

Hawthorne's brows lift. "And what reputation is that?"

Michael allows a beat of silence, then smirks. "Anti-everything. That's what they say at City Hall, isn't it?"

Hawthorne exhales through his nose—half laugh, half scoff. "Anti-everything," he repeats, turning the words over. "Let me tell you something, Mr. Schumann. People like to whine when a man refuses to follow the herd. They mistake independence for obstruction, conviction for controversy."

The stormy petrel moniker fits.

Hawthorne spreads his hands. "Tell me—if I were truly 'anti-everything,' would this city have a functioning streetcar line? A new courthouse to hold our little meeting in? I'm a key figure steering Ellington through the worst economic crisis in a generation."

Michael gives a slow nod. "And yet, somehow, they're still saying it."

Hawthorne's lips press together, for a second. Then, his expression smooths. "People love a villain, Mr. Schumann. I don't mind playing the part."

Michael lets the words sit between them. That much, he could believe.

Michael reaches across the desk, hand extended. "I've taken enough of your time. If I need anything else, I'll call."

The briefest twitch pulls at Hawthorne's cheek—something he wants to say but thinks better of it.

Hawthorne's handshake is firm, practiced, political. Michael returns it briefly—acknowledgment, nothing more.

Hawthorne presses the button on the Dictograph. "Grace, have my next appointment come in."

And all the while, the Dictograph has been listening.

As he passes the secretary, without lifting her head, she says, "People like Mr. Hawthorne sacrificed to protect the rest of us."

Of course she believes that. She's one of thousands who rationalized the CPLE's actions as serving the greater good.

Michael steps into the corridor, still thinking about Grace's words, when he bumps into someone.

A woman utters, "Oof," and papers scatter between them onto the floor.

"I'm sorry," Michael says. The woman apologizes at the same time. Both bend to the floor and in the process bump heads.

"Now I've really done it," Michael says.

The woman, rubbing her forehead, laughs.

"My fault," she says, already crouching to collect newspaper clippings—dozens of them, loose and yellow with age—fallen from what he now recognizes as a scrapbook. The kind his grandmother kept.

He gets on his knees and gathers the papers into a stack. Michael's eyes lock onto a clipping.

WARNER IS FOUND GUILTY

He doesn't speak. Just stares at the headline as she places the rest in the scrapbook like someone preserving pressed flowers.

His mind ticks. Who is she? Why does she have this? He wants to ask, but the words stick.

Instead, he hands over the clippings, his fingers lingering a second longer than they should.

Her blue eyes meet his briefly before she hugs the book, pushing stray clippings into place.

Hawthorne's office door flies open. Grace peers down at them. "Everything all right? I heard a scuffle."

"I ran into her and made a mess of things," Michael confesses and stands, offering his hand to assist the young woman.

"I was too intent on finding the office and didn't see you," she says.

Grace looks them both up and down. "Doesn't look like anyone is worse for wear. You must be Miss Kendall."

"Yes, I'm here to see Mr. Hawthorne."

Michael assesses the petite yet sturdy woman. She carries herself with a quiet confidence—refined but not pretentious.

"Good day, Mr. Schumann," Grace says and steps inside.

Michael tips his hat and waits until the door closes on a woman who seems to matter somehow—though all he can point to is his grandfather's name on the clipping's headline.

"Miss Kendall? As in Victor Kendall? What the hell?" he mutters as he jogs down six flights, mind racing, and barrels into the morning sun to finish his assignments.

Chapter Ten

Arriving at William Hawthorne's office a few minutes late for her appointment, her heels click sharp and fast on the steps as Olivia hurries to the sixth floor of City Hall. The long corridor stretches ahead, lined with frosted glass doors, numbers painted on the windows.

She scans the numbers as she walks. 616... 618... 622. She stops short, frowning.

No 620. She spins slowly in place, scanning both sides of the corridor. Nothing.

She turns back, rummaging through her handbag for the scrap of paper with the address. She's still searching when—wham. Her shoulder collides with something solid, knocking the air from her lungs.

The scrapbook slips from under her arm and thuds at her feet scattering clippings across the green marble floor. Surprised, she freezes.

"Oh," she exclaims. Without thinking, she bends down, and her forehead connects with his. Recoiling, she rubs the point of impact above her eyebrow.

The man is already kneeling, one knee planted on the marble, gathering the clippings into a neat pile. His suit jacket rides up over his shoulders, moving with quick, practiced motions—not flustered, just focused.

Olivia crouches to help but freezes when she sees what's in his hand. The headline she plans to show Hawthorne.

He doesn't move. Doesn't blink. Eyes fixed on the headline.

"May I have that?" she asks.

He finally looks up. Dark eyes. A furrow between his brows. His gaze flicks from the headline to the book in her hands—then to her face.

"Sorry," he mutters, handing it over.

His touch lingers a second too long, her fingers tingling as she withdraws the clipping.

The spell is broken when Hawthorne's secretary pokes her head out, fretting over the commotion. As Mr. Schumann turns to leave, Olivia steps into the office, resisting the urge to glance over her shoulder.

* * *

Olivia perches in the chair across from Hawthorne's desk, the scrapbook on her lap. He takes a seat, wearing authority like a well-fitted suit, hands folded with practiced ease. She wonders how many juries his posture sways.

"You're here about an endowment?" he asks, flipping through his appointment book.

"Yes. A small one. In memory of my aunt. Becky Kendall. I brought her will if that helps." She pulls it from her handbag and passes it to him.

He places a pince-nez on his nose. "Give me a moment to read through this."

As Hawthorne's attention focuses on the papers, Olivia studies his office. The walls are crowded with framed accomplishments—plaques, citations, and trophies, including one that commemorates twenty years of service on the Chamber of Commerce Board. A photograph is perched on a bookshelf. One of Hawthorne shaking hands with a man in military uniform, both smiling under an American flag.

Hawthorne taps the document. "There's nothing extraordinary here. A few bequests to charities, a few debts to clear, but the rest is yours. You mentioned an endowment. Have you decided where the funds would go?"

"I'm still considering. Perhaps a scholarship at the high school. Or something for the Ellington library. I'm preparing the house for sale now, so this seemed like a good time to explore my options." A convenient truth—she hadn't made much progress, too consumed by the past to pack it up just yet.

"If you keep the house and make an endowment, the tax implications might work in your favor," Hawthorne counsels.

"Oh, I knew you were the right person to help me." She's playing the kind of woman who needs a man to sort things out for her. Distasteful, but necessary.

"It's my pleasure. I can arrange for the transfer of monies to the charities and start the endowment process. There are a few documents you'll need to sign so I can act on your behalf."

"That's fine."

He presses a button on a box. "Grace, I need two power-of-attorney forms."

"Yes sir," comes the clipped reply.

Hawthorne clasps his hands together. "The name Kendall is familiar. I knew an attorney with that name."

He's connected the dots. She tilts her head just enough to let him think he's clever. "Well, that would be my father. Victor Kendall."

Hawthorne slaps the desk as if he's won a prize. "I knew it!"

"I'm not sure what you're happy about. He's dead, you know."

His self-satisfaction flickers out like a pinched candle flame. "Yes, I realize. It's been some time."

"1919," she says. Funny how pain refuses to age.

"An automobile accident, I believe." Hawthorne eyes the ceiling as if the answer is embedded there.

Gulping, she manages to keep her voice even and steady, though her insides are the exact opposite.

"Killed when the driver passed the trolley on the wrong side." She pays attention to Hawthorne's reaction, hoping it might reveal his participation in the accident.

"Ah yes. Very sad. A well-respected attorney and citizen."

Grace interrupts their recollections and hands him the requested forms.

Hawthorne spends a few minutes filling out the forms while Olivia opens the book on her lap. Luckily, the clipping on top is the one she intends to show Hawthorne—the same one Mr. Schumann scrutinized.

She lays it on the desk and scoots it forward until his head pops up.

"My father defended Warner."

Hawthorne puts his pen aside and pulls the article toward him. "Yes, he did. He lost, but there was nothing your father could have done."

Olivia tilts her head to the side, channeling every ounce of her debutante training—coquettish and innocent. "Why is that do you think?"

Hawthorne slides the clipping over to Olivia. "The evidence was overwhelming." He taps on the box next to him, the one used to call Grace. "This is how we caught them red-handed engaging in illegal conversations, reading from banned newspapers and singing German songs."

"Singing was against the law?" Her voice is quiet, but sharp. Her gaze flicks to the intercom on his desk. So much power in such a small machine.

"Shame it's not the same these days." Hawthorne muses, voice edged with regret.

Olivia is interested in the workings of the Dictograph but asking questions about that won't get her what she wants. "I understand that when my father died, he was handling a number of cases where the," she pauses and taps the clipping for effect, "Citizens Patriotic League were involved."

Hawthorne leans forward, a gleam in his eye that makes her harden her resolve not to be intimidated.

"Why is everyone interested in that case and the CPLE today? Is there something I should know?"

Olivia connects the man in the hall staring at the clipping with Hawthorne's comment. She's come on the heels of this Schumann person asking about the CPLE.

Her shrug is meant to throw him off track. "I just wanted to understand whether your connection to the CPLE had anything to do with my father's death."

Hawthorne shoots up from behind his desk, his chair nearly tipping.

"Young lady!" His voice cracks like a whip.

Olivia can't help but flinch.

The attorney's face is florid, his outburst rattling the windowpanes. "What are you after?"

Her pulse jumps, but she holds his gaze, weighing her next move.

"You were the state's attorney and leader of the League at the same time. That's a conflict of interest, wouldn't you say?"

The implication hits home. Hawthorne's face hardens like stone, but the purple flush creeping up his throat betrays him.

"I upheld the law," he says curtly. "That was my job."

"No," Olivia corrects, her voice steady, "your job was to enforce the law fairly. Instead, you built cases designed to convict men you already decided were guilty. You weren't serving justice. You were serving your agenda."

Hawthorne rears back as if struck, then his voice drops to a dangerous rumble. "I did my job—prosecuting men who broke the law, men who were a danger to this country."

"According to who?" Olivia challenges.

A blood vessel in his neck bulges. His hands ball into fists and he circles the desk, closing the space between them. He leans in, arms folded across his chest—a forced show of ease. Control.

"I've had enough of your charade and accusations." His voice lowers, takes on a calmer edge. Measured. Dangerous. "It's time you leave."

Keeping her gaze on Hawthorne, she slowly slides the clipping off the desk and lays it on top of the scrapbook. She rises, tucks the book under her arm, and turns toward the door. But Hawthorne doesn't move.

He's blocking her escape.

Her eyes lock onto his. Unflinching. Unyielding.

She waits.

A beat.

Another.

At last, Hawthorne steps aside.

Her pulse pounding in her ears, she steps to the door. She's won this round—a vulnerability revealed. But something in his eyes says this isn't over.

As she reaches for the door handle, she turns. He's staring at her, mouth agape—as if she's spoken a language he no longer understands.

A smirk tugs at her lips. "I won't be needing those forms. I wouldn't do business with you if you were the last attorney on earth."

Without waiting for a response, she exits, nods to Grace, and, cradling the scrapbook under her arm, slips from the office into the hallway.

Only when the door clicks shut behind her does she breathe.

Her footsteps echo in the corridor, matching her heart hammering in her chest. Had she gone too far?

A chill creeps up her spine. She may have awoken a beast—a man who believes he's powerful, though she suspects he's not.

But belief is a dangerous thing.

Hawthorne clings to the past, to a time when punishing a man for singing in German was as easy as flipping a switch.

And men like that don't go down without a fight.

But neither will she.

Chapter Eleven

Hawthorne didn't deny it. Didn't even flinch. Said the words with pride—like 1918 had been a civic duty, not a stain. Michael exits City Hall, bound and determined to expose Hawthorne.

The Kendall woman with all those clippings has him rattled. Something about her sticks—the clarity in her eyes, the way she clutched the scrapbook, like a lifeline. Her name. Kendall. Same as his grandfather's lawyer. And her presence at Hawthorne's office—surely not coincidence.

He considers waiting for her to emerge from the building, but he's got other assignments and this explosive report to write.

By early afternoon, he's back in the office, prepared to write the full story. He has facts and a quote from the City Attorney to anchor it. The only thing that niggles at him is the pretense he used to get the interview. He'll worry about that once Baxter sees what he's got.

Hawthorne's voice rings in his ears. "We must remain vigilant." Not a warning—more like a threat dressed up as patriotism.

Rolling the single sheet from the typewriter, he proofreads it.

The Citizens Patriotic League: Still at Work?

When Wilhelm Haber, an elderly German American of East Tenth Street, was assaulted under the Eleventh Street underpass, police initially classified the attack as harassment, likely the work of local youths. But when witnesses confirmed the assailants hurled anti-German slurs before fleeing, the nature of the crime took on a more chilling dimension—one that echoes the violence that gripped Ellington in 1918.

During the Great War, the Citizens Patriotic League of Ellington (CPLE) positioned itself as a watchdog against perceived disloyalty, targeting German Americans under the guise of protecting national security. The group's activities ranged from public shaming to outright physical assaults—acts that went largely unpunished due to the fervor of wartime nationalism.

Now, twenty years later, the question remains: Has the League truly faded into history, or is it quietly re-emerging?

In a statement to the *Ellington Journal*, City Solicitor William Hawthorne, once a vocal leader of the group, defended the principle behind the CPLE's actions. "Anyone who speaks against America must be held accountable."

Hawthorne did not comment on whether the CPLE was directly involved in the attack on Haber, nor did he denounce the heinousness of the assault.

The CPLE has been dormant since the early 1920s, but there is growing concern that the League—or those who share its beliefs—may be emboldened once more.

The Ellington police have no suspects at this time.

Satisfied, he hands it to Effie, who reviews reports before Baxter gets them. As she reads the title, her pencil-thin eyebrows shoot up, nearly disappearing into her hairline. "You got guts, Schumann."

He shrugs. "It needs to be told."

Shaking her head, Effie adds it to the folder for Baxter's review. "The petrel was stormy." She doesn't sound disapproving—just cautious.

An hour later, Effie taps on his desk, getting his attention without alerting other staff members. She jerks her head toward Baxter's office. "He wants to see you."

"Good or bad?" Michael asks, stubbing out his cigarette.

"I advise you shut the door." Effie's eyes are soft and focused on Michael, her mouth curved in a closed-lip smile.

"Shit."

Taking Effie's advice, he closes the door and sits before the chief whose head is lowered over the article as if his vision is impaired.

It's bad.

Michael waits, unwilling to open the conversation. There's nothing in his report that's false or without substantiation, unless you count his method of obtaining Hawthorne's quotes.

"I can't run this," Baxter raises his head, meeting Michael's eyes. "It might be true, but Hawthorne and the owner go way back. Thick as thieves."

"You should have been there, Chief! The man is so arrogant, his ego walked in five minutes before he did."

Baxter's eyebrows rise.

"Why can't you run it?" It's his finest work in years—well-researched, solid footing, a story that means something to the folks in Ellington. And to the Haber family.

Baxter presses his fingers to his temples. "You don't think I want to print this?" He slams the paper on his desk. "It's not that simple, Schumann. You don't go after a man like that without consequences."

His heart racing, Michael clenches his fists on his knees. "It's a fact that Germans were targeted in 1918."

"Doesn't mean it's happening again." He picks up the article and offers it to Michael. "And you've got no real proof."

Baxter's hand trembles, as if he's regretting his decision—but the pressure is clear.

Frustrated, Michael yanks the copy from Baxter. "I guess I misunderstood when you said to go after the story."

"You must have," Baxter mutters as Michael leaves the office.

Michael slaps the article on his desk, fingers curled into fists beside it. Pritchett leans against the wall, a satisfied smirk playing on his lips.

"What are you looking at?" Michael shouts across the room.

"You. Trying to be noble and all. You still learning how things work around here?"

Pritchett. Hawthorne's biggest fan. Baxter's sudden reversal. It reeks of outside influence.

They can kill the story. But not the truth. Not if he has anything to say about it.

And he'll turn over every rock, dig through every lie, until he finds a way to make them pay attention.

Chapter Twelve

"What a mess!" Olivia mutters, spreading the jumbled clippings on the dining room table as she sorts them chronologically, just as they were before she bumped into Mr. Schumann.

She needs order. A timeline. Patterns. Clues.

To what, she's not sure.

From her school briefcase, she grabs a notebook and writes TO DO across the top.

Her first task: Find out who that Schumann guy is.

As she picks through the news articles, frail, yellowed, and torn, an undercurrent of bias emerges. The *Journal*'s headlines are brazenly anti-German, echoing Hawthorne's own rhetoric. Is there a connection? Did the owners and editors influence the story content and flavor?

She adds another task: Was the *Ellington Journal* a propaganda puppet?

After a while, she has a list of people to contact. The three who were convicted are her top priority.

She checks the phone book.

Klare. No listing.

Vogel. No listing.

Maybe dead or moved away.

Warner. No residence, but a Warner Shoe Shop is listed. She jots down the address in South Ellington.

She underlines the shoe shop three times. She'll start there.

* * *

The next morning, with the scrapbook in her briefcase, she waits at the stop for a southbound streetcar. The ride is punctuated by passengers embarking and disembarking every few blocks until they are south of downtown where businesses fade into a residential area. At Schmitty's Corner, she descends from the car and watches the conductor and attendant turn the car one hundred eighty degrees until it faces north.

She's never ridden this far before and the area is unfamiliar. On the side of a drugstore, she spots a street sign, Eastern Avenue. The intersection is busy. Cars, pedestrians, bicycles, and motorcycles jostle for position to go in their intended direction. It's with trepidation that she steps gingerly into the street. Ever since her father's accident, she takes extra care when crossing the street.

Reaching the other side, she's in front of the Union Federal Bank of Ellington, its double doors facing the intersection.

Recalling a detail from the clippings, she heads toward the back of the building. Gold letters on the last window identify it as the Warner Shoe Shop.

She stares at the shop, imagining what it must have been like. Before the Dictograph, the trials, the convictions. Friends discussing life, their families, the war.

Exhaling, she opens the door, a bell tinkling above her as she steps across the threshold.

The interior is a welcome respite from the noon sunshine. A well-worn counter divides the shop in half. A wall of cubbies stretches across the back wall and with few exceptions are filled with shoes and bulky packages wrapped in brown paper and tied with string.

She surveys the cramped space. How had all those men met here? It's hardly large enough for a handful.

She doesn't belong here—it's as if she's stepped into someone else's memory.

"Can I help you?" A female voice startles her from behind.

Olivia turns; her face red as if caught in a crime.

"Hello," Olivia says.

A woman with brown hair pulled into a severe bun stands behind the counter, a leather apron covering her blouse. Olivia peers over the woman's shoulder searching for the shop owner.

"Cat got your tongue?" the woman says, and leans her elbows on the counter, a smile turning up the corners of her generous lips.

Olivia's shoulders loosen—something about her kind, teasing eyes settles her. She laughs. "I suppose so. I'm Olivia Kendall. I was hoping to speak to Mr. Warner."

The woman's smile fades, and her eyebrows knit over a freckle-spattered nose. "He's not here."

"I see." Olivia frowns, disappointed. "When will he return?"

The woman's eyes narrow, her tone sharpens. "What's your business with him?"

"I," Olivia falters, then exhales. "There I am again. That darn cat."

"He died a few years ago." The woman lets her off the hook, then adds, "I'm his granddaughter."

"I'm sorry he's dead." Olivia gasps and her fist covers her mouth. Oh, she's making a fine mess of this. "Can we start over?"

The woman turns and walks away. Before Olivia can figure out what's happening, the woman returns.

"Can I help you?" The shopkeeper's bright smile eases her embarrassment.

Ah, they are starting over!

Her hand shoots out and she plants an equally radiant smile on her face. "Hello, I'm Olivia Kendall. It's about my father, one of the attorneys who defended Mr. Warner in the Dictograph Case."

The woman slowly extends her hand. "I'm Clara Schumann. Perhaps I can help you."

Schumann? As in the man she bumped into at Hawthorne's office?

Olivia grips the hand, its surface rough with calluses. "Nice to meet you Mrs. Schumann."

"Miss Schumann. Call me Clara."

"I'm not married either." Olivia chuckles. The Schumann mystery remains.

"So, we have that in common. But I'm not sure what else. Have a seat." Clara emerges from behind the counter and motions Olivia to a wooden bench in front of the window.

"What were you hoping to learn from my grandfather?"

Olivia straightens her skirt and pulls the scrapbook from her briefcase. She selects a few clippings from the envelope and flattens them in her lap.

Suddenly shy, she speaks toward the newsprint. "As I said, my father, Victor Kendall, defended Bernard Warner and the other men in 1918. The case was in the appeals process, but before it could be heard, he was killed." Olivia's said this more times in the last week than in her entire life.

Lifting her head, swallowing to keep her composure, she finishes. "He was struck down by an automobile."

Clara places a hand on Olivia's arm, and though she's a stranger, it offers her comfort. "I'm sorry about your father. How awful to lose him like that."

"Thank you. I'm probably on a wild goose chase, but I have information that leads me to believe the CPLE may have had something to do with his death."

The color drains from the shopkeeper's face, her lips compress into a tight line. She squeezes her eyes shut, her head moves back and forth like a pendulum. A soft moan escapes, then her face contorts, struggling to keep her composure.

Afraid she's broken something in Clara, Olivia waits. Was it her father's death or the mention of the CPLE?

"They took everything. Our reputation. Our way of life. Our culture. Then threw it away like the entrails of a hog. I've spent years trying to forget."

Olivia would like to tell Clara that she's not alone, that she endured the fallout of the case as well. But she keeps her peace.

Clara pulls in a deep breath, letting her cheeks fill before releasing a heavy sigh.

"I'm afraid you've caught me off guard. It was a terrible time."

Olivia lays a hand on Clara's knee. "I'm sorry for pouncing on you. Now we know where that darn cat is!"

Olivia's smile is rewarded with Clara's chuckle and tiptoes her way into what she'd like to know. "Did you know my father?"

Clara shakes her head. "Recognized him in the courtroom, but never officially met him. I was eighteen at the time."

Olivia lifts the pile of clippings. "I'd like to know what happened. These tell me what the paper wanted the public to know."

Clara shrugs. "Grandfather had two or three defense attorneys. I only went to court when the case was handed over to the jury. Took them twenty-three minutes to find him guilty. Changed the course of his life in less time than it takes to bake a loaf of bread."

Olivia offers her perspective. "Everyone's trial went the same way. And from what I read, the only witnesses for the defendants were the other defendants. You'd think the defense team could have come up with more than that."

"There were reputation witnesses but not one person could refute the evidence the detectives had gathered. But honestly," Clara turns to confront Olivia, "they didn't say all that was attributed to them. I was here every day."

Olivia stands. "I saw a Dictograph yesterday. It was a box about this big." She uses her hands to size it for Clara.

"It was much smaller back then. They hid it in the bottom of the grandfather clock that stood over there, in that corner." Clara points. "I got rid of the clock after the trial. Couldn't stand to look at it and every time it chimed, it mocked me for my role in their arrests."

Olivia stands in the corner and inspects the wall, the ceiling, the floor.

Clara rises and points to a hole in the floor with her foot. "They drilled there for the wire to go through."

"They?" Olivia asks.

"The electric company. Said they were installing an electric meter. How was I to know any different?"

"And what's below here?" Olivia's shoe taps the floor.

"The basement."

"They listened there?"

"No, although that's what I thought for years until Tink told me otherwise."

"Tink?"

"Tink Evans. Porter for the bank next door."

"He was involved somehow?"

"That's... a longer story."

"I'd love to hear more. Do you have time?"

Clara sighs. "I can talk while I work. Come on back."

While she replaces the sole on a well-worn pair of men's shoes, she shares her story. Olivia listens, absorbing the details about the device and how it was installed.

When she's finished, Clara asks, "What good does digging into all this do?"

It's a fair question. So what if she finds more information? So what if the CPLE had a hand in her father's death?

What would she even do with that?

Pulling on the threads of her father's final months might unravel more than she's ready for—grief she thought was buried could rise all over again.

And before she can stop herself, a half-formed thought slips out. "What if my father was killed to ensure your grandfather went to jail?"

Clara stills. Waits for Olivia.

She presses on. "I just learned that my mother didn't believe his death was an accident." Should she tell the rest, call on this stranger's pity for her circumstances?

She hesitates. Finally, she says, "My mother died because she couldn't prove otherwise."

At that, Clara hesitates, focuses on Olivia, heartache competing with heartache.

"I'd like to help. But what can I do at this late date?"

"I tried to locate the other defendants. Are any of them still around?"

Clara's fingers tap the counter, her gaze flicking toward the front of the shop. Then, she turns back, her expression unreadable.

"There's one." She says it like a betrayal.

Olivia's heartbeat accelerates at the promise of new information. "Will he tell me the truth?"

With obvious reluctance, she says, "I think he's spent the last twenty years trying to forget it."

A long silence follows. Olivia senses that waiting is the best course of action. Let Clara process and decide without interference.

Then, Clara reaches for a tool on the workbench, fiddling with it, her hands restless.

Her jaw tight, she says, "Mr. Vogel was one of the seven men arrested. He put up bail for my grandfather and went to jail with him."

Clara tightens her grip around the tool.

"If anyone knows what really happened, it's him."

Chapter Thirteen

Albert Stone's private law office commands a spectacular view of the city.

"I appreciate you seeing me on short notice, Mr. Stone." Michael takes the chair across from the attorney, in his sixties, trim and fit.

"You likely saw the story in the *Journal*—a German man was badly beaten last week. He made the mistake of saluting Hitler in a saloon."

Stone rolls his eyes. "Not too bright, is he?"

"The men who assaulted him called him a Dirty Hun and said they'd gotten rid of people like him before."

"What's your interest, Mr. Schumann?"

"There were similar assaults during the war that lead me to believe there's a possible resurgence in anti-German sentiment."

"From what I recall, those were mostly public reprimands for not buying war bonds and such."

"True. But what if factions of groups, like the Citizens Patriotic League, don't want Germans in this town now?"

"I doubt it. It's been nearly twenty years."

"My thoughts exactly. And maybe I'm picking at threads, but from what the victim and his son described, there are parallels. What if the CPLE is behind the attack? Is it possible? Did they dissolve after the war? Or did they go underground? I'd appreciate your perspective, even at this late date."

Stone shrugs. "I honestly don't know. One comment like that wouldn't lead me to believe they've returned. How does this involve me?"

"You were the U.S. District Attorney who prosecuted the Dictograph Case. My grandfather was Bernard Warner."

Stone's eyes widen, not in surprise—with recognition. "Barney," he repeats softly. "Well now, that's interesting."

Michael puts the Haber attack aside and shifts toward a personal mission.

At fifteen, the case took over his world. His grandfather couldn't be bothered to go fishing for he had to meet with his lawyers. His mother chose not to answer his questions because protecting him was her main concern. His father kept the shoe shop running though it eventually took its toll and he died of a heart attack in 1924.

Stone has information. Details Michael can't dig up from newspapers or court records.

"Can I ask you a question unrelated to the attack? About my grandfather's trial?" Michael asks, flipping his pencil like a pendulum.

Stone folds his hands over a green felt blotter on his mahogany desk. "I suppose."

"I read the detective's testimony as reported in the *Journal*." Michael licks his lips. "Did he...do you believe he said those things?"

From below the office a streetcar bell dings. Otherwise, the office is quiet, still, anticipatory.

Stone blows out a long breath. "It didn't matter."

His head snaps up. "Huh?" He squints and peers quizzically at Stone until the attorney is uncomfortable enough to continue.

"As much as I hate to tell you this, and admit it out loud, your grandfather wasn't convicted on what he said. He was found guilty of being German."

He recalls this exact conversation with Clara a few days ago.

"Half this town is German, Mr. Stone."

"Was. No one will admit to it now." Stone's shoulders shrug, not with indifference but illustrating the pity of it all, the loss, the foolish end of a culture because of a war and people who lumped everyone under one heading: Hun.

"Look, Michael."

Stone using his first name alerts him to something new, something he needs to pay attention to.

"I'm sorry for the outcome of the trials. I did my job, and I'd do the same again under those circumstances. But Barney and the others should not have gone to jail. Efforts to free them or commute their sentences were under way six months after they were convicted."

"What?" This revelation rocks him to the core. Six months?

"The Department of Justice reviewed espionage cases and Edwin Sharp, an attorney from Evendale and assistant to the Attorney General, recommended the dismissal of all three cases. Sharp was skeptical about the truth of the alleged disclosures of the Dictograph because knowing William Jackson, he refused to believe anything the agency testified to."

As if struck in the chest by a two by four, Michael falls back in his chair. The one-two punch of Sharp's recommendation to dismiss while condemning the detectives baffles his mind.

Stone keeps talking, but his voice fades as Michael forces himself to focus, file the revelation away until later.

"After the Supreme Court denied the appeal, the only recourse was clemency. Wilson had already granted a hundred or so requests based on the Department of Justice's recommendations. Judge Colrane, Federal Pardon Attorney Brock, Attorney General Rample and I submitted our recommendations to the President."

The fog begins to lift, the words clemency, recommendation, Wilson, prick his interest.

"Wait. They, you...endorsed clemency?"

"Yes. But we were sideswiped by the American Legion and the CPLE who managed to acquire ten thousand signatures on a petition opposing their release. Amazing how fast people will sign something when everyone else is doing it. Hawthorne and Pitts went to Washington. Wilson sided with them."

CPLE. Hawthorne. Wilson.

Rising from the chair, he thinks of leaving the office, going to the nearest bar, so he can think. And drink. But instead, he paces around the small space, running a hand through his hair, pressing fingers of acknowledgment into his skull.

Stone commiserates. "I'm sorry. I, we, tried everything we knew. But Wilson wouldn't budge."

The journalist in Michael finds his feet. "Sharp. When did he make his recommendation?"

Stone thinks a moment. "Spring 1919, I think."

"Victor Kendall died around then. Could his death have impacted the appeal?"

A moment passes while Stone drums his fingers on the blotter, dull, rhythmic, thumping accompanying Michaels' emerging headache.

"The timing is close, but I can't be sure. Kendall might have told the men to strike while the iron was hot. Withdraw the appeal and go for clemency."

Michael nods. He's following the logic.

"But who knows? Kendall might have thought they had a good case on appeal. But by taking clemency, they'd be admitting guilt. It's hard to say. Have you talked to Simpson or Matthews?"

"No, but I plan to."

"You should pick their brains. See what they know."

"I'm tracking down one of the detectives as well."

Stone nods approvingly. "Beck or Johnson?"

"Beck. Johnson's dead."

"You might have luck with Beck. A down and out guy at the time. Don't imagine much has changed."

"Thank you, Mr. Stone. I came here about the attack on an innocent man and I'm leaving with a whole different appreciation for what my grandfather went through. And that you're not the enemy."

Stone chuckles and reaches a hand across the desk. "I hope they're not active again."

Michael shakes, steps away from the desk, and turns on his heel. At the doorway, a hand on the jamb, he stares at Stone over his shoulder. "I will find out if the CPLE is behind that attack. And if they are, you can be sure I'll do my best to ensure it doesn't happen again."

A nod and he's out the door, striding toward the elevator, new information flying around his head like thoughts scattered in a windstorm.

* * *

Beck's place is across town.

The streetcar conductor makes sure he deposits his nickel in the fare box. Halfway down the aisle, he drops into an empty seat and out of habit, withdraws his notebook and pencil. Stone's revelations fundamentally alter what he's believed to be true all these years. People had actively worked to free his grandfather. While ten thousand others put their names to a document ensuring his sentence was carried out.

He figures that's twenty-five to thirty percent of Ellington adults at the time. One in four.

Of the ten people on the streetcar, three of them might have signed. His barber, Mr. Patterson would have been here in 1920 - did he sign? Nick at the bar? *Ellington Journal* employees?

Effie probably did as well, to save her marriage.

At his stop, he hops off the car and walks to Beck's place, his stride quick and purposeful, infused with anger at the system, the League, even Woodrow Wilson, weak and unbending in his final days in office.

Michael pauses in front of the McKenzie Building. The limestone facade is streaked with grime and weather stains. Several windowsills have crumbled, leaving jagged gaps like missing teeth in an old man's smile.

He pushes through the brass-handled door, its hinges protesting with a screech that echoes through the dim lobby. The air is thick with mildew, dust, and something else—the unmistakable stink of neglect.

The elevator stands idle behind a folding gate, an out of order sign dangling from one side, its paper faded and curling.

He takes the stairs.

At the end of the hallway, he knocks hard on apartment seven. The door opens just enough for him to catch a glimpse of a stained, once-white undershirt and a wary pair of eyes.

"Yeah?" Smoke drifts lazily toward the ceiling from the cigarette in the beefy hand ready to slam the door in his face.

"You Stanley Beck?"

"Who wants to know?"

"Michael Schumann, *Ellington Journal*. You were one of the detectives on the Dictograph Case. I'd like to ask you a few questions."

The man narrows the crack. One bloodshot eye stares back at him. "I got nothin' to say." The door closes the rest of the way.

"You got lots to say," Michael mutters under his breath and knocks on the door again. Polite. Calm. A knock that says I know you're in there. I'll wait.

Ten seconds pass. Then thirty. Michael taps his fingertips on the wood.

"Mr. Beck. How's twenty bucks for your time?" Michael plucks his wallet from his pocket and thumbs a ten and two fives. All he has on him.

Another minute—an eternity in the dank hallway smelling of fried onions and something he doesn't care to recognize.

The lock tumbles, the door opens, and a hand creeps forward.

"Cash first," Beck says.

Plopping the bills in his palm, Michael waits while the hand retreats, the door closes.

"We had a deal." Michael says, regretting payment without a single word exchanged.

A whoosh of air flies past him as the door opens.

Michael steps into a small room with big furniture, every surface littered with overflowing ashtrays and Chinese food cartons.

Beck offers a Pall Mall but Michael declines the smoke.

"I'll only take a few minutes of your time," he says to the middle-aged man with greasy, gray hair dragged over a bald spot.

"It was a long time ago," the ex-detective says.

Michael spots his entry point and pounces. "Is that because you don't remember, or you're scared?"

Beck's chest heaves, expanding suspender stripes over a large midriff. "I ain't scared of nothin'! I remember every damn bit of it."

Michael presses his advantage. "What? What do you remember?"

Beck's eyes shift left then right, as if there's someone in the flat.

"You were hired to listen to conversations in the shoe shop and write down what was said," he prompts.

Beck nods.

"Must have been boring work, listening to a bunch of old geezers."

Beck leans against the door jamb. "It paid the bills."

"What were you listening for?"

"Anything pro-German. Against the war or the Red Cross." Beck blows out a stream of smoke.

"Was every single statement you gave in front of the judge and jury true and factual?"

Beck takes a drag and exhales with, "Yeah," yet his eyes don't meet Michael's.

"How much did you invent when you couldn't make out the words?" It's a pitch right down the middle.

The man's face reddens as he lurches to a defensive position.

Michael holds up a hand. "I'm not saying you lied. What I'm saying is maybe you wrote down what you thought you heard, or you filled in a sentence with what you were told to report."

Beck's jaw tightens. "I did my job. Reported what I heard. That's it."

He pitches his cigarette to the floor and squishes it into the scarred wood heedless of a burn.

"And you could hear everything. Loud and clear? Like they were in the next room?"

Beck's eyes roll. He's getting comfortable with Michael's questions.

"Damn thing cut out all the time. Static. Men talking over each other. That damn clock ticking and chiming every fifteen minutes. It wasn't easy."

"Then how could you be sure what was said?" Michael's jaw clenches. Beck sent innocent men to prison on static and guesswork.

Beck scowls. "I heard enough."

Michael's pulse quickens.

"You heard enough. Enough for what? To get a paycheck?"

"I'm done." Beck reaches for the door handle.

Michael jumps in, before he's pushed out. "One last thing for my twenty bucks. The testimony from the trial—it says you read your notes in court."

Beck's cheek twitches. "I read what was given to me."

"Given to you?"

Beck tenses, then opens the door. "Listen. Pitts wanted results. I gave him what I had."

He's heard Pitts' name twice in one day. He adds a large question mark next to it in his notebook.

"And that wasn't enough?"

"Your twenty bucks is up." Beck's arm sweeps across his bulging midsection, motioning for Michael to leave.

Beck gives Michael's shoulder a shove and he stumbles into the hall.

He has one more shot before the door closes and this interview is over.

"What did Pitts promise you?"

Beck shakes his head—not answering, just amused. Like Michael still doesn't understand how things are done.

Michael stands there trembling with rage. He mutters "lying bastard" under his breath, then stomps down the stairs.

Two things are now clear: Pitts, a high-ranking CPLE member, managed the Dictograph monitoring—and Beck testified to statements he didn't hear.

Michael's pulse kicks harder. If Beck didn't hear it all—if the words weren't even his—then his grandfather's conviction was built on lies.

* * *

Michael snags a booth at Dixie's and dots the pencil lead with his tongue before jotting down what he wants from John Simpson, co-defense attorney in his grandfather's case. Given Stone's directive, he has high expectations.

"Michael Schumann, I presume?"

Michael starts. The man sliding into the seat opposite him wears a custom suit, crisp white shirt, and a crimson tie—his attire evoking power and confidence.

Michael extends his hand. "Nice to meet you, Mr. Simpson. Thank you for coming."

Simpson relaxes. "I presume you're buying."

Michael nods uncertainly. Beck has the last of his cash, so this will have to go on his tab.

"Daily special good with you?" Michael asks.

"Sure. And coffee."

Michael signals Mabel to bring one special and two coffees.

"I took this meeting out of curiosity. You said your grandfather was Bernard Warner?"

"Yes, the one and only." His use of Bernard is a stark contrast to Stone's use of Barney.

"Sorry we couldn't get him off or prevent him from going to jail." Simpson appears genuinely apologetic.

Michael sighs. "Yeah. The toughest part was watching a sixty-eight-year-old man go off to Moundsville." There were other difficult times, but he won't recount them with a stranger.

"President Harding finally came through. They only did six months."

Only? Michael's head tilts, sneering at Simpson's casual dismissal. "I bet you've not spent one minute in jail."

The attorney's jaw drops.

Michael wonders if his reaction is due to his inconsiderate comment or being called out on it.

"That was thoughtless. I apologize." Simpson's concentration turns to the plate Mabel places in front of him. He cuts, then forks a bite of Salisbury steak into his mouth while Michael opens his notebook.

"Ok if we talk while you eat?"

Simpson raises his fork in approval.

"Two nights ago, a man was attacked for no apparent reason. He's German and insults were made."

Simpson chews and shrugs. "What's this got to do with your grandfather?"

"Probably nothing. I asked William Hawthorne if the CPLE is involved. He neither confirmed nor denied the League is still active."

Simpson dabs a napkin at the corners of his mouth, takes a gulp of coffee, and stabs another piece of steak. "You got nerve, Schumann. Hawthorne can cause you all kinds of trouble."

"He is an influential man," Michael says then under his breath adds, "or so he'd have everyone believe."

Simpson sputters his coffee and murmurs under his breath. "Speak of the devil."

"Well, hello, John." William Hawthorne, confident, commanding, stands at the end of the booth, smiling down on the two men.

"William," John acknowledges him.

"Look who we have here! Michael Schumann. John, did you know he lied to me? Thinks I know something about the CPLE beating up some old German man."

Michael's face reddens, but he challenges Hawthorne anyway. "Well, did they?"

Hawthorne's steely gray eyes burrow into him so long, Michael feels the burn.

"William, this is not the place or the time to bring up old grudges." John says, shoving his half-eaten meal away.

"He started it."

The interplay between these two fascinates Michael. Their tug of war defines not only their role in the courtroom, but their relationship.

"Now children," Michael says, but is ignored.

"Come see me, John. I'd love to discuss old times. We sure had fun back then, didn't we."

John's coffee cup slams onto the red Formica. Michael flinches. Hawthorne is unfazed.

"Fun? You call harassing this town's citizens fun? You're out of your mind."

"Oh, now don't get upset. I was talking about that Dictograph case. You remember. The one where I sent Michael's grandfather and his friends to prison?"

On the word grandfather, Hawthorne's lips curl into a wide grin, a snake in the grass, striking quick, without warning.

"I don't have time for your games, William," Simpson says. He pulls out his wallet and throws a dollar on the table. He tries to leave the booth, but Hawthorne blocks his exit and leans close to Michael's ear. "That little stunt you pulled has consequences."

The threat means Michael's job. He'll have to deal with that later. Right now, all he wants is to talk to Simpson.

"Mr. Simpson, perhaps another time would be best for us to talk."

A tall, rotund man calls to Hawthorne from the door. "Ready?"

"On my way, Howard."

But Hawthorne's not done.

"Have your little pow wow. It's no skin off my nose. Just remember who runs this town." He saunters to the door where his friend waits. When he passes the window where the pair sit, he slows, smiles, and winks.

Michael doesn't know what to make of it. But it unnerves him.

Simpson folds his napkin and places it neatly beside his plate. "I take it you got on his wrong side."

"I did."

Simpson scoots across the bench, but Michael grips his arm, restraining him.

"Please, one more minute of your time. Edwin Sharp, working for the Department of Justice, recommended clemency long before the appeal was denied but it went nowhere. Why?"

His question strikes a chord with Simpson. He takes a deep breath, stalling for time.

At last, Simpson exhales, slow and exaggerated. "We had a decision. Sharp's recommendation came while we were in the appeals process. We could either drop the appeal and hope Wilson granted clemency, or we could stay the course. Let the courts call for a new hearing. Neither was guaranteed. But before we could do anything, my partner, Victor Kendall was killed."

The implications dawn on Michael but he gives Simpson time.

He looks everywhere except at Michael. "We missed our window of opportunity. Wilson granted clemency to many after the war. But by the time I took over the case and decided to withdraw our appeal, he'd stopped. That petition with ten thousand signatures didn't help. Half those people probably signed it just to keep Hawthorne happy, but Wilson saw it as the voice of Ellington and decided that whoever remained on the line for jail time, would serve."

"Good Lord. If not for Kendall's death, my grandfather would have been freed."

"Nothing's for sure. I'm sorry for your grandfather and I'm sorry we lost Victor. But it's water under the bridge, Mr. Schumann. It's way too late."

Numb, Michael barely notices Simpson's departure. He sits alone in the booth, staring at the abandoned plate of Salisbury steak, the coffee growing cold.

The revelation churns in his mind. His grandfather had been so close to a pardon. Close to avoiding jail time. One man's death had sealed the fate of three innocent men.

The coincidence feels too neat, too convenient. Victor Kendall, the lawyer fighting hardest for their freedom, died in an "accident" just as clemency became possible.

Michael's hands shake as he reaches for his notebook. The pieces are starting to form a picture he doesn't want to see. If the CPLE could orchestrate fabricated testimony, pressure witnesses, and mobilize ten thousand signatures—what else were they capable of?

Hawthorne's wink through the window isn't amusement—it's a promise. Michael closes his notebook and heads for the door.

Chapter Fourteen

"Mr. Vogel is willing to see us." Clara's face breaks into a smile.

"He is?" Olivia jumps down from the stool, and unable to contain her excitement, hugs Clara.

"I'll close the shop early," Clara says, flipping the sign in the window.

The women step out into the late afternoon sunshine. After crossing Schmitty's Corner, they walk until Clara stops in front of an imposing two-story Victorian house.

On the broad front porch, an elderly man supports himself with a cane.

"Hello, Clara." His voice is scratchy as if he hasn't spoken aloud in some time.

"Hello, Mr. Vogel." Clara shifts to put Olivia in Vogel's line of sight. "This is the woman I told you about. Olivia Kendall. Victor's daughter."

Olivia climbs the porch steps to take the man's outstretched hand.

"I'm sorry for your loss. Your father was a fine attorney and a good man."

"Thank you, Mr. Vogel. I appreciate you seeing me on short notice."

Vogel moves aside and ushers the ladies to a pair of white wicker chairs.

"What can I help you with?"

Olivia pulls the scrapbook out. "I found this recently in my aunt's home. Perhaps it might jog your memory."

"Thank you, but that won't be necessary. Who can forget that awful time?"

Olivia replaces the scrapbook but is ready to rescue it should the man's memory need a boost. "Tell me about the day you were arrested."

"They came for me at home," Vogel says. "No explanation, no paperwork. Just that I'd made statements against the law."

He spends the next fifteen minutes sharing his memories of the arrests, trials, convictions, and appeal process. His temperament fluctuates with the snippets of his story and gets agitated when he recounts their defense strategy. "Our lawyers bet everything on a legal technicality—that the Sedition Act was being misused—and it failed. They argued the Act wasn't meant to punish old men chatting in a shoe shop. Said we never incited violence, never swore allegiance to the Kaiser, never did more than complain about food rations and war bonds. But none of it mattered. The judge shut down our attorneys left and right. Our good names and reputation held no merit in court."

The mention of their good names hits a nerve. Her father would've argued that character mattered, and that community standing meant something. But the court didn't care.

"And when we came home from Moundsville, half the town treated us like we'd gotten away with murder. Hawthorne and Pitts went to Washington with ten thousand signatures on a petition to make sure we went to jail and stayed there."

Clara's face goes white. "Ten thousand people wanted you in jail."

Olivia's jaw tightens. The injustice burns in her chest.

After a moment, Clara asks, "Do you remember Tink Evans? The bank porter?"

"I do," Mr. Vogel props his chin on the knob of his cane. "You know he was coerced into identifying us through that dastardly device."

Clara nods. "He told me what happened. Then he was gone." She snaps her finger. "Just disappeared. Overnight."

"There's more to that story."

Olivia and Clara simultaneously sit up straight in their chairs.

"I went by the shoe shop in February, while our lawyers worked on our appeals. Tink showed up with some misdelivered mail, looking like a scolded pup. I said, 'Tink, you're not to blame for what happened.' He let out this long, weary sigh and reached out to shake my hand—like he wasn't sure I'd take it, being a black man and all. I invited him to sit—probably the first time anyone had. He told me folks were calling him the German snitch. Hailed as a hero for turning us in."

Clara meets Vogel's gaze. "I never knew, till just before he left for California, that he did it to keep his job."

"While Tink and I sat in the shop, Barney, Clara's grandfather," he looks at Olivia, "joined us. We were talking and then, the strangest thing happened. Tink started crying. Not the bawling-out-your-eyes kind. The kind where tears run down your cheeks till you can't ignore them."

Listening to Vogel is like being there in the shop, hearing what Tink had been too afraid to say.

"Said the voices he heard weren't always clear, but they leaned on him hard until he gave them names. Then the office was cleared out, like they'd never been there. But what Tink said then, verified we were telling the truth. Half the things those detectives swore we said, never happened. He saw them write things down when no one was talking. Made it up."

Olivia blinks. "Made it up?"

Vogel nods.

The revelation sinks in, altering everything she thought she knew.

"Did you tell anyone about this conversation with Tink?"

Vogel lays his rheumy blue eyes on Olivia. "Yes, we told your father."

"And my grandfather must have told my parents," Clara says. "Mother still won't talk about what happened."

"And my father?" Olivia asks. "Do you know what he did with that information?"

Vogel sighs. "I only know he said he'd pursue it. Thought if he could get Tink to tell a judge we could get a new trial. But sadly, I never saw Tink again."

Clara's face twists with fury. "Why didn't you do more?" she snaps. "You had evidence. And still, you went to jail."

Vogel uses his cane and the porch rail to rise. He weighs his next words, studying Olivia.

"What?" Olivia stares at the old man, trying to figure out what he means.

Vogel's tone is soft, apologetic. "Because her father died. And the other attorney, Simpson, said that with the only witness nowhere to be found, there was nothing to be done."

Olivia tests the logic of Vogel's simple statement. Thinking aloud, she says, "Okay. Let me get this straight. Tink tells the truth, and before it can be used, my father is killed."

She swallows hard, blinking back tears of grief, anger, maybe both.

Raising her eyes to the old man, she asks, "Did my father die because he was looking into these allegations?"

"I don't know." Vogel's voice is drained of emotion, his shoulders sagging under the burden of the past. "At this late date, Olivia, what does knowing the answer do? It won't bring him back."

Everyone says the same thing. What does it matter? Your father is still dead.

Olivia rises from her chair and leans against the porch railing, gazing at an enormous magnolia littering Vogel's lawn with its blooms.

"No, it won't. But because my father died, my mother did too." Her hands grip the railing, struggling to keep her composure. "I lost everything. And all the evidence points to this case as the reason."

"Do you know the other attorney, what was his name? Simpson?" Clara interjects.

Olivia exhales a long breath. "Indeed, I do."

She remembers Uncle John's hesitation at Aunt Becky's, the way he dodged her questions. He knew more than he admitted, and she intends to find out what that is.

"Mr. Vogel, I'm more certain than ever that the CPLE had something to do with my father's death."

Vogel holds her gaze for a long moment, his face unreadable. "Be careful with sleeping dogs, even at this late date. I kept my mouth shut back then—figured jail was a better alternative to dying."

Olivia picks up her briefcase. "Thank you, Mr. Vogel. I realize this must have been difficult. You're a brave man."

Vogel chuckles lightly. "Young lady, I'm not brave. I'm old and have nothing left to lose. But you do."

Olivia tightens her grip on her briefcase, nodding as she steps off the porch. "Then I'd better make it count."

Chapter Fifteen

"End of the line!" The conductor's call jerks Michael from sleep. He pushes his hat off his face, checks his watch. Four-thirty. Clara should still be at the shop. The late afternoon is thick and muggy. Shrugging off his jacket, he drapes it over one finger and pushes the shop door open. Leather and beeswax polish, scents as familiar as his own cologne, greet him like an old friend.

"Hey, Sis," he shouts, passing the counter on his way into the workroom.

Clara is at the workbench running the buffer, her hand tucked into a brown shoe, turning it this way and that to shine the upper. "Hi."

She turns off the machine. The whir cuts out, leaving a muffled hum of the streets beyond the shop's front window.

The sight of a woman sitting beside Clara prompts him to remove his hat.

Clara places the shoe next to its mate, folds them into brown paper, the string hissing as she cinches it closed. "Mike, this is Olivia."

Moving past Clara, he extends his hand and stops short. A flash of memory surfaces: news clippings scattered across the marble floor outside Hawthorne's office. A scrapbook clutched tight. What is she doing here?

The woman's eyes widen, brows arching over blue eyes framed with dark lashes. The same ones he stared into while retrieving the clippings.

"Miss Kendall," he murmurs, not quite sure he's connecting the dots. "At Hawthorne's office."

Olivia smiles. "This is odd! Mr. Schumann, I presume?"

"I am. How's your head?"

Her fingers touch her forehead. "None the worse for bumping into yours."

Clara is baffled, her head switching from Michael to Olivia, and back again. "How? What? Hawthorne?"

Confused and wary, he asks his sister, "How do you know Miss Kendall?"

Before Clara can answer, Olivia straightens in her seat. "I came to speak with Mr. Warner. But Clara told me he's passed, and she offered to answer my questions."

Michael's eyes narrow slightly. "What kind of questions?"

"It's a long story," Olivia says.

Clara cuts in, blunt and to the point. "She's looking into the CPLE."

This is not what he expected. He flicks a glance at Olivia, then locks his gaze on his sister. Days ago, Clara wanted nothing to do with this. And now, she's volunteering information?

Michael frowns, but lets it go, turning back to Olivia.

She's been quiet, watching them. Now, she lifts her chin, calm but intent. "I believe they're somehow connected to my father's death."

Her statement hangs in the air. He'd wondered the same thing when he first saw Kendall's name in the papers. Meant to follow the thread. Now Victor Kendall's daughter is tugging on it herself.

"I'm sorry for what happened to him." He doesn't want to cause this woman any more pain, but he can't help himself. He's too curious. "Do you think it was something more than an accident?"

She raises an eyebrow, adjusts the collar on her perfectly tailored blouse, and answers in a voice that leaves no room for argument.

"That's what I'd like to find out."

Clara glances at the clock above the workbench and unties her apron. "It's time to close. Let's take this over to the Gaslight. I could use a cold beer."

"Fine idea," Michael says, though his mind is still spinning. "Miss Kendall, is that all right with you?"

"Olivia, please." She grabs her briefcase and heads into the shop front.

Michael tugs on his sister's sleeve, holding her back a step. His voice drops. "I thought you weren't interested in digging up dirt on the CPLE."

Clara hesitates, her lips pressing into a firm line before she glances toward Olivia. Then, after a beat, she says, "I wasn't planning on it. Sometimes you just know when someone needs help." She pauses, watching Olivia through the window. "And maybe...maybe I'm tired of carrying this alone. She's giving me a chance to finally learn what really happened to Grandfather."

Michael studies her, and suddenly her eagerness to help makes sense. Clara has carried the guilt of that damned machine for nineteen years. Olivia wasn't just offering answers—she was offering Clara a chance at redemption.

Clara exhales, his scrutiny not lost on her. "I'll tell it all over a cold beer."

"You better."

Michael follows them past a few houses, across the tracks, toward the tavern his grandfather and father frequented. Curiosity and unease jostle for space in his mind.

What is it about Victor Kendall's daughter that changed Clara's mind?

And what are the odds of crossing paths with her now—just as his own trail is circling the CPLE?

Chapter Sixteen

Ten minutes later, each has a mug of beer. The front and rear doors are propped open with cement block. A sluggish breeze stirs the stale scent of beer and cigarette smoke.

Cheers! Their mugs clink together, the dull sound swallowed by murmured conversations and an occasional burst of laughter.

Olivia swipes at a foamy mustache with the back of her hand. "Reporter, huh?"

"*Ellington Journal.*"

"That explains the way you examined my clippings after we collided."

"The headline still haunts me," Michael admits. He presses his thumb to the crease between his eyes. Olivia's not sure what he's feeling.

"I know my father did his best to get those men off. We talked about the trial over dinner more times than I can count." She lifts the mug again—part thirst, part excuse to study the handsome reporter across the table. Gary Cooper's quiet dignity with Clark Gable's masculine appeal. A dangerous combination.

"The recent attack on an elderly man and his son started my investigation into the CPLE."

She recalls the article. "The elderly man. Was his name Haber?"

Beer sloshes from Michael's mug as it halts abruptly on the way to his mouth. "Yes. Wilhelm Haber. And his son Fredrick."

"Wilhelm's grandson, Hans, is in one of my classes. I teach history at Ellington High."

"Holy smoke!" Michael exclaims and drops his own mug on the table. "This is uncanny."

"Uncanny is the least of it," Olivia says. "How about that serendipitous meeting at Hawthorne's office?"

"I got the appointment on pretense, asking him about his illustrious career. But my real goal was to confront him about the CPLE. Get him to say if it was still active or not."

Olivia leans in, forearms on the table, intrigued and attentive. "And?"

"He neither confirmed nor denied it. What did you do?"

"I pretended I needed help with my aunt's estate. I wanted to see his reaction when I asked him if he or the CPLE had anything to do with my father's death."

"You got guts, Olivia." One eyebrow raised, he asks, "And?"

"He denied it and threw me out of his office." As she recalls that moment, she's proud of herself for confronting him, because Hawthorne's not a man to be trifled with.

"A peacock," Michael exclaims. "Showing his feathers and expecting everyone to fawn all over him."

Olivia crosses her arms over her chest. "I think he's a pompous ass."

Pausing before he takes a slug of beer, a smirk crosses Michael's face. "However, a very dangerous pompous ass."

Clara sets down her beer, breaking her silence. "We talked to Henry Vogel today."

"The friend who put up bond for grandfather?"

"He confirmed Tink Evans was coerced. The detectives twisted the testimony—made things up."

Michael withdraws a pocket-sized notebook from his jacket. "Detective I talked to today said more or less the same. Even admitted to reading from a document handed to him in court."

Clara slams her mug on the table and glares at Michael. "Unbelievable!"

"Gets worse. He also told me Howard Pitts managed the whole Dictograph operation."

"Pitts? I don't know that name," Clara says.

"High-ranking CPLE member and on the prosecution team in the first trial. It's why I'm here. Figured you'd be interested, Sis."

Olivia makes a mental note. Howard Pitts. Someone else who might have wanted her father silenced.

Her attention lingers on Michael—the ease of their conversation, the way their investigations overlap like pieces of the same puzzle.

As Michael scribbles in his notebook, she studies him. His efficient movements, sleeves bunching at the elbows as he bites the pencil, flicks it. Heat creeps up her neck as she realizes she's staring.

"And you, Olivia," Michael says, breaking her trance. "You're dead set on pursuing this."

She reaches into her briefcase and hands Michael her mother's letter.

He scans it quickly, hands it back. "I'm sorry."

"She wasn't crazy, if that's what you're thinking," Olivia snaps.

"No, I didn't think that at all. I merely wonder if all this is connected. Your mother thought your father's death wasn't an accident. If he'd not been killed, perhaps my grandfather and the others would have won their appeal."

"We'll never know, will we?" Olivia stares into her empty mug on the verge of tears. But she's not weak and won't let this man think she is. Inhaling, she squares her shoulders, stiffens her spine, and says, "I want—no I need—to find out."

Clara jumps in. "Seems to me you two should pool resources and work together. You're both after the same thing."

Michael leans back, a slow grin tugging at the corner of his mouth, the challenge gleaming in his eyes. "I'm game if you are."

"I'm in," says Olivia and covers Clara's hand with hers. "How about you, Clara?"

She folds Olivia's hand into hers and faces her brother. "One condition."

Michael arches a single brow. "Name it."

"We never, ever, tell Mama. Not until we know the truth. She doesn't need to know we're stirring the pot."

Michael nods solemnly, but a trace of unease lingers in his expression.

"Remind me never to cross your mother," Olivia says, hoping her glib comment is taken in the spirit intended.

The CPLE left scars on everyone. Olivia understands why some scars never heal, why covering them or pretending they don't exist is easier than confronting them. Why Michael and Clara shield their mother. Something she tried to do. But failed.

As the streetcar sways along its tracks toward Aunt Becky's, Olivia presses her fingertips to the place where she tucked her mother's letter. The past had always felt like a burden she carried alone.

For the first time in years, her past feels manageable.

Chapter Seventeen

Meeting Olivia has sparked something he hasn't felt in a long time. He catches himself smiling at the memory of their drinks at the Gaslight. Despite her polished, society-girl way, she's easy to talk to. That sorrowful smile of hers tells him her grief still hovers, but there's something undeniably charming about it.

"Call for you." Effie shouts from across the room.

He grabs the receiver. "Schumann."

"Michael?" A woman's voice he recognizes floats through the receiver. For a second he thinks it's Olivia, but the tone is different. Softer. It's the nurse from St. Boniface.

"Nurse Franklin! How are you?" Michael leans back in his chair, places his feet on his desk, crossed at the ankles.

"I'm fine." Her reply is quiet and subdued.

"You don't sound fine." Michael reverses his relaxed posture and swings his feet down, angling away from the newsroom.

"I'm calling to let you know that Mr. Haber was released yesterday. He's not fully recovered but doing well considering his injury."

"That's good news," Michael says. "I appreciate you letting me know."

A moment of silence puts him on alert.

"You see." Her voice lowers. "A man came in a few minutes ago asking for him."

Michael props the receiver between his ear and shoulder, snags his pencil, and opens his notebook to a blank page. "Oh?"

"I told him he'd been released. Then, he wanted his address."

A pause.

"I wouldn't have given it to him even if I could."

Another pause.

"The guy gave me the heebie-jeebies."

Michael's pencil moves on instinct. Scribbling helps him think. "Did you get a name?"

A soft scrape rustles through the receiver, as if she's put her hand over the speaker. Her words are muffled, unintelligible. He waits while she takes care of business on her end.

"I'm sorry. It's gotten busy here. Can you meet me on Monday? I don't want to talk about this over the phone."

"Yes. Yes, of course." Michael locates the date on his desk calendar. "What time?"

"I'm done at six."

He jots down her name and the designated meeting time on June 22. "I'll see you then."

The Habers need to be told about this.

Olivia will know how to talk to the Haber family—how to warn them without escalating their fear.

But that's not the only reason.

He wants her there.

Without another thought, he dials her number.

Chapter Eighteen

Olivia agrees to meet Michael at the Haber's in an hour.

She can't decide what to wear, shoving hangers aside until a pale pink button-down with a belted waist catches her eye.

She takes extra care with her hair and makeup, tries on her favorite straw hat—but it's too jaunty. Too cheerful. She unpins it and smooths her hair.

The Habers live within walking distance, but the street offers no shade. By the second block, her powder melts and sweat slides down her back.

Michael is at the corner. Removing his hat, he greets her. "Good afternoon, Miss Kendall."

"Hello. Please call me Olivia and for pity's sake put your hat back on. It's too hot to be so formal." The words fly out of her mouth without thinking and she regrets her tone. The heat, the purpose of their visit have her short tempered. She pretends to check house numbers.

Replacing his hat, Michael points to a small, wood-framed house, its white exterior dulled with dirt and age. "I called ahead."

Knocking on the front door, he warns Olivia about Mrs. Haber. "She's gruff, but I believe it's because she's afraid. Don't take it personally."

The door opens and a middle-aged man greets them.

"Please come in."

Even though the parlor is warm and stuffy, Olivia is grateful to escape the intense midday sun.

Michael introduces Wilhelm Haber, Fredrick, and Mrs. Haber.

Mrs. Haber offers cool drinks but doesn't mince words when, in a heavy German accent, she exclaims, "I no like you come here."

"Es tut mir leid, Frau Haber."

Mrs. Haber's demeanor shifts slightly at Michael's apology. The German words mean nothing to Olivia. She tugs at Michael's sleeve. "What did you say?"

Mrs. Haber cuts in, a smirk pulling at her lips. "You not staying long."

"Is Hans here?" Olivia asks. "How is he doing since school let out?"

"He's working," Fredrick says. "Has a summer job at the market. He told me how you handled the class and that you took a personal interest in his well-being. Thank you."

"No thanks needed," Olivia says. "It's my job to make sure students feel safe in the classroom—mentally and physically. Please tell him I said hello."

"Wilhelm, how are you feeling?" Michael asks, taking a seat across from where the elderly couple sit side by side.

"He has nightmares," Mrs. Haber interrupts.

"I'll speak for myself if you don't mind, Mama." Wilhelm pats her knee to take the sting from his reprimand.

To Michael, Wilhelm says in his thick accent, "I get headaches and sleep is difficult."

"I'm sorry that happened to you, Mr. Haber," Olivia says.

"We're here to check on you," Michael says, "and to let you know something unusual happened this morning at the hospital. A man, unknown to the nurse, asked after you. Wanted your address."

At this, Mrs. Haber turns to her husband and pokes him in the shoulder. "I tell you this happen. We are not safe."

"Settle down, Gretl," Wilhelm says and pats her knee again. To Michael, he asks, "Do you know who the man is?"

Michael shakes his head. "I'm meeting the nurse to find out more, but wanted you to keep watch, maybe stay close to home."

Fredrick, who's been peering out the window, drops the curtain back into place. "I heard them."

Mrs. Haber's inhale is sharp.

Fredrick continues. "I went back to get Papa's slippers. As I started to leave the room, I heard a man ask for our address. The nurse said no, and I thought that was the end of it. But he leaned over the counter, growled in her face. 'Give me that German's address. Now.'" His tone mimics that of the threatening man.

Fredrick licks his lips and glances at his parents. "Papa, I recognized the voice. The one who gave the orders."

Mrs. Haber's hand comes to her mouth as she collapses with a sob on her husband's shoulder.

Mr. Haber ignores her; his gaze holds steady on his son. A muscle twitches in his jaw, fingers gripping his thighs like claws.

"Don't worry Papa, I didn't confront the man." Fredrick stoops beside his father.

Wilhelm cups his hand over his son's cheek. "He didn't see you, did he?"

Fredrick covers his father's hand with his. "No. I stayed in the room till I was sure he was gone. Truthfully, my legs were so shaky, I could hardly move." His forced laugh does nothing to lighten the mood.

"Can you give me a description?" Michael interrupts the father-son exchange.

Olivia's surprised by Michael's question. She'd have offered comfort first, acknowledged their fear before prodding into the incident.

But Fredrick is unfazed. "I only saw his back as he walked away from the nurse's station. He was about my height, but heavier. "shoulders, short neck, gray hair, slick like he's used too much Vitalis. Had a bald spot." He pats the back of his head.

Michael's already scribbling, posture sharp with purpose. There it is—the hunger, the rush.

She wants to tell him to slow down, to sense the tension in the room.

But he doesn't.

And then Mrs. Haber explodes.

She surges to her feet, throwing off her husband's comforting arms and stands in front of Michael looking down on him. "Enough! You," her finger stabs his shoulder, "put us in danger. You write this in your paper, how will we be safe?"

Michael freezes. His shoulders round, notebook clenched like a shield. The light in his eyes—gone.

Olivia rises, voice firm but gentle. "Michael, I think it's time to go."

But he doesn't move. A flicker of shame, then regret, crosses his face.

For all his chasing the truth, Olivia isn't sure he's considered the cost. His eyes widen and his shoulders sag as understanding hits.

"I didn't mean for it to come to this," Michael whispers, his voice cracking under the strain of his confession.

Wilhelm's gaze softens. "You were doing your job," he says, though his unease is evident in his trembling hands.

Mrs. Haber points to the door, her finger shaking, "You go! Never come again!" Her voice wavers—not just from anger, but from something worse. Fear.

Olivia doesn't move. Michael opens his mouth, then closes it, realizing he's making things worse.

Michael nods, turns to Wilhelm, and lays a reassuring hand on his forearm. "I'm sorry. I promise to make this right."

"Mrs. Haber," Michael tips his head respectfully to the woman who shows him her back.

"Fredrick." The men shake hands. "I'll treat what you've told me with respect and consideration for your family. But do be careful."

Fredrick opens the door. His gaze moves deliberately from Michael to Olivia. "You do the same."

As they step off the porch, the door clicks shut behind them. Olivia glances over her shoulder. The curtain shifts, then stills, as if someone has stepped away.

Michael rolls his hat in his hands. "What have I done?"

Olivia exhales, staring at Michael for a long moment. He's done more than just his job.

"I'm not sure," she admits. "But you can fix it. You can make it right."

They walk in silence.

She doesn't know what making it right looks like—but they will have to figure it out.

Chapter Nineteen

Michael escorts Olivia home but declines her invitation to come in and talk. He needs distance. And a drink.

Nick's is dim, cool, and empty except for the bartender. He orders a whisky, neat, downs it, and signals for another.

The second sits untouched, condensation forming a wet ring on the bar's dull surface. Michael stares into the amber liquid, not seeing the drink, but Wilhelm Haber's face—tired, scared, dignified.

The anonymous man asking for the address—he's real. Would his visit to the Haber's' home lead the fox into the hen house? What if he was followed?

His hand curls around the glass, fighting the urge to drown his guilt.

Professional persistence has always been his strength. Follow the thread. Uncover the truth. But this isn't just a case anymore. These are people. A family already walking a razor's edge in a community with a faction that has turned on them.

Am I hunting the threat—or creating it? Is it so important to know, to see my name under an important headline that I'm risking more than I have a right to?

His thumb traces the rim. Olivia's face flickers in front of him, her voice steady even when Mrs. Haber's rage pressed into her. Not once had she shrunk from the woman's fury. Because it isn't about her. That's what makes her different. And why Clara changed her mind.

He caves and gulps the whiskey.

"Schumann!" A boisterous voice calls.

Kellerman.

Michael indicates the empty stool beside him and hails the bartender.

Abe tosses back a bourbon, slams the glass on the bar, and signals for another.

"Did you hear?" Abe asks.

"Hear what?"

"Another old man was attacked. German." Kellerman's tone lacks inflection. Just another day on his beat.

Michael's glass halts halfway to his mouth.

"When? Where?"

"Eleventh Street underpass. Same M.O. as Haber. Three men. Last night near dark. The man, despite the beating he got, gave us a description of one of them."

Michael's two-whiskey buzz vanishes. "Haber's son said there was a guy at the hospital whose voice he recognized."

Kellerman's brows raise along with his shot glass. "Give it to me."

"Six-foot, heavy-set, graying hair, bald in the back."

Kellerman nods. "I got the same. Except for the bald spot."

"Same gang as Haber?"

"Possibly."

"We need a name, Abe."

Kellerman guffaws. "Only a thousand men in this city match that description."

Eager to move the needle on identifying the man—and despite endangering the Habers—he brings Nurse Franklin into it, knowing full well this could put her in jeopardy.

"I know someone who saw his face."

Kellerman yanks his notebook from his back pocket. "Who's that?"

"I have a meeting with her on Monday."

"Her?" Kellerman's brows wrinkle, his pencil stops mid-air over the blank page. "You're doing police work, Schumann. That's not your job. I let you chase your theories because I thought they might help. But you start pulling civilians into this, especially women, and it's on my desk when it goes sideways."

Michael holds Kellerman's gaze. If he reveals Nurse Franklin's identity, he's pretty sure she won't talk. Then all he's got is a dead end.

"I'll do it. She trusts me." As he says the words, he isn't so sure. They haven't had more than passing conversations.

But this is big. And he'll protect the nurse. Make sure she's safe.

Kellerman merely looks at him while he twirls his half-empty glass. "If I talk to her, I get a lead that could mean an arrest. What's in it for you?"

Michael contemplates the question. After this morning's rough conversation with Wilhelm, he decides he's not doing it for the byline or the glory. He's doing it for the old men under the underpass, the Haber family and every person who's been silenced by fear. And maybe, to prove to himself that the truth still matters.

He shoves his untouched whiskey over to Abe. "You get the men who committed the heinous attacks. I get the story that exposes whoever's behind it. You and I both know the CPLE is the likely suspect."

Abe scratches the back of his neck, his face shadowy with doubt. "You're not wrong about the CPLE. But you're asking me to sit on my hands while you do my job."

He sighs, empties his glass, then side-eyes Michael. "Fine. Bring me something solid, and I'll get it in front of the other guy."

This "other guy" has a name, bruises, and probably a hospital bracelet. "Who's the victim? Motive?"

Abe shares eagerly. "Karl Doller. Doller with an e. Older guy. Retired baker or something. Has no idea why. Said he supported the CPLE in '18 so being German may not be the reason."

"How did that come up?"

"I figured you'd want to know."

"If he supported them then, why target him now? What's he been saying lately?"

Kellerman shrugs. "I got nothin.'"

Michael strides out of the bar, already turning over how to identify the man at the hospital.

If this doesn't stop soon, someone may not survive.

* * *

At the office, Baxter's door is closed, and through the window, a man is gesturing wildly.

Effie curls her forefinger, inviting him to her desk and to lean in. Her eyes dart around the newsroom. Then her head jerks toward the editor's office. "Hawthorne."

"What?" He casts a wary glance across the room. "Shit!"

Realizing he's used profanity in the presence of a woman, he says, "Beg your pardon."

"None needed. My sentiments exactly." Effie hands him a sheet of typing paper, an excuse to congregate at her desk as they watch Hawthorne emerge from Baxter's office, joking and laughing like two old buddies.

Michael suspects Hawthorne's here about his prominent citizen ploy and is demanding some retribution.

Baxter spies Michael. "Ah, here he is. Ears burning, Michael?"

He touches one ear. "Nope, can't say they are."

Hawthorne glides down the narrow aisle toward him. As neither give way, their shoulders collide. The contact spins them both around, forcing them face-to-face.

Crossing his arms over his chest, Michael defies Hawthorne's pretentiousness, as if to say: *You don't scare me.*

The attorney's chin is high, nose tipped up, snooty.

"What makes me worthy of your time, Hawthorne?"

As if Michael is a ghost, Hawthorne ignores him and says over his shoulder, "The owner expects a full report, Baxter. I've been protecting this town's interests since my county attorney days—they know what real leadership looks like."

Michael grimaces. The owner. The town's interests. Like 1918—work through the system, let others do the dirty work.

His stomach tumbles, a sense of dread rising in his throat. Hawthorne strolls toward the exit, his face impassive—a man used to getting what he wants.

His shoulders slump as Hawthorne exits, taking his livelihood and career with him.

"Schumann." Baxter's anger slices through the newsroom, which falls silent immediately. "My office. Now."

Not bothering to sit, Michael stands in front of the desk, bracing for the inevitable.

"You tried to pull a fast one," Baxter growls, dropping into his chair. "That little stunt—pretending to set up interviews with 'prominent citizens.' There was only *one* citizen you wanted. And now he's breathing down my neck."

The barest flicker of a smile plays on Michael's lips before he tamps it down. No sense denying it.

"You've been sniffing around the CPLE again, haven't you?" Baxter's voice drops. "I told you that story was dead."

Michael's mouth tightens. "It's not dead. And you know it."

Baxter huffs, shaking his head. "You never learn, do you?"

Michael leans in. "Chief, I'm fishing in a puddle—no depth, no meaning—a fluff piece meant to fill the page. This story has teeth. Kellerman just told me that another man was attacked. Let me check that out. Please."

Please tastes like ash on his tongue.

"Too late. I gave it to Pritchett."

Stunned into silence, Michael can't think of a worse person for that story. But Hawthorne's visit is the answer. Pritchett was in his pocket before and obviously still is.

"I've got a decent lead on the man who ordered the attacks." Revealing that fact is like handing over a match to someone standing in gasoline—but he hopes it will sway Baxter.

"Give it to Pritchett," Baxter repeats.

If he does that, he'll be playing right into Hawthorne's hands. If he doesn't, Baxter can do irreparable harm to his career. Michael stands mute at the corner of the desk.

Baxter sighs. His face is a canvas of conflicting emotions, furrowed brows and tightly pressed lips betraying a simmering anger. Yet, beneath the stormy exterior, his eyes soften, revealing a glimmer of understanding and compassion.

"The only reason I don't throw you out on your ear is because I expect you've learned your lesson. You'll quit this crusade to right every wrong from the past. You don't know what that story will do. Hawthorne's on the Chamber board. I run that story, half our advertisers cancel. I told you to drop it. Last chance."

The air in Michael's lungs whooshes out. He struggles to breathe. Frozen in place, Baxter's face blurs as Michael tries to focus. He wants to sit. He wants to run. All he can do is nod—like one of those toys with the bobbing head.

Either unaware or unwilling to acknowledge Michael's reaction, Baxter picks up the phone and dials. "Glad we're in agreement. Now, get to work."

Baxter's words release his body, but not his thoughts. Michael walks woodenly to his desk, staring at his hands. Might as well be encased in concrete. Useless. Trapped in a fight he can't win.

I can't lose this job.

I'm doing the right thing.

I am a good reporter.

He wants to go back to Nick's and drown himself in a bottle, but that won't do any good. He has a lead and he'll be damned if he gives it to Pritchett.

Job or no job.

Some things matter more than a paycheck. The truth is one of them.

Effie, her purse tucked under her arm indicating her workday is ending, stands beside him. She taps on his desk and a slip of paper falls into his lap. He sweeps it up and tucks it into his coat pocket.

Heading home, he reads it. The words are simple. "You are not alone."

He clenches it in his fist. He isn't alone. And he's not done. Yet.

Chapter Twenty

Olivia picks up the receiver.

Michael's voice is clipped and urgent. "There's been another attack. Can you meet me at the morgue?"

Did the man die? She pictures a room with dead bodies on tables and shudders at the thought.

Her silence cues him to his mistake. "Sorry. Not the dead people morgue. The newspaper archives. Here at the *Journal.*"

"Whatever for?"

"The cop that covered both attacks says if I can find a description or sketch—anything that matches the man Fredrick described—he'll show it to the other victim. And I can show it to the nurse at St. Boniface."

"I suppose." Clearing out Aunt Becky's closet can wait. "When?"

"After lunch." Michael pauses. "But listen. I need a cover for our research. Hawthorne came to the office yesterday to ensure I halt my investigation. I can lose my job if we're caught."

"He threatened your job. Can he do that?" Olivia realizes how innocent she sounds. Of course he can. He's got half the town in his pocket.

Olivia chews her lower lip. "I have an idea. What if we say I'm researching the founding families of Ellington and you're helping. That way you aren't looking into the CPLE, and I get a history lesson out of it."

"Perfect. See you at one o'clock. Meet me outside the main door to the paper."

* * *

133

At the *Journal*, Effie Winslow introduces herself as the three of them descend the stairs to the basement. Michael gives Olivia a quick tour while Effie stands watch at the door.

Michael selects *1920* for his research. Olivia chooses *1919*—the year her father died. As she turns the brittle yellow sheets, dust and paper particles tickle her nose, causing her to sneeze three times in succession.

"Gesundheit!" Michael says.

Finding nothing of note in January or February, she moves on to March. "What exactly are we looking for?"

"A face the nurse can identify," Michael says. "As you can see, front pages carry sketches, sometimes photographs. With the CPLE so prominent, perhaps we'll get lucky. Once I get her description, I'll be able to tell if Hawthorne is a match."

Standing over the newspaper is the only way to scan the pages. She digs in her briefcase for something to guide her eyes down the columns. The scrapbook and envelope full of clippings is still there.

"I have clippings." Olivia announces as if she's unearthed Tutankhamen's tomb.

"What?" Michael's head jerks up.

"The same ones that went flying when you bumped into me."

"You've had them the whole time?"

"I forgot about them in the drama of the last few days." She extracts the envelope from her briefcase.

"I'll look through those." Effie takes the envelope from Olivia. "You stick with *1919*."

Effie makes sure the door is locked, grabs a clump of clippings and starts rifling through them.

Scanning the newspapers is difficult in the uneven light of the single lightbulb swaying above the table. The shifting shadows make Olivia feel watched, though she knows they are alone.

In a late March edition, a headline announces, "Verdict in Sedition Case Expected Today". Running her finger down the lines of the article, she halts at the fourth paragraph.

"Michael, listen to this. Another disloyalty case my father defended. John Schroeder. Sound familiar?"

He halts his progress, waits for her to continue.

"In his closing argument for Schroeder, Victor Kendall was full of wit and humor and oratorical highlights. He ridiculed several Government witnesses and their testimony, and discussed politics, the war, the Wilson administration and its critics, German music, women and their frailties. Schroeder's state of mind and the "hysteria" growing out of the war were touched upon. He closed with a plea to the jury for his client, in which he incorporated an entire chapter of the Bible."

A laugh catches in her throat. That was Father—commanding, theatrical, devout.

Michael leaves his work and stands beside Olivia. Looking over her shoulder, she inhales the faint scent of tobacco and ink. His breath warms the space between them, and she subtly studies his face, the shifting light casting it in sharp relief—a strong jaw, high cheekbones, a shadow of stubble.

The air between them is thick, charged with something like electricity running through her stomach, her chest, her throat. He turns his head. Reflexively, she drops her chin as heat rises to her cheeks.

If Michael notices her discomfort, he doesn't show it. Perhaps his journalistic tendencies block whatever sensitivity he has to others. In any event, she's glad he's not responded to the moment; any acknowledgment would unravel her completely.

Olivia spots one line at the end of the article. "Victor Kendall warned that sedition was the easiest charge to make and the hardest to disprove."

Michael snorts. "I'd say he was right."

"Two weeks later, he was gone."

"I'm sorry." Michael lays a hand on her forearm.

There it is again. His touch flutters her heart, warms her face.

"I'm going to look for the Schroeder verdict," Olivia says.

She searches the following days but finds no mention of Schroeder's guilt or innocence.

Talking to herself, she taps her fingers on the table. "It's odd. Of all the clippings, there are none about Schroeder."

Michael snaps his fingers. "That's because Schroeder was tried in Evendale. If the *Journal* didn't cover the verdict, maybe the *Post* did."

"That makes sense. All the ones Aunt Becky saved came from the *Journal*."

"Hey, you two," Effie says, holding one of Olivia's clippings aloft. "This says there were seven men accused."

Michael doesn't look up. "Yeah. So?"

"As I remember, there were eight."

Michael stops reading, lifts his head and peers at her across the gloomy room. "An eighth man?"

"Want me to check it out?" Effie's eyes glint with curiosity.

"That'd be great," Michael exchanges a glance with Olivia. "How's your search going?"

"I'm about half-way through *1919*," Olivia says.

"Let's wrap it up. I want to get to the *Post* today." Turning to Effie, he asks, "Can you handle the rest of *1919*?"

"I'll do it over lunch while I'm searching for our mystery man."

"I finished *1920* and *21*. Mentions of the CPLE peter out after that. Did you know that Hawthorne was presented to the King and Queen of Belgium—for leading the greatest patriotic organization in the country?"

Olivia can't help herself. "That man makes me want to vomit."

"Well let's not do it here."

Michael checks his watch, tapping it absently as if that could slow time.

"I need to show whatever we find to Nurse Franklin at six when her shift ends." Michael closes the books and restacks them.

As they exit into the street, Effie lights a cigarette, inhaling deeply.

To Effie, Michael says, "Tell Baxter I'm following up on that warehouse fire near the rail yard. That should keep him happy for a couple hours."

"Will do. Want me to call Max and warn him you're coming?" Effie asks.

Michael squeezes Effie's arm and plants a kiss on her cheek. "You're a doll."

She swipes a hand over her cheek as if in disgust, but her playful smile and blush give her away.

Turning to Olivia, she says, "I hope you find what you're looking for, young lady. But beware," she crooks her thumb toward Michael, "this one's up to his eyeballs."

"I will. Thanks for your help today."

Effie opens her arms, and Olivia steps into them. The older woman's scent is faintly sweet, like gardenias, reminding her of Aunt Becky. She lets herself lean in.

With Clara and now Effie, she's rediscovering something she didn't realize she'd missed: female solidarity. A sisterhood forged in shared purpose.

Chapter Twenty-One

A diminutive man, compact in stature but exuding energy, strides up to the front desk at the *Evendale Post*.

"Michael!"

The men shake hands. Michael can't recall the last time he saw Max, but they run into each other every so often. He couldn't call him a friend. More a professional acquaintance.

Michael moves aside. "This is Olivia Kendall. She's a history teacher and is researching the founding families in the county."

"No need for pretense. Effie filled me in. And this pretty lady can have whatever she wants."

Michael hadn't expected Effie to do more than tell Max they were coming. Now someone else is aware of their search.

Max's lopsided smile and bright blue eyes endear him to her almost at once. He reaches for her hand and raises it to his lips.

Olivia blushes and lets the man have his way with her fingers. "Enchanté," she says.

Their interplay puts Michael off. He'd never kiss a woman's hand. Max's brand of charm irks him—cheap, rehearsed. The ease with which Olivia responds to Max's attention pricks at something raw inside him, a weakness he hadn't realized existed until this moment.

"Can you get us access to the archives?" His gruff tone earns a confounded stare from Olivia, but Max merely smiles.

"Follow me."

Like the *Journal*, the archived newspapers are in the basement. Max unlocks the door and switches on the lights. "You got a date, topic, or name? We've organized a set of index cards."

"*1919.*" Olivia and Michael speak at the same time. They laugh and look at each other. Michael is struck by the symmetry, not just in the search, but in what drives them to keep digging.

Olivia sets her briefcase down on one of the tables, while Michael reels off his needs. "Looking for defendants charged under the Espionage Act. The attorney was Victor Kendall. And anything on the Citizens Patriotic League of Ellington, and William Hawthorne."

Max points to a long box of index cards. "I'll pull *1918* to *1920.* Those are the prime years for your search."

Michael and Olivia agree on who's searching for what so they can divide and conquer. Max's eyes flit from one to the other, and he shakes his head as Olivia extracts a card and pages through *1919.*

While Michael flips through the card file, Max hovers close.

To keep Olivia from overhearing, Max whispers, "I hope you know what you're doing. That young lady has no business being involved and you know it. Hawthorne's the kind who won't take kindly to people poking in his business, past or present."

Sheepish, Michael lowers his voice. "I have it under control. We just need to find something that ties one of the attackers to Hawthorne or the CPLE."

"The ones under the underpass? You think they have something to do with it?" A spark of curiosity flickers in Max's eyes.

"They did it before, and there are too many similarities to ignore." Michael's whisper is frantic, conveying an intentional fear to Max.

"Nice of you to drag me into your investigation," Max adds irritably. "You've got an hour till I have to lock up."

Michael nods. "That works for my deadline."

Max shuffles to where Olivia is hastily turning pages. "You have everything you need, Miss Kendall?"

She glances up. "Olivia. This indexing will save tons of time. Thanks, Max."

The small man turns the door handle. "Schumann, put everything back. I'm not your maid."

* * *

An hour later, Max saunters into the room. "Any luck?"

Michael speaks first. "Nothing." Nothing to show the nurse, but he can't leave her waiting.

"Now what?" Max asks.

Peeling back his shirt sleeve, he peers at his watch. "I've got to meet my witness. Empty handed. Let's clean up."

"Wait!" Olivia counters. "I'm still looking for the Schroeder verdict."

"Ah," Michael's forgotten her mission. He glances at Max. "What if Max stays with you and I go meet Nurse Franklin?"

She tilts her head. "That would work. I'll keep an eye out for a sketch or something. Max, you have time to watch over me in this creepy basement?"

"I'd die before I let anything happen to you." Max mimes rolling up his sleeves, then examines his thin arms with mock disappointment. "On the other hand, perhaps my razor-sharp wit will suffice."

"Your theatrics are way too much for me." Michael stuffs his notebook in his breast pocket and climbs the stairs to street level. Nurse Franklin's description will either rule out Hawthorne or put him squarely at the center of his investigation. He's not sure which he prefers.

* * *

He reaches the hospital just as Nurse Franklin exits the building. His suit is rumpled, his collar damp with sweat, and his empty pocket threatens to stop his investigation cold.

He hesitates before calling out and scans the street. Two men linger outside a barbershop, one of them lighting a cigarette. A woman with a paper sack steps off the curb.

Nothing suspicious. But his gut twists all the same.

"Nurse Franklin!" Michael strides up quickly and lowers his voice. "Let's talk over here."

She gives him a once-over. "You look like you've seen a ghost."

He takes her arm, guiding her around the side of the building where a tree casts a long shadow against the wall.

"This isn't exactly proper," she says, but her tone softens when she sees the worry etched in his face.

"I know. I'm sorry," he whispers. "There was another attack. Like Mr. Haber."

She covers her mouth, eyes wide.

"And it was important that I get something so you could identify that man, stop these attacks." Michael looks off into the distance. "But I have nothing."

"Oh." Nurse Franklin focuses on the direction where Michael's gaze is focused, as if he's watching something. "Don't you want a description?"

He's been so focused on bringing something to her, he's forgotten what she has to offer. His notebook in hand, he poises his pencil. "Yes, of course."

Focusing on the sky, she lists his characteristics. "Your height. Belly so big he couldn't button his suit coat if he wanted to. His nose had a huge bump on the end. Bug-eyed, like he knew what I looked like under my uniform." She shivers.

"What about his hair?"

"Thin on top. Mousy brown. Gray at the temples."

"Anything else?"

She shakes her head.

Definitely not Hawthorne. But who?

She stares at him. The seconds stretch between them while a streetcar bell clangs in the distance. "I'm hoping this is the last thing you need from me. I think I should steer clear of whatever evil you're chasing."

He scuffs his shoe on the ground and nods. She's right.

"Can I walk you somewhere?"

"My stop is a block from here."

"Lead the way." Michael crooks an arm and Nurse Franklin steps beside him and curls her arm through his.

* * *

As dusk settles over the city, the southbound streetcar rattles along the tracks toward home. Michael stares out the window wondering if Olivia found what she was looking for.

Stepping into the street, the atmosphere shifts. The cool evening air brushes against his skin, and with it comes a sense that something is off. He quickens his pace, a subtle reaction to an inexplicable sensation that he's not alone.

With each step, his senses sharpen. The sound of footsteps, light but deliberate, trail behind him. He glances over his shoulder casually, but it's only a pedestrian on the other side of the street.

No visible threat. Just a knot in his stomach and a prickling sense that he's being watched. Or followed.

The streetlamps flicker to life, casting yellow pools of light, both welcoming and ominous. He picks up his pace, heartbeat thumping, rationalizing his anxiety. Each time he looks over his shoulder, he half-expects a shadow in a doorway to materialize into a person.

At his door, he kicks himself for leading whoever is following him to his home where his mother and Clara are inside. Too late now.

He enters the parlor and peeks through the curtains. Sounds from the kitchen tell him dinner will be ready soon.

The house is too exposed. Too vulnerable. He slips out the back and ducks into the narrow slot between his house and the one next door. At the end, leaning against the wall, he wants a cigarette, but its glow will reveal his position. He glances up and down the street, berating himself for jumping at shadows.

He stays alert to night sounds until he's certain his family is safe, but knows that sometimes, it's not just about what you see—it's about what's lurking just out of sight.

Chapter Twenty-Two

With Max opposite her paging through *1920*, Olivia flips through *1919* and finally finds the Schroeder verdict. Guilty. Her father lost—why would the CPLE go after him if they got what they wanted?

Her eyes scan the rest of the page—then her father's name jumps out. Victor Kendall represented Leopold Adelmann in a lawsuit against a judge for calling him a German spy during a League meeting.

He lost two high-profile sedition cases involving the CPLE—then went after a judge. "That's pretty high stakes, Father," Olivia says aloud.

Max lifts his head. "What's high stakes?"

"Take a look at this."

Max climbs on a chair for a better view. She points at the article about the judge and crosses her arms while she waits for Max to finish.

His head twists. "Kendall's your father."

Olivia nods. "He also defended this man." She redirects Max's attention to the headline about the Schroeder verdict.

Max scans the article. "I'm not following the connection."

"My father defended Michael's grandfather and was killed by an automobile during all these trials. Michael and I think these recent attacks are connected to the CPLE."

Max heads back to his volume of newspapers. "So, this is personal."

"Very," she says and rounds the table to peer over his shoulder.

He flips a page, then another, too quickly to read anything more than a headline or two.

"Wait!" Olivia cries. "Go back." A single word in the headline grabs her attention. League.

Max turns the page back.

"There!"

Under the headline, "Principals in $50,000 Suit Against Patriot League Member" is a courtroom sketch. Olivia searches for identification. Her finger stabs at a man with a mustache. "Hawthorne."

"Pretty good likeness," Max says.

"It is. That means the rest of these men might be just as recognizable." Olivia straightens, hands on hips. "This is what we've been looking for."

"This is what Michael needs to show the nurse?"

"Yes, and you've just found it!"

Olivia puts a hand on each of Max's cheeks, turns his face toward hers and plants a kiss on his forehead.

He reddens from the neck up, but his lips part, showing a row of straight white teeth. "Why Miss Kendall! If I didn't know better, I'd say you were trying to seduce me."

Olivia's cheeks burn. To distract him and herself from her spontaneity, she points to the paper. "I need that."

"Well, you can't have it."

"I'll bring it back."

"No. Documents don't leave the morgue."

Olivia studies him. "I'm taking that, Max, even if I have to knock you down."

"All right, wait a minute." Max scuttles to the shelves. A chair scrapes, something rolls, then a grunt.

She contemplates tearing the sketch out and making a run for it, but that only happens in the picture shows.

"Here." Max extends a folded newspaper to her. "We had another copy."

Olivia grabs it, opens it to the front page, and stares down at the sketch. A buzz of energy flows through her as she realizes what it means if the man in the hospital is in this sketch.

She folds the paper. "Thank you, Max. I'm eternally grateful."

"What now?"

"I'll get this to Michael in the morning."

"Where does this nurse work?"

"St. Boniface."

"Well, I can save you a trip and leave it with him at the newsroom."

"You're kind, but I'll do it."

"Olivia, can I point something out?"

She's stuffing her briefcase with her notes. "What?"

"There are people who probably don't want this sketch circulated."

"What people?" As soon as she says it, it dawns on her and Max confirms it.

"Hawthorne. The others." He points to the paper.

"You mean...I didn't..." Olivia sits abruptly.

Would she be in danger if she carried this sketch across town? Take this potential bombshell home with her?

"I guess I didn't think it through. But I don't want to put you in danger either."

"Those men don't know about me. I'm aware of what the CPLE was capable of back then. Can't imagine they're still in operation. It's been too long."

She really wanted to be the one to give Michael the ammunition he needed, but Max's warning weighs heavily on the side of caution.

"Will you tell him to call me after he meets the nurse?"

"Cross my heart." Max makes an exaggerated X on his chest.

"All right." She picks up her briefcase and hands him the paper. "Let's get out of here."

Chapter Twenty-Three

The next morning, as Michael approaches his office, Max greets him.

"Morning, Mike."

"This is a surprise." Michael slows his pace.

"Hey, can I get a minute? Before you go in?" Max shoves his hat off his forehead so he can see Michael as he tilts his head upward.

"Uh, yeah." Michael stares down at the shorter man. "You stalking me?"

A chuckle escapes before Max clutches Michael's arm and guides him along the sidewalk away from the entrance to the *Journal*. "Olivia and I found something last night. I think it's what you need."

Michael stops dead in his tracks. "What?"

"Not here."

With unspoken agreement, they walk down the block until Max steps into an alley. He extracts the newspaper from his suit coat pocket and unfolds it. He flicks the sketch with his forefinger, hands it to Michael, and waits for his reaction.

Michael's eyes widen as he scans the sketch. "Oh, Max. This is perfect!" He grabs Max by both shoulders. "You have no idea what this means! This could be exactly what we need to—"

"Whoa there," Max interrupts, grinning and stepping back. "You're not gonna kiss me, are you? Because Olivia already claimed that honor."

His elation at the sketch is overshadowed by hearing that Olivia kissed Max. He's not sure why it bothers him, but it does. Perhaps he's been too lackadaisical about the woman, and Max's charm is already getting results.

Brusquely he asks Max, "May I keep this?"

"Yeah sure, but may I ask what you plan to do with it?"

Michael exhales, his lips tight as he thinks about what he is going to do next. "I need to go to the hospital."

"What? Are you sick?" Max asks.

"The nurse works at St. Boniface. But first, I gotta check in at the office." Michael's mind reels through scheduled assignments, but Effie will have more. "Max, I can't thank you enough."

"Olivia and I were happy to find it. Let me know how it goes, will you?"

Michael senses Max wants something else but he's already planning his trip to the hospital. He murmurs as he turns to leave, "Sure. See you later."

* * *

Michael eyes the address in his notebook and matches it to the house number on Eighteenth Street. After the hospital said she'd called in sick, he'd borrowed a phone book and looked up her address.

He steps onto the porch and knocks.

"Who is it?" echoes from inside.

"Charlotte. It's me. Michael."

"Go away."

The two words are slurred, her tone tired and aggravated.

"I heard you were sick. Can I do anything for you?"

At this, the door opens. Charlotte Franklin supports herself with one hand on the door, the other on the jamb as if she needs it for support. Her hair is disheveled, her clothing wrinkled, almost slovenly. But it's her face that nearly brings Michael to his knees. There's a bruise above one eye, with adjacent scrapes on her forehead and nose, raw and angry. Her bottom lip is swollen and split down the middle.

"Oh no..." He swallows pitiful refrains of sympathy. A sneaking suspicion of what happened —and why—rattles him to his core.

"You did this." She hisses from her broken mouth. "Know what you can do for me? Leave me alone!"

But she contradicts herself by walking away, leaving him standing on the porch.

He steps tentatively inside and finds Charlotte alternately holding an ice pack to her lip, then her eye.

This is his fault. He'd dragged this poor woman into his crusade for justice. "I'm sorry."

"As a reporter, I'm sure you want to know what happened. So here it is. I'll tell you, then you get the hell out. Understood?"

Michael nods mutely at the prospect of information, but his notebook stays tucked in his pocket.

"I got off the streetcar like always, turned onto my block. Heard footsteps behind me—didn't think anything of it. Lots of folks going home after work, right? When I got to my door, I was searching for my key, when the next thing I knew, my face was kissing the wall. He pinned me, then wrapped his arm around my neck. I couldn't breathe. Couldn't move." Charlotte touches her throat.

"I'll never forget his aftershave. Piney—like cleaning solution. Whispered in my ear: 'You and that reporter need to stop worrying about things that don't concern you.'"

She closes her eyes, concentrating. "His voice. I've heard it before. Not sure where." She pauses, then continues. "Asked if I understood. I nodded like a fool. He released me and disappeared."

Michael absorbs her terror, her helplessness. He swallows hard before he asks, "Did you call the police?"

"No. He said to keep my trap shut."

Kellerman was right. He'd jeopardized an innocent woman.

"Anyone else see what happened?"

She shrugs. "Probably not."

He's got a list of questions as long as his arm, ones that identify the thug, but one look at her face stops him. This is no time for a victim interview.

A knock on the door startles them both. Charlotte shrinks, her body curling on the sofa in a protective ball.

"Want me to check it out?" He stoops beside her, gazing into eyes like a deer with the hunter's gun aimed.

She nods vigorously.

He looks around for a window he can peer through, but there's none with a view of the porch. He decides to do what Charlotte did.

"Who is it?" He waits, and hopes it's not the guy who beat her up last night.

"Michael. It's me. Max."

Max? What the hell?

From the front room, Charlotte's voice is weak, questioning. "Who is it?"

"It's a friend. I'll be right back," Michael says over his shoulder as he steps onto the porch. "What are you doing here?"

Max flinches. "I came to check on you. And her."

Michael's hand freezes on the doorknob. How did Max know he'd be here? He closes the door, ensuring Charlotte can't hear them.

A knot forms in his stomach. He's seen Max twice in one day. Is he involved in this?

"You just happen to show up? What's going on Max?"

Shifting his weight foot to foot, Max stares up at Michael. "I didn't follow you, I swear. It's just that after you left, I got to thinking. Were you safe? I warned Olivia last night and thought maybe you could use a hand, or a friend, with all," his hands spread out encompassing the house, "this."

"Go on." Michael is intrigued with Max's thought process.

"I called the hospital to check on her," he nods at the house. "And they said she was sick. That's when I really got worried. You saw her last night and even if you had nothing to show her, what if they didn't know it?"

Blinking, as if to fix blurred vision, Michael says, "They?"

"I don't know who they are, but what if they thought you'd gotten something from her, something that would put you both in danger."

Michael nods, seeing Max's logic.

"So, I came here."

Blowing out a long breath, Michael says, "She's been hurt. Badly."

"Ah, geez. I hate it when I'm right."

"No more than me."

Max flicks a glance at Michael. "Did you show her the sketch?"

Michael shakes his head, slow and regretful. "No. I don't dare. She's already scared half to death."

"Then your sketch idea is dead in the water?"

Michael thinks a moment. "Not completely. Kellerman said he'd show the other victim. And her description fits two of the men."

"Well, that's something," Max says.

Silence stretches between the men, both lost in their own thoughts at the circumstances.

"Who's he?" Charlotte's scratchy voice comes from behind Michael.

He hadn't heard the door open, and he grapples with what to tell her. Or not to tell her.

He sees his own reaction to Charlotte's injuries mirrored on Max's face. Eyebrows pinched, eyes soft with pity, as if he's witnessed this kind of hurt before. Then, just as quickly, the look vanishes. Max sweeps off his hat in an easy bow.

"Max Ingram at your service, ma'am. Looks like you could use some ice for that eye. Do you have any? If not, I can run down to the corner store?"

"That's kind of you," Charlotte says, "I just ran out."

He tips his hat. "Back in a jiffy."

Michael watches him leave, wondering again about the timing of Max's arrival.

Chapter Twenty-Four

On the porch, Olivia holds a tin of cookies. Effie has a casserole. Michael taps on the door, soft, respectful.

"Who is it?" A woman asks from within.

"Michael."

A sharp click, a soft creak, the door swings wide. A young woman beams at Michael, then freezes when she sees the strangers flanking him. Olivia's hands tighten on the tin as she takes in the woman's bruised and bloodied face—Michael's description hadn't done it justice.

Nurse Franklin's hand shoots to one hip. "You got more friends than I have nylons. Who are they?" She nods toward the group.

"I apologize for coming unannounced." He turns to Effie. "Charlotte, this is my colleague at the paper, Effie Winslow."

Effie steps forward. "I thought you might enjoy a home cooked meal while you're recovering." She removes the lid. "Chicken and rice."

Charlotte's features relax. "That's kind. I haven't been to the market in a couple days."

Not to be outdone, Olivia jumps in. "I'm Olivia and I've brought cookies. I know when I'm not feeling well, a sweet helps." She berates herself for sounding like a puppet.

A smile begins, but halts abruptly as Charlotte touches her lip. "Still hurts."

Michael takes charge. "We'd like to talk to you. Can we go inside?"

Olivia's glad he's asked. Standing on the porch makes her feel naked—someone could be watching them.

"Yes, of course. Please, come in."

Effie turns left toward the kitchen. Olivia follows the nurse and Michael, placing the tin on a side table in the front room. Charlotte yanks a sheet and blanket from the sofa, rolls them up, and stashes them behind a chair.

"Sorry, the place is a mess."

"We're sorry for barging in." Effie says from the doorway.

"You look a little better today," Michael says.

"I am, but let me tell you, every bump in the night wakes me, and it takes hours to get back to sleep."

"I've been a little jumpy lately myself," Olivia offers solidarity. "This whole thing with the men who attacked Mr. Haber is weighing on all of us."

"That's why you're here, isn't it? You found something."

Olivia holds her breath, the tension in the room thickening when no one denies it.

"You're right. I do have something. But," Michael raises a hand as Charlotte opens her mouth to speak. "It's on your terms. Not ours."

"What's that mean? My terms?" Her gaze lands on Olivia as if she's got the answer, and she does because they've rehearsed what they would say and ask, when they'd decided to visit.

Olivia sits next to Charlotte and lays a hand on her knee. "Miss Franklin, I won't claim to understand how you're feeling. But at one time, I was deathly afraid."

Effie is over Charlotte's shoulder, and her tiny smile gives Olivia courage.

"My father was hit by an automobile when I was sixteen. He died from his injuries."

"Oh geez, I'm sorry." Charlotte tucks her hand over Olivia's.

"Thank you." Her voice catches but she continues. "I was there when he was struck down. I couldn't cross a street for a year. Every time I went to dismount from a streetcar, I was paralyzed for fear of it happening to me."

"But that's nothing like this." Charlotte says, waving her hand around her face.

"No, no, of course not. You're in a much different situation. But here's the similarity." Olivia clasps the woman's hand. It's smooth, elastic, the hand of a woman who heals.

Charlotte waits, her hand tightening in Olivia's grip.

"Now, I'm chasing whoever killed my father. The one who ran him down is still out there. And I think he's connected to the same men who attacked Mr. Haber."

Charlotte's eyes widen like saucers and she jerks her hand out of Olivia's grasp. "No."

"Yes. Michael and I both know Mr. Haber. His grandson is in my class in high school. The attack on them was senseless and as there's been another attack recently, you are our best...our only hope, to connect the same men to those who killed my father."

"But they'll come after me again. I don't want to live like this. I have to work, but I'm afraid to leave my house."

"That's where I come in," Effie leaves the doorway and stoops next to Charlotte. "I have an extra room at my place. You can stay there, and I'll arrange to get you back and forth to the hospital. Until this gets resolved."

Shock registers on Charlotte's face. "You'd do that?"

"I would. And mostly it's because I like this big oaf over here." Her head jerks toward Michael. "He's got a good heart, just kinda clumsy when it comes to thugs and bad guys."

"Yeah, that's him." Charlotte groans when she tries to smile at Michael.

Michael slips the folded newspaper from his suit coat pocket. Olivia hopes he doesn't pounce, that he goes easy so as not to spook her.

Charlotte eyes the paper. She touches her eye then her lip.

Olivia clasps her hand. "You don't have to do anything. But I, er we, are worried that even if you don't look at what Michael has, you aren't clear of danger. So, no matter what you decide, Effie's offer stands."

Her chin lifts ever so slightly. Then it dips.

Olivia crosses her fingers on her unoccupied hand, a silent prayer of hope.

"All right."

The tension breaks, and everyone breathes again. Michael, Effie, and Olivia make eye contact. They aren't done yet. They got permission. Now they need a positive identification that one of the men in the sketch is who they are looking for.

"Give it to me," Charlotte extends her hand to Michael who gives her the folded paper.

"Front page," Michael says. Outside, cars rumble down the street and a woman calls for her kid, the sounds drifting into the room.

Laying it flat on her lap, Charlotte stares. Her eyes move from man to man, studying each as if her decision is life or death. Because it is.

She spends a few seconds on one image. Her finger points. "Him. Howard Pitts. He was the man looking for Mr. Haber."

Olivia wants fireworks and a band playing to celebrate this milestone. But in the next moment, she realizes what needs to happen next. Take this to the police so they can stop Pitts from doing any more harm.

Chapter Twenty-Five

At his desk the next morning, Michael sifts through his assignments. A cutest pet contest, local bakery celebrates fiftieth anniversary with free cupcakes, and a high school band prepares for national competition. He makes the calls. Schedules the stops. Maps the route. All in the name of fluff—and keeping his job.

Catching up with Kellerman is a priority. He adds him as his final stop at Nick's.

His notebook has one page left. He pulls a fresh one from his desk drawer, tucking the old one away.

Effie hunches over her typewriter, a cigarette dangling from her lips, the ash long, threatening to fall.

"You have the report on the second attack?" he asks.

Her head jerks up and the ashes drop into her lap. She swipes them away and fumbles through a stack, finds the copy she wants and hands it to him.

The report has no new information. Michael wanders over to Pritchett's desk.

"Chief took me off the attacks on those German men, as I'm sure you're aware," Michael says.

Pritchett glances up, adjusting his glasses. Scraggly hairs protrude from his nostrils.

"I'm aware. Dead end if you ask me."

"Tell that to the guy in the hospital." He can barely control his irritation at Pritchett's snotty dismissal. "Did you get a description of the attackers?"

"What's it matter? Not your concern. Go write about dancing dogs or whatever they've got you on today."

Michael's jaw tightens. He's getting nowhere. "At least I can look forward to free cupcakes." He backs away from Pritchett.

He hands Effie his assignment slips confirming what he's covering.

"Meet me at the Five and Dime on Lincoln at noon. I have information on that eighth man. And bring me a cupcake, Cupcake."

* * *

"How's Charlotte?" Michael says, sliding onto an empty stool at the counter, glad to sit after running around town all morning.

"She's better. Called in sick again." Effie taps an ash into a cup of cold coffee on the counter. "What's next, cub reporter?"

"I hope to find Kellerman at Nick's after work."

"Is he on your side?"

"He said he'd take whatever I found to the second victim. I've got no choice but to trust him."

"Glad you're not trying to find him at police headquarters. There are too many big ears that run straight back to Hawthorne and Pitts."

Silence settles between them, thick with smoke and consequences.

Effie reaches into her purse and slides a newspaper onto the counter, her finger tapping the headline.

Eighth Suspect Held by U.S.

Michael straightens and scans the article. Jimmy Rowe—a jockey from Louisville—charged with making statements against Red Cross workers and nurses.

"I did a little digging. They arrested him two weeks after the others. And confessed," Effie says, voice tight.

Michael's gaze snaps to hers. "Confessed? To what?"

"Told the judge he'd made those statements in the shoe shop as bait to get evidence. Timing's interesting too. Detectives verified they heard his statements in late June."

Michael stares at the paper. "And the other seven arrests were made days later."

Effie nods. "The trail goes cold after that. My bet is the charges were dropped."

Michael stiffens. Something's off. His fingers curl around the edge of the paper, dragging it toward him.

"They were scrambling." His thumb presses into the newsprint as if he could force out more answers. "They needed more for indictments. Before their July Fourth deadline."

Michael lets out a hollow laugh, his head thrown back in disbelief. "A goddamn setup, and nobody saw it."

Pitching his cigarette into the coffee cup, he shoves his hat on his head.

"I'll be at the office after this last story. Main Street's fresh look," he says. *Would a coat of paint hide Ellington's scars?*

"All right, I'll go to Nick's and hold Kellerman till you get there."

Michael turns left. Effie makes a right.

She doesn't look back. Neither does he.

* * *

In the office Michael rummages in his desk drawer for his old notebook. He shuffles the contents until he's so frustrated, he yanks the drawer out and tips it onto his desk.

It's gone. Everything was in there—Hawthorne, Stone, Simpson, Nurse Franklin. A flash of heat surges through him, and his pulse thrums in his ears.

Instinctively, he checks Baxter's office. Pritchett is waving his hands in animated jerks as he talks.

Pritchett took it. Michael's certain of it.

He clears the debris and slams the drawer shut. He glances at his desk calendar, checking any appointments for tomorrow. In the box marked June 22, his mistake stares back at him.

Six P.M. St. Boniface. Franklin.

That's how they knew. The connection to him—right there on his calendar.

The realization hits like a sucker punch. He never thought twice about what he jotted on his calendar. It never occurred to him someone would go looking.

Pritchett. Again.

He marches across the newsroom, glancing at the clock—4:45. If he wants to catch Kellerman, he'll have to move fast.

As he nears Baxter's office, the door opens and Pritchett steps out, smiling like the cat that swallowed the canary.

Michael blocks his exit, his jaw working as he weighs his options. Part of him wants to pin Pritchett against the wall until he talks. But he forces himself to think like a reporter, not a street brawler. Confronting Pritchett now would only confirm that the notebook information is important.

"Finished for the day chief," Michael says, his voice steady despite the anger simmering beneath, his gaze fixed on Pritchett's beady eyes. He is enjoying the old man trying to escape, moving to one side to get past, and Michael mirroring his move.

Baxter looks up from his desk, his expression a mix of irritation and caution. "When you two finish your little dance, close the damn door."

"Sure thing." Michael stands sideways just enough for Pritchett to pass him, eyeing each other until the old man scurries away like a rat looking for its hole.

* * *

Michael spots them. Effie leans casually against the bar while Kellerman nurses a whiskey.

He drops on the empty stool as Effie signals for her tab.

"I've got it." Michael waves her off.

Snapping her purse closed, she slides the handle up her arm. "Thanks for the company, Abe. See you tomorrow, Michael."

Still seeing red from his missing notebook and kicking himself for the stupid note on his calendar, he's in no mood for small talk with the cop.

He removes the paper from his pocket, unfolds it, lays it in front of Abe, and pokes an accusing finger on the sketch. "Here's the proof."

Kellerman leans in, eyeing a half-dozen members of the CPLE. "Damn! You weren't kidding."

Pointing to the man in the middle of the sketch next to Hawthorne, Michael says, "My witness identified Pitts as the man asking about Haber at the hospital."

Kellerman exhales through his nose, fingers drumming against his glass. "So?"

How could he be so dense?

Michael spells it out like he's teaching a stubborn child. "If Pitts was looking for Haber, he must have something to do with the attack."

Abe sits back and signals for another drink. The men in the sketch don't blink—just wait, daring him to act.

"And I'm supposed to show this to the second guy. Doller."

Michael exhales—relieved the cop finally gets it.

Kellerman tips his whiskey and downs half. "Pitts was a nobody till Hawthorne came along. Pulled him up through the CPLE ranks as his sidekick before demoting him to toady. I don't want to go back there, Michael. It's too dangerous. The League's gone, but look who still runs things—same men, new name: the Chamber."

"Look Abe," Michael says, an undercurrent of urgency in his voice. "I know you stayed under the radar back when the CPLE was having its way. But it's 1937 not 1918. Whether it's the CPLE or the Chamber, things haven't changed. People should feel safe in this city."

"It might be a long time, sure, but elephants don't forget." Abe's tone carries a hint of fear.

"Then I'm an elephant too!" Michael slams his glass on the bar. He wants to scream at the top of his lungs, but that won't get him what he wants.

Instead, he lowers his voice to a whisper. "Abe, my grandfather lost everything because of the CPLE. Many others in this city were harassed, beaten, and humiliated. Everyone was so afraid of them, that no one said anything, did anything. This whole damned city was paralyzed by this group who used terror to reach their goal. If everyone was too afraid to speak out, they had free rein. I don't want that to happen again and if we," Michael points to Abe, then himself, "do nothing, and someone else is hurt or, God forbid, dies, it's on us."

His pulse hammers—whether from whiskey or fury, he doesn't care. He's said what had to be said.

Abe stares at him, shifting his gaze to the mirror behind the bar. He studies his own reflection, a man divided between what's right and what's smart. The whiskey glass lingers in his grip. He turns it slow, deliberate.

Finally, he downs the last of his drink, folds the paper, and tucks it in his coat pocket.

"I'll check with Doller," he says, quieter now. "If he can identify Pitts, I'll take it to my superiors."

Chapter Twenty-Six

At Uncle John's office, Olivia greets Adeline Able, secretary to the firm John and her father ran for more than twenty years. They spend a few minutes catching up until the intercom buzzes on Adeline's desk, and her uncle's voice is in the room as if he were standing next to her.

"I'm ready for Miss Kendall."

Briefcase in hand, Olivia rises and reaches for the doorknob and hesitates. Memories of past visits squeeze her heart, but she swallows them down and steps inside.

Uncle John rises at her entry and comes around the desk. "Olivia! Imagine my surprise when I saw you on my calendar. You certainly brighten up an old man's boring day."

He kisses her cheek and ushers her to one of two green leather chairs facing his oversized walnut desk. Her seat in front of him evokes painful memories of difficult decisions and heartbreak when he and Aunt Becky discussed the details of her parents' estate.

John barrels straight to the point, missing her melancholy entirely. "What can I do for you? I know you've got Becky's estate in hand. Is there something else you found while clearing the house?"

"I've been going through Father's old cases...and I need your help understanding what happened back then." She reaches into her briefcase and pulls out a yellow pad of paper with her notes.

John's expression shifts, from easy warmth to a chilly smile. He leans back in his chair, an attempt at indifference. He tilts his head, considering. "Olivia, if this is about those old sedition cases—"

"It is."

His jaw tightens.

Her gaze does not waver. In fact, Olivia hardens her resolve and braces for his objections.

"Not again," he says, shaking his head. "That theory of yours has no legs. We lost those cases, life went on." His voice drops, weary. "That's all there is to it."

She's glad she prepared her approach this morning because she's got a ready response.

"Is that really all there is to it?" Her glare challenges him to say otherwise. "You and father had two high-profile cases. One in Ellington. The Dictograph case. And another in Evendale," she glances down at the pad. "John Schroeder, I believe."

"We did." John places his elbows on the desk.

"Why did you and father take those cases? Did you believe you could win?"

Her direct question, meant to put him on the defensive, hits home. John wriggles in his chair as if adjusting his backside from sitting too long.

"There weren't many attorneys willing to take on those cases. Those men were doomed from the start—no one wanted to be associated with them."

Olivia nods as if in agreement. "But you and father were a winning combination before those trials. That must have hurt your reputation."

"Your father wanted the cases. He liked defending the little guy, the one who got the short end of the stick."

"And you went along."

John nods. "It paid the bills. Seven times our usual fee. Pretty good money."

Olivia extracts a news clipping from the legal pad and lays in on the desk. It's déjà vu from her meeting with Hawthorne.

C.P.L. MEMBERS SUED BY GOETZ

John picks up the clipping, briefly scans it. "Goetz came to us for representation. Victor was itching to take the CPLE down. Offense instead of defense. Your father worked on the pre-trial motions and jury selection. Unfortunately, he died before we could go to trial."

"Why didn't you handle the case afterwards? That's a decent fee for winning fifty thousand dollars."

"I was overloaded. Overwhelmed after Victor was...gone." John sits back in his chair, looking everywhere but at Olivia.

Plowing on, she says, "Then the firm signed Leo Adelmann. A city official suing the police court judge for, coincidentally, fifty thousand dollars. You didn't take that one when Father died either." Olivia cocks an eyebrow. "Overloaded?"

"It was just me," John says. "I had other work. Cases I could win."

Olivia catches his slip on that last—he didn't think he could win Adelmann's case. Or worse, he didn't want to try. It was too risky. Too public. Too connected.

"The same day Schroeder was found guilty, Adelmann began his suit. While the Dictograph Case was in appeals, Goetz hired your firm to go after the CPLE. Is it possible that Father's ambition rattled a few cages?"

John sighs. "I suppose if you stack them all up like that it's damning, but trust me Olivia, that's nothing more than timing. Coincidence."

He glances at the clock on his desk. "I've got another appointment. Have you got what you came for?"

He wants to be done and she wants to quit making this man squirm like a witness on the stand. The irony is not lost on her.

"One more thing," she says and unconsciously uncrosses her legs, planting her feet firmly in front of her.

"Do you remember Tinker Evans?" Her chin lifts enough to let him know she's intent on answers.

John frowns, his mouth tightening. "Who?"

"The bank porter. Black man, mid-twenties. He testified multiple times. Identified the men to the detectives by their voices."

A pause. A fraction too long.

"Doesn't ring a bell," John says, shaking his head.

"That's strange." Olivia flips a page on her legal pad, keeping her voice neutral. "Because I have it on good authority that he told you and father that the detectives fabricated evidence."

John's face is stone. Not a muscle twitches.

"Now Olivia. It's been a long time. I have notes from the case somewhere. I can look and get back to you."

What is he hiding? Grabbing her briefcase, she peers at him. "You do that, Uncle John. Check your notes on how the CPLE manipulated *everything*, from the statements and the witnesses to the bribery and blackmail that got them what they wanted. Did they get to you too? I know they didn't get to father. He was a better man."

She shoves her yellow pad into her briefcase and stands.

His head droops, and when he finally looks up, there's something in his eyes—guilt? Fear?

"I'm sorry, Olivia," he murmurs.

"For what?" Her voice is sharp.

He hesitates.

The clock ticks, measuring the silence between them.

"I just am."

She waits, hoping he'll clarify. He doesn't.

"No, I'm sorry." She says without a trace of sympathy. "Sorry for you and the men in this town who let, no, wanted to hurt innocent men, to fulfill an agenda."

She yanks the door open, then stops. Over her shoulder she says, "I want to trust you. But I'm not a little girl anymore, Uncle John."

And then she leaves. No slamming. No theatrics. She moves with deliberate, unhurried steps, ensuring she appears to be in control. Outside John's office, she leans against the wall, pressing her fingers to the bridge of her nose. A quiet, steady exhale—then she squares her shoulders, lifts her chin, and steps back into the real world, composed as ever.

* * *

The interview saps her energy, but she wants to share it with someone. Michael is her first choice, but Effie says he's out of the office.

"Can you tell him to meet me at the shoe shop? I've got something to tell him."

Then she dials the *Post*.

"Olivia! Love of my life. What can I do for you?"

Max's charm is just this side of ridiculous. "You can meet me at Warner Shoe Shop after work."

"Shoe shop? I don't believe I'm in need of any such services."

She rolls her eyes. "I'm meeting Michael and his sister there. And there's something I need you to do."

"Oh, Am I your knight in shining armor?"

"Let's just say the armor is heavy, dull, and won't protect you from harm."

"I am thoroughly intrigued. See you at six."

* * *

The bell over the door tinkles as Olivia steps inside, the pleasant scent of leather and polish greeting her. Max follows, his gaze sweeping the tiny lobby of the shop.

From the rear, Clara's voice calls out. "I'll be right there."

"No rush," Olivia replies, absently running her fingers over the countertop.

"Is this where they talked?" Max asks glancing around the shop.

Olivia points to the corner. "That's where the grandfather clock was."

"Clever."

"What's clever?" Clara asks, wiping her hands on her apron as she steps from behind the counter.

The two women embrace like old friends.

"This is Max Ingram."

Extending a hand, he says, "Pleased to meet you. Clever—how they hid the device."

Clara fixes him with a hard look, unimpressed. "More like dirty tricks. But sure, call it whatever you want."

Clara crosses her arms over her chest and eyes Max with suspicion. "Why'd you bring him along?"

"Max is a reporter with the *Evendale Post*," Olivia says. "I was thinking he might be able to help us find Tink."

"Um, pardon me, I'm in the room here. Who's Tink?"

Olivia explains the connection, then, "After my uncle just denied knowing him, I'm thinking Tink might have a few more pieces of the puzzle." Raising her eyebrows, she asks Clara, "Where did you say he went?"

"California."

Max scoffs. "That narrows it down."

"You didn't let me finish." Clara's glare could spark kindling. "Los Angeles, I think."

"Sorry," Max scuffs a shoe on the floor, and with a hangdog look says, "I'll behave."

"It's a big city," Olivia states the obvious. "A needle in a haystack."

"I have a pal at the Times. But before I contact him, can I get a bit more information?"

Clara tells him what she can about Tink, then, eyeing the clock above the workbench, removes her apron. "Let's close up and head over to the Gaslight."

"I assume you're inviting me to tag along," Max says.

Olivia glances at Max, then Clara, "I trust him."

A subtle frown pulls at the corners of Clara's mouth, "All right then. Let's go, Shorty."

"How quaint. However, I much prefer Max." His tone is light and teasing, but there's steel beneath the words.

"I think I'll call you Maximus," Clara announces, and winks at Olivia over Max's head.

"Much better than Maxwell," he says. "Parents named me after the coffee or the Nashville hotel. Tennesseans have odd naming conventions."

And despite everything, they have a reason to laugh.

As they head toward the saloon, Olivia follows Max and Clara's interplay with quiet amusement. Max's jokes are harmless, and Clara has a quick wit. But knowing Clara even for a short time, her guard won't drop easily.

For one moment Olivia thinks Max's grin is the same—easy words laid over something harder to read. As they walk, she's glad to be quietly observing a moment that's not fraught with danger and suspicion.

* * *

The Gaslight is busy. All the barstools are taken, and a foursome play cards. The rear door is propped open but does nothing to alleviate the stink of an ancient saloon filled with sweaty customers.

Max buys a round. They sip their beers and chat while they wait for Michael—no point starting without him.

The lively conversation, fueled by Max's natural energy and Clara's pragmatism, allows Olivia to relax. Her thoughts drift toward Michael and all she has to tell him since she last saw him at Charlotte Franklin's home.

She lifts a stack of mail from her briefcase she's been ignoring. Flipping through the envelopes, one gets her immediate attention. The return address is the Board of Education, postmarked last week.

It must be confirming her position at the high school for the coming year. She slides a finger under the flap, unfolding a crisp white page inside.

Miss Kendall:

The Board of Education has received concerns regarding discussions in your classroom that may be deemed controversial or inappropriate given current community standards. While we encourage academic freedom, we also recognize the importance of ensuring that educational material aligns with our district's values and expectations. We trust you will exercise good judgment in future lessons and avoid any topics that might be considered divisive. Failure to do so may result in further review.

It's signed by Theodore Varney, a man she's never heard of. No title below his name.

The words blur. She reads it again, then once more, as if repetition would make it clearer. Concerns? Inappropriate discussions?

A creeping heat rises in her chest, the paper shaking so violently she flings it onto the table, rejecting its message. It's not just a reprimand. It's a warning. A muzzle.

"What is it?" Reaching for the letter, Clara asks, "You mind?"

Olivia pushes it toward her.

Clara scans it and Max reads over her shoulder.

"I'm a history teacher!" she snaps. "It's my job to have discussions with my students on divisive topics."

Her outburst makes heads swivel toward their table. Max's hand inches across the table, palm up, offering a wordless apology.

But she's too upset to be coddled and ignores Max's gesture. She doesn't understand. They've had these kinds of discussions all year. Why now?

Then an ugly thought hits her. But before she can spend any time analyzing it, Michael stands at the entrance to the bar, backlit by fading daylight. She observes this man who means something to her, she's not sure what, but his slumped shoulders and shuffling steps indicate he's had a tough day, and she wants to make it better.

As he drops into the vacant chair next to her, she slides her mug toward him. "You look like you need this more than I do."

Without meeting her gaze, he drops his hat on the table, lifts the mug, and drains it. "You have no idea."

She hadn't noticed his hair—deep brown and wavy, a half inch too long over his collar. It's the kind she'd like to sink her fingers into, then gently tug on to pull him toward her.

"Jesus, Michael. You look like hell." Clara says, jerking Olivia back to reality, quickly looking down to find her hands curled into combs.

Running her fingers through his hair probably won't mend his troubles.

Max goes for another round.

Olivia is anxious to hear about the cop and the sketch.

Michael puffs air from his mouth, rolls his eyes skyward till they settle on Olivia. His Adam's apple bobs. "He's going to ask the other victim."

Max raises a glass. "Cheers to good cops catching bad guys."

Olivia grasps his forearm. "This is fantastic, Michael. Progress."

He wrenches his arm from her grasp. "Will you stop? It's not all flowers and ribbons."

She flinches. It's not just the words—it's the dismissal in his voice. The way it turns her support into a crime.

"Go to hell, Michael," Olivia snaps, the words bursting out of her before she can stop them. She doesn't care if it's harsh—he has no right to treat her this way.

His head shoots up as if he's been slapped. He meets her gaze, his jaw tight, muscles strained, as he runs a hand through his hair.

"I'm sorry," his voice falters. The words seem to scrape against his throat. "I didn't mean it, it's just that her getting bushwhacked is my fault."

Olivia leans back, putting space between them, her own fear rising.

"I wrote the meeting with Charlotte on my desk calendar. And my notebook came up missing. I can't say for sure, but my money's on Pritchett, who has a direct line to Hawthorne."

Glasses tinkling and low murmurs of conversation cover the silence at the table.

"I'm sorry, Michael," Clara says.

"Yeah, me too. It's all my doing. First the Habers. Then Charlotte Franklin gets in their line of sight, and now I have an enemy in the office."

"I hate to say it, but it means you're getting too close," Max says. "You're on to something."

"A very dangerous something," Clara says.

Olivia hesitates to add to all the bad news, but she hands Michael the letter.

His eyes narrow then he reads.

"You too? Geez."

He wipes a hand down his face, scratches the stubble on his chin. "I guess it's time to throw in the towel."

"You don't mean that," Clara whispers.

Max asks, "What about the cop? What if he gets an ID?"

Elbows on the table, Michael cradles his beer. His voice is quiet, forcing the others to lean in to hear him.

"If he does get an ID, he'll go to his boss which will likely result in the police at least having a conversation with Pitts. Which sounds good but might lead him and his cronies back to us."

A heavy silence follows.

It's over. It has to be. Olivia doesn't want to end up like her parents.

But if she quits now, she may never know if her father was murdered.

How badly does she want to find out?

Max frowns. "I guess I'll put my hunt for this Tink guy on the back burner."

Michael straightens. "What do you mean?"

"Clara says he's in Los Angeles. I should be able to find him."

"Finding him won't keep us safe," Clara says and now everyone is looking to Michael for what to do.

Olivia wants to walk away. Put the clippings back where they came from. Bury the scrapbook—bury all of it. Pretend she never opened it.

But the past doesn't stay buried. Not really. Her mother's letter is proof.

Her grip tightens on her briefcase. Maybe the sketch will lead to finding the attackers. Maybe Max will find Tink. Maybe the letter from the Board is a bluff.

But what if the truth doesn't fix anything?

What if it only makes it worse?

She tells herself to let go.

But she can't. Not yet.

She swallows, forces the words out. "Michael, are we safe?"

He doesn't answer right away. His gaze is distant, unreadable. Finally, he exhales. "What if we lay low until we either have a confirmation from Kellerman or Max finds Evans?" His voice is steady, practical. "If one or the other happens, we'll figure out what to do next."

His words settle over the table like dust. No promises. No reassurances. Verbalizing the cold reality of their situation. And a choice.

Though it's not the answer she wants, Olivia says, "Okay."

"I will find Tink," Max assures them.

Clara acknowledges with the barest nod.

Max taps the letter from the Board. "And this? What do you want to do about it?"

Olivia hesitates, her fingers brushing the edge of the paper. The letter is meant to rattle her. But if she runs to the Board of Education demanding answers, she risks playing right into their hands.

"I'm going to sit on it for a few days. There's no urgency."

Her decision presses them into silence. The bar's background noise hums—a shuffle of cards, the occasional burst of laughter.

Max breaks the silence. "Come on, Olivia. I'll get you home."

The idea of walking alone on dark streets, her mind tangled in the night's revelations, is suddenly unbearable.

"I'd appreciate an escort."

Pressing his hat on his head, Michael's eyes dart between her and Max. "No, I'll do it."

"You will not!" Clara stands, one hand on her hip, daring him to argue. "Finish your beer and take me home."

Olivia catches the flicker of something in Michael's expression before it vanishes—a moment of frustration or something sharper. Heat rises to her cheeks, though she can't say why.

"It's fine, Michael." To take the sting out of her refusal, she touches his arm. "Max is more than capable."

Max grins, tipping his hat. "At your service, Miss Kendall."

As Olivia stands, she senses Michael's eyes on her, tension crackling between them. She wants to meet his gaze, but something stops her. Something she can't identify and isn't ready to name.

Max places a hand lightly on her elbow, guiding her toward the door.

Outside, the cool evening air relieves Olivia's flushed face. She glances back through the bar's smoky window and catches a glimpse of Michael watching them, his face shadowed and unreadable. The need to comfort him surprises her, like a small ember sparking to life.

"You all right?" Max asks, his tone light, but observant.

Yes," Olivia says quickly, pushing the feeling aside. "Let's go."

Chapter Twenty-Seven

They don't speak on the way home. The last forty-eight hours have chewed Michael up and spit him out. He's too numb for idle chit-chat.

Suddenly, Clara throws an arm across his chest, stopping him in his tracks. She points at the shoe shop with lights ablaze and people gathered on the sidewalk.

They break into a run. Clara leads the way through the narrow aisle to the workroom, where a man in a dark, city-issued jacket peels a thick sheet of paper from his clipboard.

"Who are you? What are you doing?" Clara asks as the man bumps past her.

He plasters it on the door and smooths out the wrinkles. "Your wiring is faulty."

Through the window Michael spies his mother pushing past neighbors and gawkers. Lips pressed into a thin, bloodless line; she reads the notice.

The inspector, his thinning hair slicked back, a self-satisfied air about him, tilts his chin to Clara. "For your safety, ma'am."

Michael grabs the man's arm, yanking him around. "What the hell is this?"

The inspector hesitates, but he tucks his clipboard under his arm, adopting the cool detachment of a man who's done this a dozen times before. "Routine check. Loose wiring and frayed insulation. Fire hazard. City can't allow it."

Michael doesn't buy it for a second. He glances at Mama, but she gives the barest shake of her head, a silent warning to keep his temper in check.

Clara gets in the man's face. "Who ordered this inspection?"

The inspector smirks as if the question is beneath him. "City safety regulations. Inspections happen all the time."

Michael isn't sure what infuriates him more—his smugness or the fact that arguing won't change a damn thing. "And what happens next?"

"Now I turn off the power. Eliminate the possibility of a fire breaking out." The man ducks back into the workshop, and a moment later, it goes dark. A flashlight beam illuminates the inspector's exit path.

He pauses on the steps and speaks to his mother. "Make the necessary repairs and request a follow-up inspection. Once the violations are cleared, you reopen. And if you become a member of the Chamber, these visits don't happen." He tips his hat.

In the shop doorway, Clara grabs his arm. "Hold on. I know you."

"What do you think you're doing?" He yanks his arm from her grip.

"You did the wiring! For that Dictograph thing." Her chest heaves with anger and memory.

"I thought this place was familiar. Have a good evening."

The man scurries off like a weasel slinking away, leaving them with nothing but the sharp sting of helplessness. He turns to his mother, searching her face, but her expression is neutral. Only her hands, twisting the hem of her apron, betray her emotions.

The shop—their family's livelihood—is in trouble. And looking at his sister, so is Clara.

And Michael has no doubt who's behind it. Hawthorne or Pitts. Maybe both. Even the letter from the Board has their fingerprints on it. Too much to be coincidence.

Clara stares at the sign. CLOSED UNTIL FURTHER NOTICE. She grips Michael's sleeve. "They could have sent anyone. But they sent him." Her whisper carries both fear and fury.

Deliberate torture on top of deliberate loss of business.

"Mama, what are you doing here?" He helps her sit on the steps.

"He came to the house. Said the shop had a past-due inspection. I thought nothing of it, so I gave him the key and said I'd come along in a few minutes."

"You gave him a key?" Clara stands over her mother, hands on hips. "You should have waited for me."

"It's my shop." Their mother halts any further complaints from her daughter with sharp eyes and pursed lips.

"But Mama," Clara starts.

"But Mama, nothing. I did what I thought was right." Her tone demands respect.

Michael spins on his heel and assesses the bystanders. A new wave of onlookers has taken the place of the first, surveying the drama, tittering behind their hands.

He spies the man who owns the hardware store adjacent to his house. "Sam, do you know an electrician?"

Sam jumps at his name, his expression flickering with unease before he answers. "Yes, I do. Let me get his number. I'll be right back." He dashes to the corner and disappears.

His mother rises from the steps with a ragged breath. Michael holds her up though she doesn't wobble or stagger. Her backbone stiffens as she sloughs off his support to stand alone.

Moments later, Sam bounds up with a slip of paper.

"Thanks, Sam," Mama's voice catches. "Let's go home, Clara. Michael, take care of this." Her hand flits toward the shop.

Clara locks the door. Brother and sister stare at the white warning which they both know has little to do with electrical wiring.

* * *

At home, Clara cries uncontrollably, her face buried in Mama's shoulder while she rubs her back murmuring, "There, there."

Michael stands in the parlor, rooted in place, hands hanging uselessly at his sides. Everything comes crashing down on him. The shop closure, the electrician, rethinking their zeal for answers. He should say something. Fix things. But how?

Finally, Clara's sobs quiet into small, shuddering breaths.

His feet move and he kneels in front of Mama, looking up at her, searching her face for the words, the reassurance, the absolution he so desperately needs.

But when she meets his eyes, there's no comfort there. No anger, either. Something worse. Disappointment.

He drops his gaze, swallowing hard against the lump in his throat. His hands clench on his thighs. He draws in a sharp breath. He won't cry.

Then Mama's hand touches his hair, like when he was a boy.

Something inside him breaks.

The first tear escapes before he can stop it—a betrayal. Then another. The pressure in his chest snaps, and suddenly, he can't help it. He's crying.

Mama's hand on his cheek twists the spigot, opening him up until he's buried his face in her lap.

"I'm sorry," he hiccups, his voice raw. He lifts his head, desperate for her to tell him it's all right, to tell him they'll fix it, that it's not his fault.

But she only shakes her head, slow and heavy.

He's never felt so vulnerable, so insecure.

Clara wipes her eyes. Dragging in a deep breath, she screams at Michael. "This is your fault. You had to keep digging, so they sent their expert, the one who already knows where every wire runs. The message is loud and clear, Michael."

"I know. I'm sorry." He has only one response to the evening's events. To everyone he's hurt.

His apology does not appease his sister.

"If you'd just left it alone." Clara throws up her hands. "You think you're some crusading journalist, but all you've done is put a target on our backs."

Michael sits back on his haunches, gaping at Clara. "You were in it too. Don't act like I forced you into this. You wanted answers as much as I did."

"I was, but not anymore. I've worked too hard to watch the shop go down the drain. We're already running on a shoestring. The bills are piling up."

Mama shoots an alarming glance at Clara. "What? Are we in debt?"

"I'm sorry, Mama. I've tried everything to keep it going, but people without jobs don't need shoes repaired, and if they do have a job, they put off fixing them."

"Michael," Mama asks, "What do we do now?"

It's the second time this evening, he's been asked this question.

If he moves forward with his investigation, he could lose his job, and his family depends on his income.

If he backs off, he's leaving a story on the table. And the victims without a perpetrator.

Has he been selfish? Has he chased this story for his own ambitions, ignoring the risk to his family? He thought he was doing the right thing—exposing the truth, holding men like Hawthorne and Pitts accountable.

But at what cost? He can fix wires. He can call an electrician. But how do you stop the CPLE? How do you fight when you don't know who's pulling the strings?

Mama's hand lingers on his cheek, her fingers warm but trembling. She's looking at him like he has the answers.

"Mama, Clara," Michael faces his family and the demons he's resurrected with his investigation. "I had no idea things would go this far."

Mama's shoulders slump as she withdraws her comforting touch, nudging him off her lap.

"Figure it out, Michael. And that better be the last time this family is harassed by the CPLE. I'm going to bed." She lingers in the doorway. Her forehead wrinkles with expectation.

Clara joins her.

And Michael is held captive by the love he has for these women. He really has no choice.

"I'll back off."

A stern nod of Mama's head acknowledges his promise.

Michael replays the night—Clara frozen by the sign, the electrician, Olivia on the edge of backing away, her job in jeopardy.

Then her question. Tossed out in uncertainty, now echoing with meaning.

Are we safe?

The pieces snap together.

He bolts upright, his voice cutting through the stillness like a blade.

"Olivia!"

Chapter Twenty-Eight

Olivia wants to tell Max she's fine going the last two blocks alone, but she's not, really. The quiet night is bathed in moonlight, the glow mixing with street lamps as they navigate the cracked sidewalk. The brick house is set back from the road, large expanses of lawn surrounding it.

Olivia digs through her pocketbook, fingers catching the sharp edge of her keys. She fits one into the lock. At the pressure, the door inches open. As if someone is waiting for her. As if unseen fingers draw the door inward, welcoming her into the unknown.

Did she forget to lock it when she left? No, she never forgets. She backs away, her keys dangling, and whispers, "Max."

Quietly observing his surroundings at the bottom of the stoop, he asks, "What?"

She backs away. "The door. It's unlocked."

Max scrambles up the steps and scoots in front of her, his presence small but mighty. "Stay here."

Max steps into the foyer, one stealthy foot at a time. "Could have left a light on."

"I didn't know I'd be out this late," she counters, but adds a mental note to leave one on in the future. "The switch is on the wall to your left."

A click floods the stoop, momentarily blinding Olivia's view beyond.

"This is one of those times I wish I had a gun." Max moves further into the hallway.

Stepping into the house, Olivia presses the button for the hall light, startling Max.

"Can't a guy get a warning?"

"Sorry." She glances around. Everything looks as she left it.

Dropping her briefcase and pocketbook on the sofa in the parlor, she lights a table lamp chasing shadows into corners. She twists the knob on the matching one and breathes easier.

Max stands at the archway. "Let's light the whole place. Then we'll check upstairs."

After they've inspected the first floor, Max asks if everything looks all right.

Her nose wrinkles. "I smell cigarette smoke."

It reminds her of Michael, the acrid smell clinging to everything, tickling her nostrils.

"And you don't smoke," Max states the obvious. "You got a back entrance?"

"This way." She leads him to the kitchen, lets him check the lock and the bolt. It's secure.

"Let's check upstairs." Max's head tilts toward the ceiling.

On the landing, between the first and second floor, a heavier tang halts her progress. "It's really strong here."

Olivia's heart is rocketing around her chest. She puts her back against the wall, letting Max take the lead.

His footsteps echo on the hardwood floors. First Aunt Becky's room, then hers. At the top of the stairs, he beckons. "Can you come up? I don't smell anything, but you might."

The thought of someone invading her privacy, going through her things, terrifies her.

At the doorway to her room, she takes a breath, sniffing audibly. "Nothing." Her voice is mouselike, tiny, and inconsequential.

Max crosses in front of her into Aunt Becky's room. Reluctantly she follows and once Max is in the room, she halts at the doorway and repeats the process. She takes a deep breath through her nose until her lungs are full. The stench of cigarette smoke, sharp as burning leaves, assails her nostrils. The realization that a stranger has been in her aunt's room slams into her chest, squeezing the air from her lungs. Her stomach clenches, and before she can stop herself, she stumbles into the bathroom and kneels over the toilet bowl, the sharp tang of beer in her throat.

Max smooths her hair as she retches. His voice is steady, almost cheerful. As though this isn't the first time he's comforted a woman in distress.

Thank heaven he's here. What if she'd come home alone? What if she'd been here when the smoker entered her house?

Oh, dear Lord. What's happening?

She lets go of the toilet and flops onto her bottom, lying her forehead on the cool porcelain tub, not ready to leave the proximity to the bowl. Reliable, steady, absurdly comforting. Like Max.

Giggles bubble up as she compares the comforting presence of her new friend to the commode.

Then comes a hearty chuckle, sharp and brittle, rising in bursts that shake her shoulders—until the past crashes over her.

Kneeling beside her father's crumpled body, his blood soaking her taffeta dress—pink shadow blooming into deep crimson across her lap.

Her laugh dies mid-breath, breaking into hiccupping sobs.

A moment ago, Father had been telling her a knock-knock joke, the one about Dwayne the bathtub, I'm dwowning. Now, she's clutching his hand, cold, damp, limp. The ambulance. The hospital. The end.

The past shifts into the present. Someone took her everything. And it can't be replaced.

Max rolls off a ball of toilet paper and hands it to her.

She blows her nose.

"Got anything to drink?" Max asks.

"Brandy." It comes out thick and nasal, like she's talking through cotton.

"Perfect."

Max gets up, brushes his pants off and extends a hand to Olivia.

She hugs herself a little tighter. "I'll stay here."

"No, you won't," Max tells her. "Being up here is not good for you, till we can figure things out and air out the house."

Olivia relents and takes Max's hand. She's unsteady, but holding the handrails, she manages the stairs. Flopping on the sofa, she points to the rolling cocktail cart, crystal glasses with a matching decanter, half full of soul-soothing brandy.

Max pours a good amount into two glasses and hands one to Olivia.

She sips the drink, giving her fragile stomach a thimbleful at a time to avoid heaving again. "Do you think it's them?"

Max's right eyebrow shoots up. "Them? As in the CPLE?"

"Who else would break into my house? What did they hope to find?" Her hand gestures around, the brown liquid sloshing in the glass.

"Tomorrow," he hesitates and waits for her to meet his gaze. "Tomorrow, you need to look around. See if anything is out of place or missing."

"And if something's missing? What then? Call the police? Move back to my apartment?" Then it dawns on her. "Speaking of police. Shouldn't we call them?"

"And tell them what? That you smell cigarette smoke. They'll mark you down as hysterical."

"But someone was in my house!"

"Without any evidence of forced entry or theft? They won't take it seriously."

The wall phone rings in the kitchen, startling them.

"You want me to get it?" Max asks.

"No, I will." She rises from the sofa. "But come with me." She's not about to go it alone.

Olivia lifts the receiver and stands next to the mouthpiece. "Hello?" Her voice is shaky, rough like she's been coughing.

"Olivia, it's Michael."

"Michael."

"Is Max there?" He speaks quickly, his voice loud and demanding.

Is he jealous? She recalls his distress at her leaving with Max. "Yes. Why?"

"Can I talk to him?" After what she's been through, she dutifully hands the receiver over, willing to let Max handle whatever Michael wants—because she's so tired and doesn't want to talk or think any more. The brandy is working.

She wants to pull aside the sheer lace curtains and peek outside, but she's afraid of what she'll see. She sits on a kitchen chair and rubs her hands on the glass, warming the drink.

Max places the earpiece in its cradle. "I'll be right back. You want another?"

"No. What's going on?"

Decanter in hand, he returns and sits at the table.

"What did Michael want?" The brandy tricks her into relaxing and she leans into it.

Max adds a half inch to his glass, takes a gulp. "The shoe shop was shut down tonight. The city ordered it closed for electrical violations."

Olivia blinks, as if trying to process the words in a way that makes sense. But of course, they don't. The shoe shop. The letter. The cigarette smoke in her house. The realization coils in her chest.

She exhales, slow and controlled. "Let me guess. Just like that."

Max hovers over his glass, props his elbows on the table. "After I told him about what happened here tonight, he's thinking of pulling out of the investigation." His tone matches the seriousness of his words.

She stiffens. "Pulling out?"

Max nods.

She squeezes her glass so tightly a sharp pain runs up her forearm. Michael Schumann, pursuing this story with unwavering determination, who helped her see the truth for what it was—is now considering giving up? After everything?

She almost walked away earlier tonight. But now her anger sparks inside her, smoldering there for years, pushing back against the smothering fear.

Her jaw tightens. "If I can't, he can't."

Max studies her, his brows knitting together. "He has a family. His mother and sister rely on the shop to survive. You can't blame him for—"

"I don't." She swirls the brandy in her glass, watching the liquid catch the light. "But if he backs down now, what does that mean for the people who've been hurt? The Habers. Charlotte Franklin."

Max exhales. "You're not wrong."

Olivia sets her glass down carefully, deliberately. "And what about me? Someone was in this house, Max. Maybe they were just looking, maybe they weren't—but do I just pretend it didn't happen?"

Max doesn't answer.

"And that letter. Threatening my job." Her voice rises. "We just let them get away with it? Let them harm innocent people? Let their threats become reality?"

Olivia closes her eyes, presses her fingertips against them. This is the kind of thing you read about in the paper, in Dick Tracy comics—threats scrawled in red, intimidation in the dead of night. But it was always someone else. A name in the headlines. A face in the ink.

Now, it was her. And Michael.

Max's voice snaps her back. "I'll sleep here tonight." He says it lightly, almost flippant, but his eyes are fixed on her bruised dignity. She almost asks him if he had done this before. Watched over someone too afraid to be alone. But that's too personal.

She throws the rest of the brandy back. To hell with her stomach. "That's all well and good, but what about tomorrow? And the day after that?"

"We'll figure it out." He gives her a half-smile, but his eyes are serious. "I promise."

Olivia raises her empty glass. "Thank you, Max."

"Not the worst gig I've had. I hope you don't mind if I tell my buddies I slept here."

His playfulness takes the edge off and she's grateful again for his presence.

With all the lights on and after another round of lock checking, they head upstairs. On the second floor, the faint remnants of cigarette smoke linger in the hall, but she pushes past it, refusing to let it get to her.

She locks her door, sets the key on the nightstand, and fully clothed, lies on top of the quilt. The house is quiet, but she can't shake the feeling she's been defiled—her sanctuary debased, her safety shattered. Everything is the same, yet nothing is.

She stares into the dark, flinching at the tiniest sounds. Every creak, every whisper of wind against the glass becomes a presence lurking in the shadows. She tells herself they're nothing. But what if they're not?

Chapter Twenty-Nine

Effie eyes Michael as he lumbers into the office. "You look like something the cat dragged in."

He rubs a hand across his jaw, the rough scrape of stubble a reminder of how little sleep he got. He spent half the night obsessing over what to do about the shop and forgot to shave.

"Shop's closed," he mutters, half to himself. "Electrical violations."

Effie stills. "You're kidding."

"To top it off, it was the same guy who installed the Dictograph."

Her gaze sharpens, lips pressing into a firm line. "And that just happened? Out of nowhere?"

"Yeah. Real convenient timing, isn't it?"

Effie glances around, then leans in. "I know a guy at the inspection bureau. I'll make a call."

"How's Charlotte?" His tossing and turning included her welfare.

"Went to work today. We took the streetcar together, but she refused to let me walk her in."

Michael's grateful for this woman who has dared to stand beside him. But she's the kind of gal who jumps in and thinks later. He's not sure how he got this lucky, but he's not taking it for granted.

"Let me give you some money. Cover meals and such." He reaches for his wallet.

She stares him down. "You do that, and our friendship is over. If I need something, I'll ask."

He removes his hand from his wallet.

"You need to see this." She hands him this morning's edition, taps below the fold, middle of the front page.

Michael reads it at his desk.

BARTENDER STABBED IN LATE-NIGHT ATTACK

Phil Hupfeld, 30, employed at Figgy's Tavern at Seventh and Baker, is in stable condition at St. Boniface Hospital following a brutal assault. The incident occurred at closing time when two assailants approached Hupfeld requesting a light. As he struck a match, one man plunged a knife into his ribs. The pair fled, leaving their victim bleeding until discovered by a passing citizen. Money left in Hupfeld's wallet indicates robbery was not the motive. Officer Kellerman heads the investigation.

Hupfeld is a German name and Figgy's isn't far from the underpass. Nothing taken. Another attack.

It's obvious Pritchett filed this story, but it's useless trying to get any information out of him and any inquiries would have him in Baxter's office in the blink of an eye.

What about Kellerman? He'll give him the straight story.

But he can't. He promised.

He drops the paper. The need-to-know nags at him like a hen pecking at his brain. His hands rake through his hair, fists clenching. Who's going to stop them if he doesn't? How many more before someone dies?

Stay away. Stop. Or else.

Effie rifles through proofs, prepping stories for the afternoon edition. The thought strikes before he can shove it down.

One small favor. One question for Kellerman, that's all. Then he'd be done.

No. Don't put her in any more danger.

A tiny ask. See if Kellerman believes this attack is related. If so, he's got another shred of evidence that the CPLE is using old methods to squash new threats of anti-Americanism in Ellington.

What he swore to Mama and Clara last night was a lie the moment it left his mouth. He can't let this go. Even if it means throwing his family's safety out like yesterday's trash. He'll just have to be more careful, strategic.

He should wash his hands of it all.

But the headline blares an ugly side of Ellington. Daring him to take one more shot at the truth.

"Screw it," he mutters, tearing the article from the paper. He scratches a quick note, drops it on Effie's desk and makes his way to the water cooler. Filling a paper cup, he watches her read the note. An imperceptible nod of her head means she'll come.

Michael circles back to his desk, snags his notebook, assignment slips, and shoves his hat over his mussed hair.

Outside the office, he lights a cigarette, stepping into the narrow strip of shade along the sidewalk, grateful for any shelter from the heat.

A few minutes later, Effie joins him. She leans in for a light, shielding the flame from the breeze with her hand.

"Can you ask Kellerman if that attack is related? And if Doller identified Pitts from the sketch?"

Michael shifts, scanning the street, the storefronts. Too many windows. Too many eyes.

Effie picks a bit of tobacco from her tongue, pauses before replying. "I'll meet Kellerman. But we need to proceed with caution. Powerful folks in this city are worried."

"Yeah, the cockroaches are all stirred up."

She taps her cigarette, watching the ashes fall. "It's difficult to get rid of cockroaches."

Michael snorts softly, but there's no humor in it.

Effie studies him. "You know what you're doing?"

Michael flicks his cigarette to the ground and grinds it under his heel. "Not a damn clue."

* * *

Michael paces the tiny yard behind his mother's house, cigarette in hand, waiting for Effie's call. Butts pile up in an old flowerpot—the cost of worrying. He kicks himself for not doing what he told his mother. That he was finished. That he was done digging up old dirt.

The screen door creaks, and he whirls around.

"Effie's on the phone," Clara says, holding the screen door open.

Michael pitches his cigarette into the pot, bolts up the steps, and snatches up the receiver.

"Effie."

"Can you talk?"

A horn honks and a streetcar bell dings. He pictures her in the phone booth near Nick's, twisting her head, checking for anything, anyone out of place.

Her voice is just above a whisper. "That attack is probably connected, but he's not positive. And, Doller identified Pitts."

Michael straightens. Three assaults, two positive IDs.

Effie's next news makes the tally meaningless. "Police Chief laughed him out of the office. Said a twenty-year-old newspaper sketch doesn't mean squat."

Of course it doesn't.

Michael clutches the receiver, his lifeline to answers.

"Kellerman's done, Mike. He said he lived through this last time. He won't push it."

Michael sees red, his anger rising, displacing exhaustion, displacing everything. "Until someone dies."

A gasp behind him.

He whirls, and there's his mother—hand over her mouth, the whites of her eyes visible behind wire-rimmed glasses.

"If it comes to that, Ellington has a whole different kettle of fish to fry," Effie says.

Michael swallows hard, distracted, his mother's unreadable expression making his chest tighten.

"Yeah. Thanks, Effie. I've got to go." He drops the receiver into place without waiting for a response.

His mother whispers, "Who's going to die?"

Her question catches him off guard. He doesn't want to lie—but he can't tell her he's already broken his promise. That he's still chasing the CPLE. The truth could break her.

"No one, I hope."

She stares at him.

"I need to talk to you, Mama." He's got to be honest with her now that there's a third victim and the second has identified Pitts.

"I've got to finish the dishes." She turns toward the kitchen, as if that will end the conversation.

"The dishes can wait." Michael takes her hand and leads her to the parlor.

Sitting next to her on the sofa, he clasps her hand, his thumb stroking her knuckles. Her hands are gnarled, spotted, her veins visible under paper-thin-skin. When did this happen? When did she grow old?

A lump rises in his throat. How often had he leaned on her without thinking? Expected her strength without gratitude? She'd endured so much on behalf of him and Clara. Her father's tragedy, her husband's early death, never complaining, never asking for pity, never expecting sympathy.

"Mama." He squeezes her hand, voice quieter now. "You're my hero."

She peers at him as if he's spoken in a language she doesn't understand.

"I'm not sure I could have done what you did."

"Whatever in the world are you talking about?"

"I felt awful about grandfather getting arrested, being humiliated, going to jail. How was it for you? I never asked."

Her head drops back onto the sofa, eyes focused on the ceiling. A flicker of something crosses her face—pain, sorrow, fear.

"I did what I had to do. That's a woman's duty."

"And what did you do?"

Unexpectedly, a tear slips down her cheek. She swipes at it as if she's shooing a fly.

Then, barely above a whisper, she says, "Someone died because of me."

The words hit him like ice water, but Michael doesn't move, doesn't change his expression.

"Who?" His tone is patient, as if he's asking a child to explain a riddle.

"Victor Kendall."

Chapter Thirty

Pre-dawn light and a songbird drag her from tangled dreams into the reality that she slept on top of the covers in her room in Aunt Becky's house. Any other day, she'd leap out of bed, get moving to fulfill a packed agenda. But after the break-in last night, she lies there, taking stock of her situation.

Before finally falling asleep, sometime in the wee hours of the morning, she decided it was time to stop fearing ghosts and start talking to the living. Someone had thought to frighten her by threatening her job and entering her home. She refuses to let them win. Cowering in a corner gives them power, leaving her with none.

And that is not an option.

She pads downstairs to find Max sipping a cup of coffee and reading the morning edition of the *Journal* at the kitchen table.

"Rough night?" he asks.

"Yeah. Wonder why." Olivia pours a cup and sits at the table.

"I've got to go home and change, then go to work. You all right here?"

"Yes. But can you come back when you're done for the day? Before dark?" She despises the timid tone of her voice. The break-in threatens her independence.

"At your command, milady."

"You're such a flirt."

"I'll take that as a compliment." At the doorstep, he says, "Lock this behind me."

Hugging herself, she follows Max's progress toward the streetcar stop. Fingering the dining room sheers, she wishes they were heavier. These only blur the view, not block it.

Upstairs, she opens windows to air out the lingering smell of smoke, then sets the fan in the hall to sweep the bedrooms.

Back downstairs, the quiet is oppressive. With nothing else to distract her, she empties her briefcase onto the coffee table.

In addition to the scrapbook, slips of paper with random notes from her conversations with Uncle John, Hawthorne, Matthews, and Vogel peek out. Skimming each, she sets them aside but pauses on the Vogel notes. 'Simpson wouldn't touch it.'

Uncle John confirmed that he'd stepped away from the case.

She reviews her call with DJ, who was full of animosity, demanding she 'let it go.' Maybe his gruff manner disguised a warning, not a dismissal.

Without thinking, she dials his number.

"DJ?"

"Yes?"

"This is Olivia Kendall." She rushes through the greeting. "I know you told me to stop looking for answers about my father's death, and maybe I should. But there's something I need to know."

A long pause stretches. "Fine. What is it?"

"I'd appreciate the truth."

Silence screams in answer.

"Did you know the detectives fabricated evidence?" The quiet lengthens, punctuated by a door slamming in the background. Olivia pictures DJ pacing, weighing his words.

"Yes," he says finally. "We all knew."

Olivia's stomach turns. "And you did nothing?"

"John and I thought it was too dangerous. But your father drafted a motion to supplement the appeal with the tampering as newly discovered evidence and asked us to support it. We tried to talk him out of it, but Victor was willing to face whatever consequences came from calling out the detective agency, and therefore, the CPLE."

Her heart twists painfully. Her father had been right and stood alone.

DJ sighs. "A week later, your father called, furious. The motion hadn't been filed. Told him I signed it and sent it back to his office. Probably a timing issue."

Olivia's breath catches. "And then?"

"That was the last I heard. A few days later, Victor was dead. After his death, things fell apart." DJ's voice is flat, tired. "John didn't want to fight the CPLE. Said our reputations would be ruined no matter the outcome. I didn't disagree."

Her thoughts race. "Is it possible John stalled the motion by not signing it?"

DJ is quiet for a long moment. "It's possible. John was scared, Olivia. I was too. But Victor..." He trails off.

"But Father wasn't."

"No. And I wouldn't dismiss the notion that your father's pursuit of justice might have put him in harm's way."

The implication hangs between them—deliberate, chilling.

"DJ, when my mother wanted to investigate his death, did you help her?"

A pause. "I did. She was so confident his accident was CPLE related. I met with the driver and his wife, checked them both for connections, but found nothing. I shared that with her not long before she died."

"I never knew any of this. Did she stop looking?"

A long silence. Then DJ's voice, softer: "I think she believed her search was fruitless."

Understanding the reason her mother jumped into the well doesn't shock her. Olivia presses a hand against her chest. Her mother hadn't been broken by grief—she'd battled against silence when no one else would listen. And when DJ gave her an answer, she chose escape over continuing a search that no longer held hope.

She swallows, holding back tears of resignation.

"One more thing," she chokes out. "I received a letter from the school board. It threatened my job. Said I needed to 'exercise good judgment' in my lessons going forward."

"Goddammit, Olivia!"

She jerks the receiver away from her ear, pulse spiking. The force of his anger crashes through the line, sharp and unexpected. Her grip tightens, bracing for what comes next.

"I..." she starts, but DJ barrels ahead, growling.

"These bastards never change!" His voice is like a live wire, crackling with outrage. "They play by their own rules, and when someone questions them, they push back. Hard."

He's not angry at her. He's angry for her.

"Who signed it?"

"Theodore Varney."

"Varney?" His voice sharpens. "He's not on the board any longer. I know him. And if he's involved, it's fake, but still a warning."

"So, what do I do?"

"I'll handle it!" DJ snaps. "I've had it with their intimidation tactics. Think they can scare you? Not happening."

His outrage crackles through the receiver, a sharp contrast to the guarded tone he'd used earlier. This isn't just concern—it's personal.

"Thank you, DJ," she says. "For everything."

"Olivia. It's obvious you won't stop poking your nose in where it doesn't belong, but can you promise," he hesitates, "to be careful?"

"I will."

She leaves it at that. But she's not done. The CPLE cannot be allowed to rise from the ashes of the war and start their vigilante justice again.

The questions pile up, pressing against her ribs, anxious to be asked and answered. What happened to the motion? Did John sign it? Or did it quietly disappear, swallowed by the chaos of her father's death?

There's only one way to find out.

She reaches for the telephone, brushes aside indecision, and dials.

* * *

Adeline Able answers the phone. "Simpson Law Office."

"Addie, it's me, Olivia."

"Oh, hello. I'm afraid John's not here. Can I take a message?"

"No. I want to talk to you."

"Me? Well, all right. How can I help you?" Adeline's creaky voice has a wary edge.

"I need you to think back to the days before my father died. He had a motion to introduce new evidence in the Dictograph case. Do you remember it?"

"Biggest case of the decade."

"That motion. Did it ever get filed?"

"Let me think." Adeline hums softly.

Olivia doesn't dare breathe.

"Wait! I have a checklist for all papers coming and going to be sure they all get executed. Let me see if I can find it. Hold on."

A thud, a flurry of paper, then Adeline's voice returns.

"Here it is. Victor and DJ signed. But I don't have a check next to John's signature, nor do I have a check next to Motion Filed."

Olivia is mute, unsure what to think.

Adeline adds, "According to this, DJ returned the documents one week before your father died."

Before she can ask about John's missing signature, Adeline cuts in.

"We had a method for getting things turned around in one to two days. I guess I never followed up. But we were busy with a few high-profile cases at the time and after your father...."

The realization hits. John didn't sign. The motion was never filed. One man stalled it. The other died. Was that just tragedy—or strategy?

A surge of heat floods her chest.

"May I ask why you want this information after such a long time?" Addie asks.

"Tying up loose ends," Olivia says lightly, though her heart is pounding. Then she adds, casual but firm, "This conversation never happened."

A beat of silence. Then Adeline's voice, steady and knowing. "What conversation?"

"You know, Olivia..." the secretary adds, "I felt terrible for those men. They seemed like decent family guys. But after we lost the case, people would look at me funny at the grocery store - like I'd been helping traitors. Made me wonder if maybe the CPLE was right all along, even though..."

Olivia's hand trembles as she hangs up the receiver. The house is unnervingly quiet, the silence pressing against her chest.

John hadn't just failed her father. His silence had helped bury him.

The truth sits before her, undeniable.

The phone rings, loud and jarring.

It's Michael. A thrill rushes through her at the sound of his voice.

"Hello. How are you?" She smooths her hair as if he can see her.

"I'm fine. An electrician is coming later this week. Should be back in business by the weekend."

"I have news," she blurts out, excited to tell him about her conversation with DJ and Adeline.

"I do, too," he adds.

"Oh, good." She waits for his news.

"Can you come to dinner tonight? I'd like you to meet my mother. There's something she thinks you ought to know. About your father."

Her breath catches. After everything today, he wants her to meet his mother. And what does she know about her father?

"Oh?" She straightens. "What is it?"

"Let's save it for dinner." His tone is light, but the meaning is clear. "What's your news?"

"It can wait till I see you."

"I'll come get you," Michael offers.

She's grateful for his protectiveness, though a part of her balks at needing it. "Can Max come too? He's promised to stop by after work?"

"Hmm," Michael utters, followed by a pause long enough for her to wonder if he objects. "Yeah, sure. We've got room at the table and Clara might enjoy Max's company."

"It's a date." She cringes. Not a date. Absolutely not a date.

"Be here at six," he says, giving her the address. "And I hope you like pot roast."

"One of my favorites."

* * *

Michael ushers them into the parlor, a quaint room made smaller by an oversized sofa lined with antimacassars. A pair of brocade armchairs and walnut end tables complete the cozy space.

A flicker of warmth sparks in Olivia's chest at the sight of Michael. For a moment, she nearly leans in—just a friendly peck on the cheek—but the moment slips away as Max steps forward, taking Michael's outstretched hand.

Clara hands glasses of water to everyone. "Hello!"

Olivia sniffs the rich aroma of a hearty meal. "Something smells heavenly."

A stout, gray-haired woman pauses in the doorway examining the strangers in her home.

"Mama," Michael acknowledges her presence.

Max offers a hand. "Mrs. Schumann, I'm Max Ingram. Thank you for having me."

She shakes his hand. "Please call me Minnie. That's what all Michael's friends do."

"I'm afraid my mother would disapprove. Thank you for having me, Mrs. Schumann."

Olivia catches the mention of his mother, layered uncomfortably between courtesy and something heavier.

Michael guides Olivia to his mother, who can't be more than five feet tall. Sparkling blue eyes, crow's feet, and time's wrinkles adorn her face like embroidery on well-worn linen. A double strand of pearls twists at the neckline of her apron-covered dress.

"I'm Olivia Kendall. It's lovely to meet you." She's genuinely delighted to meet the other third of the Schumann family.

"You have his smile."

"A lovely compliment. Thank you."

"Dinner is ready," Mrs. Schumann announces and scurries away.

Between bites, talk drifts from the meal to the heat of the summer, to how much food Mrs. Schumann insists everyone take. Olivia savors the warmth of shared company.

"I've missed meals with family," Olivia says. "You've made me feel welcome and filled my stomach with wonderful food."

"I'm happy you came, Olivia. You must miss them."

Tears threaten, but she pushes them back. "Eighteen years since Father passed. Mother, seventeen."

"Your father was a good man. He did the best he could for mine."

Olivia focuses on Mrs. Schumann. "I'm sorry it didn't turn out differently."

Mrs. Schumann adjusts her plate, moving it back an inch indicating she's finished.

Clara rises, but Minnie lifts a hand. "No. Let it be." She gestures around the table. "I'd like to tell Olivia what happened, and you all should hear it, too."

Clara sits. Max places his hand on the table, palm up. Clara eyes him, confused as to his intent, but when he inches it toward her, she lays hers in his.

Olivia wishes Michael would take her hand—not to ease her fear of the unknown, but of finally knowing. A tremor runs through her fingers before flattening them on her thighs.

Minnie swipes at crumbs on the tablecloth, then folds her hands, and rests them on the table. When all is silent, she begins.

"I'll start after the verdict. Father came home from the shop one day in late February. He told me Tinker Evans came by to apologize for his part in the mess, that he'd been forced into the identifications. And, that the detectives made up many of statements."

Clara jumps in. "That aligns with what Mr. Vogel told us."

Her mother gives her an evil eye. "You talked to Vogel?"

Clara hesitates because she can't lie, but doesn't want to get in trouble. Hanging her head like a child caught in the cookie jar, she mutters. "Yes."

"There's a lot you don't know, Mama. We'll fill you in later, but please," Michael checks with Olivia, who nods. "Please continue."

"Yes, well. I told Papa he needed to tell his attorneys, maybe something could be done. But he said Tink was frightened, and it wouldn't do any good because it was unlikely that Tink would ever go in front of a judge and jury again. It was only the man's good nature and morals that he told my father at all.

"I got it in my head that maybe I could help, do something to get the case reopened or whatever they call it. I went to your father's office, Olivia, and told him what Tink said. He said he'd talk to Tink on the sly and check into the allegations."

Olivia knots the napkin in her lap.

"Knowing I didn't want Papa to find out I'd asked Victor to help, he came here a few weeks before he died. He said he'd talked to Tink, but hit a wall when he couldn't find the detectives."

A tear slips down Minnie's cheek. "That was the last time I saw him."

Her face tightens as another tear follows. She presses a hand to her mouth, her voice catching. "Oh, God, I should have left it alone."

Olivia rises and kneels beside her, wrapping her arms around the woman who tried to do right by her family. "It's not your fault."

Nodding through trembling lips, her guilt spills out in a whisper. "I'm sorry, I'm sorry."

Olivia puts her forehead to Minnie's, cradles her cheeks, and gently wipes her tears away with her thumbs.

"Wait," Clara says. "Mr. Vogel said he and grandfather told Mr. Kendall what Tink said."

She looks at her daughter, then at Olivia. "If that's true..."

"Then you have nothing to regret," Olivia says. "I'm betting Father kept your secret, just like you kept his all these years. It's no wonder you thought you were the cause of his death."

Minnie's shoulders loosen.

Olivia returns to her chair. "Thank you for telling me. I know that was hard. I'm proud of my father for going after what he believed in. And I'm proud of you for doing the same. What you've told me ties into what I learned today."

She pivots to Michael. "DJ Matthews said my father drafted a new motion for the appeal. But it was never filed."

"Why not?" Michael asks.

Olivia explains her call to Adeline. "Uncle John didn't sign the motion."

Minnie asks, "Uncle?"

"Oh, he's not really my uncle. It's what I call him, being my father's law partner for years."

"I remember him. Not as enthusiastic as your father. Passive. Almost dismissive."

Michael's gaze is steady on Olivia. "What are you planning to do with that information?"

The corners of her mouth turn down as she returns his gaze with an intensity that conveys both vulnerability and quiet desperation. She doesn't want to. But she must finish this. She inhales deeply, closes her eyes, releases her breath. "Confront him. Again."

Max clears his throat to get their attention. "I've yet to share my news."

Michael's head twists toward him, brows raised, a hint of frustration in his narrowed eyes.

Max exhales, setting his glass down. "While you two have been chasing ghosts, I've been digging in Los Angeles."

He leans in. "I found Tink."

A beat of stunned silence.

"And he's ready to talk."

Chapter Thirty-One

Michael meets Max at Aunt Becky's house where they make the call to Tink. Multiple clicks and whirrs suggest the connection is being made across the country.

"Mr. Evans? This is Max Ingram. We spoke yesterday."

"Hello, Mr. Ingram."

"I've got Olivia Kendall and Michael Schumann here with me. We know your time is limited so we'll get right to it."

"This is the one and only call we'll ever have," Tink says, his voice carrying a southern lilt. "And my name must never appear anywhere. I'd like the folks in Ellington to think I'm dead."

They agree, and Tink gives them ten minutes.

"I'm Olivia Kendall, Victor's daughter. You remember him?" She leans in, her head nearest the receiver.

"Yes, Ma'am, I remember him well. He listened to my story, didn't judge, and offered to help me find a new job when I quit. Would have quit sooner, when the manager threatened me, but I had a baby boy and a wife to support."

Michael tips his head in an inch, indicating his turn to speak. "Tink, this is Michael Schumann, Barney's grandson."

"Michael!" Tink exclaims. "You were hardly more than a pup, running errands for the shop, bringing deposits over to the bank. How's Clara? Your mama?"

Touched by Tink's kind memories of him and his family, he tells them they are well, and that Clara sends her regards.

Michael leans toward the receiver. "We've been told the detectives fabricated evidence. Can you confirm that?"

"I can do better than that," Tink says. "That Johnson detective didn't know any German."

Michael and Olivia exchange glances.

"Why is that important?" Michael asks.

"Because more than half the time, when he was writing stuff down, the conversation in the shop was in German. One time, I tested him. Said 'Es regnet heute, oder?' He replied, 'Ja.'"

"It wasn't raining, was it?" Michael asks.

"Hadn't in a week." Tink chuckles grimly.

"They turned in statements they couldn't have understood," Olivia whispers.

Michael's stomach drops. Nineteen years, and none of them had questioned this. They'd been fighting a battle they didn't understand.

"You left Ellington not long after you told the attorneys," Michael says.

Tink lets out a long breath, a sound more resigned than bitter. "After I met with Victor, they came for me in my own yard. Knocked me down before I even saw 'em coming. Kicked me so hard, I thought I'd never stand again. That's when I knew, we had to leave. My wife packed what she could, and we were gone the next day."

"Any idea who the men were?"

"One was Pitts. I'd never seen the other."

The three look at each other, shock registering on their faces.

"Look, I wish I had more time, but I need to go. You got what you need?"

"Thank you," Max says. "We'll keep all this in confidence."

"Good. I left everything behind to be free of the CPLE. I don't ever want to hear of Ellington again."

A breath, then a soft click.

The men collapse into chairs around the kitchen table.

Olivia moves around the kitchen making coffee. "Why didn't we consider that the men spoke German? It's so obvious," she asks and stares at Michael. "Did your family ever question that?"

"Not that I know of."

"Beck must know something," Michael says. "He was tight-lipped when I talked to him a couple weeks ago. Maybe this twist about the men speaking German will get him talking."

"Pitts is the key. Is he acting alone or is he still Hawthorne's flunky?" Max asks.

"The million-dollar question," Michael says. "But the police don't care, the *Journal's* stonewalling me, and we've been threatened on multiple fronts."

Olivia looks at Max, then Michael. "This gives me one more reason to confront John. He doesn't know I know about the motion. Maybe he'll crack."

"That's pretty risky," Max says.

"He's not telling me everything," Olivia insists. "I'm sure of it."

Michael turns toward her in his chair. "If you get a meeting with him, I'd like to be there. Not that you need a backup—just another witness to his explanations."

"That's fine," she says.

"You want to help me interrogate Beck?" he asks Max.

"Sounds like fun. I'm in."

"What about Pitts?" Olivia asks.

"We're stuck without Kellerman. He's under orders to leave it alone."

"I'm so tired of people saying that. Leave it alone."

Without thinking, Michael reaches across the table and pats her hand. "I gather you're not willing to do that."

"No way in hell."

Michael catches the determination in Olivia's eyes and something lifts inside him. Maybe, just maybe, they were closer than ever to the truth.

Chapter Thirty-Two

"Hey! It's me!" Olivia shouts as she passes the counter into the workroom where Clara is hammering a heel plate onto a work boot.

"It's a lovely day. I thought we could get lunch and catch up."

Clara wipes the sweat from her upper lip. "I wish I could. We passed inspection, and now I've got a backlog of orders to fill." She lifts her hammer by way of apology.

While Clara works, Olivia slides onto a nearby stool. "I have a meeting with Uncle John."

Clara's hammer stills for a beat. "When?"

Olivia's stomach twists with dread. "Day after tomorrow."

The bell tinkles and Clara's eyes dart to the front. "I'll be right back."

From the open doorway beyond the counter, Olivia glimpses a man wearing a dark gray suit.

"May I help you?" Clara asks.

"I'm looking for Michael Schumann."

There's steel behind the innocent question. Olivia stiffens.

Clara answers. "He's not here."

"Not in the newsroom either," the man says.

"What do you want him for?" Clara challenges.

Olivia edges closer to the workroom doorway, careful to stay out of sight.

"He's been asking the wrong kind of questions."

"I, I don't know what you're talking about."

"I bet you do." His voice oozes mockery. "One. He's your brother. And two, your little meetings with your friends at the Gaslight guarantee it."

Olivia gasps, clapping a hand over her mouth. Who is he and what business is it of his what they do at the Gaslight?

"I must say," he muses, his voice carrying a hint of malice. "Didn't expect to see this place open again so soon." He pauses, then adds, almost lazily, "I guess electrical problems were too easy to fix. Hawthorne's not happy."

"Too bad," Clara quips.

Olivia peeks around the corner. The man is tall, broad-chested, suggesting wide girth beneath his suit coat. Under a head of thin, graying hair, a bulbous nose sits between cold, calculating eyes that bulge from their sockets, beneath fuzzy caterpillar eyebrows. There's something familiar about him.

The man chuckles, but it lacks humor. "He needs to back off."

His eyes fix on Clara's hammer beside the cash register. His hand moves to it slowly, fingertips brushing the worn wooden handle before wrapping around it.

Watching the threat to Clara, fear grips Olivia by the throat. Without thinking, she grabs an awl from the workbench, hides it in the folds of her skirt and steps through the doorway, planting an innocent smile on her face.

"Oh, Clara. Those shoes are divine." She stops abruptly, feigning surprise as she looks from one to the other. "Oh, I'm sorry. You have a customer."

The man straightens, but his hand stays on the hammer.

"Yes, he's just leaving," Clara says stiffly. Behind her back, she sticks out her hand. Olivia clasps it and stands beside her. Two against one. But he's twice their size with a weapon in his hand. The odds are not in their favor.

"I haven't finished," the man says and picks up the hammer and examines it casually.

Clara squeezes Olivia's hand. In the other, she grips the awl, the metal cool and menacing against her palm.

He taps the metal head on the counter, once, then again. "Funny thing about your grandfather. He wasn't a bad man, he was just...too German. A perfect example for our purposes."

He was in the CPLE! Olivia can't imagine how Clara is taking this.

Her question is answered when Clara drops her hand, pushes past, and grabs the door handle.

"I don't know who you are, but your days of threatening my family are long gone. I don't care to hear your confession—I'm not your priest." She opens the door, the bell tinkling joyfully.

They face off like gunfighters on a dusty street at high noon.

Olivia doesn't move. Even a breath will break the stalemate.

The hammer slams down on the counter. Olivia skitters backward into the farthest corner. Clara flinches but holds her ground.

A deep indentation mars the counter, the strike so heavy, it splinters the wood. Olivia swallows and moves the awl into her right hand behind her back.

"I'm not done. Your brother needs to stop sticking his nose where it doesn't belong." He taps the hammer in his palm, each rap emphasizing his words. "And the other one too. That schoolteacher."

He means me!

Her knees threaten to buckle.

But Clara is composed, still holding the doorknob, her face drained of color, but manages an angry glare.

"You have the count of three to get out or I'll run onto the street screaming. Then what will you do?"

He slams the hammer against the wall next to the counter, white specks of plaster spit onto the floor.

Wincing, she readies the awl, should it be needed.

"One." Clara shifts, bracing for escape. "Two."

He pitches the hammer over his shoulder, and it thuds onto the floor.

At the door, he gets nose to nose with Clara. "Last warning! I won't be so nice next time."

He shoves Clara's shoulder so that she stumbles and loses her grip on the door. He glances over his shoulder at Olivia then stomps down the steps to the street.

As he turns away, she catches a glimpse of a bald spot on his head. The nose, the bulging eyes—she gasps.

The sketch. Fredrick Haber's description.

Clara slams the door, throws the bolt, and locks it.

"What the hell just happened? One minute I'm mending a boot, the next, I'm staring down a member of the CPLE." Clara arches her eyebrows at Olivia, looking for answers.

Olivia shows Clara the awl. "I had you covered."

Clara chuckles. "If only I'd known."

The two women stare out the window onto the empty street.

Quietly, almost under her breath, Olivia tells Clara the truth. "That was Howard Pitts. The one in the sketch that Nurse Franklin identified."

Clara's eyes widen. "Then I should have been scared to death. Not just scared."

"I know I was."

"I need a drink."

"Gaslight's out of the question."

"Mama's got beer at home."

"Let's go."

Chapter Thirty-Three

The elevator in the McKenzie building is still out of order. Michael trudges up three flights with Max huffing along behind.

After three tries, no one answers the door.

"What now?" Max asks.

Michael kicks the doormat aside and picks up a key. He glances around the hall and over the banister. Quiet and empty.

Michael inserts the key into the lock, his palms damp, fingers shaking.

"So, now we're breaking and entering?"

Rethinking his spontaneous action, he removes the key, slips it back under the mat. What would breaking into this guy's apartment do for him? There's no physical evidence after all this time and it sure as hell isn't worth going to jail for.

He slaps Max on the shoulder. "Thanks for being my conscience, buddy."

"What the hell are you doing?" A bark from behind startles them into turning, red-faced for being nearly caught.

Michael plants a smile on his face. "Mr. Beck! I'm so glad we caught you."

The burly man, one hand on his hip, the other hefting a grocery bag, spears them with his eyes. "You're that newshawk."

"Michael Schumann. *Ellington Journal.*"

Cocking his head toward Max, he asks, "Who's the shrimp?"

Michael opens his mouth to defend his friend.

But Max, ever quick on his feet, smirks and adjusts his hat with exaggerated care. "The name's Max Ingram. You must be Stanley Beck—legendary gumshoe, snitch extraordinaire."

Michael's hands curl into fists in case Beck takes offense.

But he brushes it off. "What do you want?"

Surprised they haven't been summarily ushered out of the building, a boot on backsides, Michael jumps in. "Did the men you monitored speak mostly in German?"

"Huh?"

"You told me you had difficulty hearing. The clock. The static. I don't recall you saying the men spoke in German."

Beck frowns and shifts the grocery bag to the other arm. "What the hell does it matter?"

Michael stays patient. "The men spoke German half the time. You and Johnson didn't understand it. So how did you write accurate reports?"

Max glances around the hallway. "Would it be best if we take this inside?" He indicates the apartment door.

"Um, yeah." The keys rattle on the ring as Beck unlocks it, drops his groceries on the kitchen table, and starts storing them.

Deciding an honest appeal for information would yield better results, he says, "Mr. Beck, I know this is difficult, and I understand what it means for you to reveal your part in the monitoring. But we're in a bind. Some elderly men have been attacked in ways reminiscent of that era. We suspect the CPLE."

Beck freezes. "If the CPLE's involved, I ain't talking."

Max edges into the kitchen, craning his neck to meet Beck's stare. "So, you're fine letting innocent men take the blame. Or is it only folks weaker than you that get the short end?"

"Listen, pipsqueak!" Beck snatches Max's suit coat, pulling him toward him up on his toes.

Michael rolls his eyes. Trust Max to mouth off at the worst moment. He'd heard him crack jokes, play the charmer, but never spit fury like that.

He clamps a hand around Beck's arm, digging his fingers in hard enough to lower Max to the floor.

"Let's settle down. Both of you."

He gives Max a warning look.

Max yanks his coat back into place on his shoulders and dusts off the lapels.

"All we want to know is if the reports were fabricated. If half of what you heard was in German and neither you nor Johnson knew the language, it makes sense the statements were fudged or totally made up."

Beck raises his eyes to the ceiling and exhales, his lips fluttering. "If I give you something, will you leave me alone?"

Swift as an eel, Max extracts his notebook and pencil. "Ready."

Beck stops his grocery sorting, leans against the kitchen counter, and speaks slow and deliberate.

"Pitts came by every night, like clockwork, to collect our notes. Half the time, we had jack shit to give him. After two weeks, we only had a couple decent statements.

"Then he blew up. Said we had to do better, or he'd have us pulled from the case. I told him straight up—we can't just make this stuff up. And you know what he said?" Beck lets out a humorless chuckle. "Why the hell not?"

Michael's stomach tightens.

"Believe it or not, I had some damn morals back then. I fixed up a few statements just to keep Pitts happy. Johnson did the same. By mid-June, we had about a couple dozen comments Pitts considered worthy across seven speakers.

"But Pitts needed more. He took me and Johnson to the track, introduced us to a down-on-his-luck jockey who agreed to bait the men in the shoe shop. We set up a schedule to be at the Dictograph while he hung out.

"He'd go in, act like a customer, make pro-German comments, trying to get a rise out of the men. It worked, too. Made Pitts happier than a preacher with a church full of sinners."

"Rowe got arrested," Michael says, barely containing his disgust. "If you knew his statements were false, why write them down?"

"Pitts told us he wanted both sides—in case he needed context. But I think he wanted something on Rowe in case the truth came out. Cover his tracks. Have a patsy."

Michael's pulse pounds in his ears. "And at the trial, you read what was given to you. Not all of which was what you heard."

Beck holds his gaze. "Pitts had sheets of comments prepared. I had to read the thirty-two counts against one man alone. I didn't recognize much of it."

"So...you lied?"

Beck snorts. "Hawthorne's a tricky bastard. He didn't ask me if I wrote those statements. He asked me to verify that the paper I held contained reports of what the men said. Then he asked me to read."

Beck shrugs. "So yeah, I lied."

Michael's fist curls so tight, his nails bite into his palm. He pictures his grandfather in prison stripes and Victor Kendall's blood seeping onto the cobblestones beside the trolley. Beck's cheeky admission hits like a slap—flippant, but devastating.

He sucks in a sharp breath, pulse hammering. Hat back on, he's suddenly itching to get out—to process, to think, to figure out what the hell to do with it.

Beck's eyes flick to the door, like he's already regretting every word.

"Look," Beck mutters, rubbing a hand over his jaw, "I shouldn't have told you any of this. Leave me out of whatever you're planning. I ain't going to jail for those crooks."

Michael's jaw tightens. "That a warning?"

Beck scoffs. "It's a fact." He steps forward, gripping the edge of the door. "You two ain't got a clue what you're up against."

Max snaps his notebook shut with a flick of his wrist. "Yeah? Well, facts don't scare us."

Beck grunts. "Then you're dumber than you look, shrimp."

"And you're just as washed-up as I thought."

Beck glares. Holds his tongue, shaking his head like they're a couple of fools.

The door closes behind them as the men descend, footfalls heavy on the worn steps.

"Well, that was fun," Max says. "Thanks for letting me tag along."

"You got pretty fired up in there. Now that we're working together, is there anything I should know?"

Max clomps down the steps ahead of Michael. He can't see his face when he says, "Let's just say I've got no patience for men who pick on helpless folks. Grew up with it. Swore I'd never look the other way again."

Michael doesn't answer. He feels the same, and it may explain Max's overabundance of charm with Olivia and Charlotte.

His mind turns to Beck who'd given him definitive proof of what he's suspected all along: Hawthorne publicly punished respectable men to achieve his goal of ridding Ellington of all things German.

The courthouse banners. The jeering crowds. The law twisted into fear.

His grandfather staring through the train window—brave but frightened, hoping for a Presidential pardon that took six months to arrive.

They stole everything from him. His freedom. His name. His dignity.

Michael tightens his jaw, steadying the fire in his gut.

He doesn't know how yet. But he'll make them pay.

Chapter Thirty-Four

Olivia paces the parlor, pulling the curtains aside every thirty seconds to check on Uncle John's arrival.

Michael arrives and she motions for him to sit, offers him coffee, and resumes pacing.

A maroon car pulls up to the curb. "He's here." Olivia hurries into the hall, straightens her skirt, fluffs her hair, and lengthens her backbone. A quick glance in the hall mirror ensures she's calm and relaxed, but her insides are churning like a storm-tossed sea.

The knock is sharp.

Uncle John steps in, the afternoon sun behind him, obscuring his features.

"How are you, Olivia?" he asks and leans in to kiss her offered cheek. He hands her his hat, which she settles on the rack.

"Please come in." She gestures to the parlor.

Michael stands beside the sofa, hands buried in his pockets.

"Uncle John, I think you know Michael Schumann."

John's step falters as he examines Michael. "I don't think we've met."

He's already lying!

Michael offers a hand. "We met at Dixie's a few weeks ago. I'm with the *Ellington Journal*. We discussed the Dictograph case."

John arranges his face as if a light bulb comes on. "Ah, yes. Schumann. I remember now."

He sits on the opposite end of the sofa from Michael, perched on the edge, ready to escape. Olivia arranges herself in a wing chair directly across from him.

"I thought this was a dinner invitation." He locks eyes with her.

Olivia tilts her head toward Michael. "He's here for moral support. Let's talk about why I invited you, Uncle John. Since we last met, I've learned a few things that lead me to believe you've been lying to me."

"What are you talking about? I've been a family friend for decades. I'm your Godfather."

Her palms dampen and her resolve wavers. But his earlier lie sticks in her craw, pushing her forward.

"Well, you've just lied about meeting Michael. And both times we talked, you lied."

John scoots forward on the sofa, inching closer to Olivia, though the coffee table is a barrier between them. "I never. I don't know what you're talking about."

"When I showed you Mother's letter, you told me it was the meanderings of an unwell woman. Another lie."

He leaps to his feet. "Your mother was not herself after Victor died. You'd believe her over me?"

Her fists pound the arms of the chair. Her eyes blaze. "You bet I would."

John's face drains of color, but she's not backing down. She's done tiptoeing around the truth.

"When I asked about Tink Evans. You said you didn't remember. Lie number three."

"I told you—"

"You're a liar." Her voice hardens.

John opens his mouth, but no sound comes out.

"You knew there was evidence tampering. Knew the CPLE was after him. Didn't you?"

"They had a lot of power. I couldn't—"

"What did they have on you?" She's shaking with rage. "What was worth more than my father's life?"

John bites his lower lip, pacing the length of the sofa. When he finally opens his mouth, a breath stutters on his lips.

"I," he falters, "I didn't think it would go that far."

He sits again, clenching his hands between his knees. His breath comes in short gasps.

"Tell me!"

"Delia." The word breaks from him like a sob. "At fifteen, she had a baby. Out of wedlock."

Olivia reels as if struck. "What?"

"Marrying the boy wasn't in the cards, so we sent her upstate under the guise of an extended visit with relatives. She gave the baby up for adoption. When she got engaged in 1918 to a prominent young Evendale man, the CPLE threatened to expose it. Her marriage, our reputation—everything would be ruined."

"So, you protected your daughter and let Father go it alone. And when it came time for you to sign the motion for the appeal, you didn't. Why?"

Simpson's entire body deflates, shrinking visibly. His head moves side to side.

"He was so excited when that Tink fellow told him what the detectives did. He said we finally had them. But all I could think about was what they'd do to us for exposing them.

"I put him off—told him I'd lost it while I bought time to get the CPLE to back off. Then they went after Tink, and I came clean about the blackmail. Said I'd sign the motion. A few days later he was dead."

The world tilts beneath her, a free fall into a bottomless pit of betrayal. She grips the arms of the chair, her knuckles white. "He died because of you."

"No, that's not true. I figured it was them." He exhales, his voice hollow. "I turned over every stone, every rock, trying to link the driver with them. But I came up empty. I found nothing. Perhaps they were that good, but Olivia, I couldn't prove foul play. Please believe me, I tried."

"Mama tried, too. And look what happened to her." She jumps up, tears running down her cheeks.

"And your life was ruined," he says quietly.

"My life wasn't—" She stops, hands clenching into fists. "It didn't turn out how I thought. And yes, I carry wounds. But my father's compass pointed north. So does mine."

Olivia stares at him, exhausted and resigned.

"I'm sorry, Olivia. Sorry for my weakness, for my part in your father's death, your mother's too."

"In your office the other day, you said you were sorry but wouldn't say why."

He closes his eyes and speaks. "Becky came to me with that letter. Wanted answers, just like your mother."

"And you passed it off as the ramblings of a grieving woman. Why didn't you just tell me that?" Her rage rises—an ocean of red throbbing behind her eyes.

"I thought you'd let it go. Thought you agreed your mother was unstable. What good would it do to dredge it all up again?"

There it is again. Let it go. What everyone wants.

"Would you let it go if it was your family, your daughter?"

John stands alone. Shoulders heaving. Chin on his chest.

Olivia can't trust him. Can't talk to him. Can't stand to be in the same room with him.

"I can't call you Uncle anymore," she sniffs and digs in a pocket for a handkerchief but comes up empty.

Without looking at him, she runs upstairs, and on her return, Michael is talking to John.

"Mr. Simpson, those attacks are real. People are being targeted for their German heritage. Howard Pitts is the leading suspect, but the cops won't do anything."

Olivia adds, "Pitts threatened me and Michael's sister. Said we needed to stop poking into CPLE."

"What?" John's head snaps up.

"I, er, we," Michael motions to Olivia, "need to tell this town about these attacks." Michael edges closer and puts an arm around Olivia—a steady pressure she didn't know she needed. "With your knowledge of their mechanics, you can show the similarities to what happened during the war. Ellington should not have to live in fear while the power of influential men close off avenues of recourse."

Uncle John goes still. He swallows hard, hands clenched into fists.

"Do you really want another Victor Kendall on your conscience?" Michael's voice is ice.

John's jaw tightens. His fingers curl and uncurl as if gripping something invisible. He opens his mouth, but no words come out. He looks out the window.

Michael presses. "That's exactly where this is headed. The same men who took him down are at it again. Maybe you couldn't stop them then. But you can't stand by now and do nothing."

Uncle John sways slightly. A flicker of something breaking crosses his face, then vanishes.

And just for a moment, she remembers him as he was.

John on one side, her father on the other, both beaming with pride at her graduation.

That man is still in there.

Then he speaks.

"What do you have in mind?"

Chapter Thirty-Five

Simpson puts down the pen and hands the paper to Olivia. She glances at it, then passes the handwritten letter to Michael. "You're the journalist."

One hand accepts the document, the other rubs his chin. He clears his throat and reads aloud.

To the Editor:

Ellington has recently borne witness to a series of troubling attacks against individuals whose only perceived crime is their heritage. These acts, while alarming, carry with them an unsettling echo of our town's past—a past I know all too well.

Nearly two decades ago, Ellington was at the heart of a nationwide fervor to root out so-called disloyalty during the Great War. As one of the attorneys in the infamous Dictograph Case, I saw firsthand how fear and suspicion can cloud judgment, leading to actions that, though legal, were profoundly unjust. The scars of that time remain etched on our community—and on my conscience.

The Citizens Patriotic League of Ellington operated with the law behind them. I understand that many who participated in those events did so believing they were serving their country. Others felt they had little choice but to go along. All deserve compassion as we reckon with what occurred.

We must ask ourselves, does legality absolve us of moral accountability? Can we, as a community, truly thrive when we permit fear and prejudice to dictate our actions?

Ellington has a choice. We can turn a blind eye to these attacks, rationalizing them as isolated incidents, or we can confront them head-on as a community determined to learn from its past. Let us not repeat the mistakes of 1918. Let us instead strive to be better—to treat our neighbors with the respect and dignity every person deserves.

As someone who has carried the burden of Ellington's past, I urge us all to choose a better path forward. Let us reject fear, embrace empathy, and ensure that Ellington's heritage and its future are ones we can be proud of.

John Simpson

Attorney at Law

Ellington, June 1937

The implication of Simpson's words linger, settling over them like a heavy fog.

Michael lowers the paper, looking directly at Simpson. "You're putting everything on the line..."

"And places you in a precarious position," Olivia interjects, her voice measured. "Are you prepared for the fallout?"

A slight shrug contradicts John's raised brow and darting eyes. "I'll send Mary to her cousin in St. Louis till this blows over. I'll be fine."

Olivia rests a hand on his shoulder. "Thank you."

"Actually, I found that to be quite liberating." A small, almost imperceptible smile tugs at the corner of his mouth. Then, quieter, he adds, "I know I'm responsible for what happened to Tink. And I should have helped Victor."

"This sends a strong message to certain CPLE members that their actions are being scrutinized," Olivia says.

"A fair turn of events, since they've been surveilling us," Michael says.

He glances out the window, scanning the street as if expecting eyes to be watching. "This will add fuel to the fire."

Simpson leans forward, resting his elbows on the dining room table. "They believed they were invincible then. I imagine nothing has changed."

Michael's mind reels. Print the letter, and he'll expose a bit of the truth. But at what cost? More threats or real consequences? If Baxter fires him, he has no platform to tell the story. Either path risks someone's wellbeing.

The phone rings, and Olivia calls Michael into the kitchen.

"It's Effie."

Michael's stomach tightens on the way to the kitchen. Effie wouldn't call unless something was wrong. "What is it?"

"Baxter's having a fit. He's screaming about the holes in today's edition due to your lack of reporting."

When Simpson agreed to write the letter, Michael completely forgot about filing his stories for the day.

"Yeah, I've got one story. I covered the new Dodge release this morning."

"Give it to me," Effie says.

Michael flips open his notebook and rattles off the details.

"You're lucky I have a soft spot for lost causes, Schumann."

Then her voice softens, and Michael imagines she has her back to the office. "I have news on Rowe."

Michael perks up. "Good or bad?"

Effie sighs. "Bad, I'm afraid. The guy died of a broken neck at Beulah Park in Ohio. Fell off a horse. Go figure."

"That's the end of that trail."

There's a pause, static crackling faintly over the line.

Michael leans forward, lowering his voice. "We have a breakthrough."

"Let me know how I can help. I'm one Baxter tantrum away from cleaning out my desk. Not my fault you guys don't file on time."

"Sorry, Effie. I'll be in tomorrow. Promise."

The phone goes dead.

Back in the dining room, Max is shaking hands with Simpson.

"Oh. Hello, Max," Michael says.

"I came by to take this young lady to dinner." Max's straight white teeth gleam in the dusky dining room.

Michael's eyes flicker toward Max, whose easy charm is beginning to grate.

"Oh, well, I had the same thought." Why didn't he think of that?

"Well now," Olivia teases, glancing between them. "Quite the competition."

"Before anyone goes to dinner, I need help making two copies of this." He waves Simpson's handwritten pages. "Olivia, do you have a typewriter?"

"No. Sorry."

"Max, can I go to your office?"

"Depends."

"Michael," Olivia says, her mouth pursed, a puzzled look in her eyes. "What's your plan? You haven't told us what you want to do with the letter."

Michael exhales, rubbing a hand over the back of his neck. He glances out the window. What he does next can't be reversed.

"I want to test the *Journal*. Hawthorne has my editor in his pocket, essentially banning me from working on the story. I think we should submit the letter to the *Journal*." Then, turning his attention to Max, "and the *Post*."

Max nods appreciatively. "Smart move. Force Baxter's hand."

"Could cost me my job," Michael sighs.

Olivia shoots him a look of concern.

Simpson snaps his fingers. "I've got two typewriters in my office. What if we go downtown, get this typed up, then take Olivia to dinner?"

All eyes are on him, waiting for a decision.

Folding the letter, Michael tucks it into his jacket.

"What are we waiting for? Let's make it official."

Chapter Thirty-Six

At his office, Uncle John switches on the lights, uncovers the typewriters, and pulls a bottle of whiskey from his desk drawer. Michael moves the typewriters side by side so he and Max can share the document. As the keys start clacking, Simpson pours the amber liquid into four tumblers and offers one to Olivia.

Nodding at the other two, he says, "Their reward for finishing."

He takes a sip, then glances at her. "We've not had a chance to talk privately."

It's the first time she's had to examine her own feelings since his revelation hours before. Over the rim of her glass, she studies her uncle. Smaller somehow, the weight of his choices diminishing the presence he once commanded—yet larger for owning them.

"I don't understand why you lied to me." Clearing up this last mystery holds the key to her future relationship with John.

"I could chalk it up to stupidity," he admits, swirling his drink. "But the truth is, I underestimated your perseverance." His gaze flicks toward the anteroom. "And I never connected you with that reporter."

"He's a part of this, yes," Olivia concedes. "But there's a more compelling reason."

"I'd love to hear it."

She exhales. "I have a student in my history class. Hans Haber. Grandson of Wilhelm Haber, a recent German immigrant, and a victim of the first attack."

Simpson closes his eyes briefly, as if bracing against the impact of it.

"That boy was terrified in school," Olivia continues. "Among peers who don't always respect his heritage."

She sips her drink, gathering her thoughts. "I felt just like he did when Father defended the men accused of disloyalty. I got the cold shoulder. Backs turned when I joined conversations. Invitations that never came."

"Victor never said anything."

"He wasn't the kind of man to lay his burdens at someone else's feet." She offers a faint smile. "The dinner table wasn't for grievances. It was for lessons—ethics, tolerance, trusting the system. His values. Mother's, too. And mine—whether I like it or not."

The clack of dueling typewriters drifts into the room. Olivia lets it settle before speaking again.

"I wouldn't be here if I hadn't found Mother's letter. And I know why Aunt Becky never showed it to me."

John exhales. "Because you'd go off and do exactly what you're doing now—only younger, and not as wise?"

Olivia lifts her glass in acknowledgment.

He studies her for a long moment, until a smile spreads across his face. "You're not the same girl I remember." He exhales, almost amused. "Back then, you were just trying to survive it. But now? Now, you're facing it."

Olivia stares into the amber liquid. "I had to. Thought I could count on you. But that didn't work out, did it?"

"What you said, about me not being your uncle any longer, I get it. I brought that on myself by lying to you. I'm sorry." He chuckles under his breath. "Seems that's all I'm saying these days."

Olivia sips, ponders an answer. "Might be awhile before I forgive you, but by helping us stop these attacks, you'll get preferential treatment." She lets a tiny smile curl the corner of her lips.

John nods, understanding her hesitation. "Are you regretting your search?"

If she had never found the letter, she wouldn't have met Michael, or Clara, or any of the others who had risked something to tell their stories. And maybe she wouldn't have found her own voice in the wreckage.

"No," she says softly.

She sets her glass on the polished walnut desk and leans in. "Your letter won't be the end of this. You know that, don't you?"

He says nothing—neither confirms nor denies.

"It will provoke Hawthorne. Pitts. Maybe others. Once it's out in the world, there's no taking it back."

The typing stops. Uncle John shouts, "Come in. I've got a reward for your work."

Max spots the bottle first, crosses the room in a flash, and knocks back a drink. "I like the wages here."

Michael, slower, more deliberate, ignores the other glass and lowers himself into the chair next to Olivia. He looks directly at her. "Hawthorne won't sit still for this."

John lifts his glass in a mock toast. "We were just saying."

Olivia's fingers tighten around her whiskey. She wants this to be over. Wants the attacks to stop. Wants safety for everyone. Peace. And closure.

But wants don't change anything unless you're willing to fight for them.

She exhales, steadier this time. "We have to finish this, Michael."

Michael's lips curve into a smirk. "And how, pray tell, do we do that?"

Her gaze lands on the box on John's desk, and an idea clicks into place.

She straightens, her eyes finding Michael's with unmistakable mischief. "What if we turn the tables?"

The room is silent, anticipatory.

"Let's say the letter draws Hawthorne out. He challenges John. And let's assume," she glances at Simpson, "that my good uncle agrees to a meeting. One we can observe."

"Secretly," Michael finishes and cocks his head, a slow smile creeping onto his lips. "If you're thinking what I think you're thinking..."

"It would be poetic justice," she says, with the faintest lift of an eyebrow.

Michael's eyes are alight with something dangerous. "How wicked, Miss Kendall."

His words carry an intimate undertone, verging on flirtatious.

Olivia freezes, tumbler halfway to her lips. This is new, unexpected, but not unwelcome. Her heart trips over itself.

Despite her racing pulse, she manages a playful response. "You've yet to experience the depths of my guile, Mr. Schumann."

Max frowns, oblivious—or pretending to be. "We can't be the ones mailing the letters. If we do it, our objectivity is compromised."

Simpson sets his glass down. "I'll post them in the morning. Keep things on the up and up."

Olivia rises, finishes her drink in one smooth motion, and sets the tumbler down with a satisfying thud. Is it the whiskey warming her insides or Michael's spontaneous comment?

She flashes a big smile, masking her nerves. "Now, gentlemen," she says, "I believe you owe me dinner."

Chapter Thirty-Seven

Michael jumps off the streetcar, flips the newsboy a coin, and rifles through the *Evendale Post*. Simpson's letter is on page two, printed exactly as submitted. The thrill of seeing it in print is tempered by the fear of powerful men reading it.

Tucking it under his arm, he heads to the office. Waltzing into the newsroom, as if he hasn't a care in the world, he comes to a dead stop in front of his desk. It's bare. Naked. The desk calendar has disappeared, his pencil holder has no writing implements, and his nameplate is missing.

Effie tips her head toward a small cardboard box on the floor beside her desk containing his meager belongings.

"The letter arrived yesterday afternoon," she says.

Michael lets a smile play on his lips. He grabs the Post and strides into Baxter's office without knocking.

Michael slams the newspaper on Baxter's desk, folded to Simpson's letter. "You failed the test, Chief."

Baxter's eyes dart to the paper, then narrow. "You're done, Schumann."

"Because I found the connection you won't let me print?"

"You disobeyed my direct order to kill the CPLE story."

Michael leans over the desk, bringing himself eye to eye with Baxter. "Your order? Or Hawthorne's?"

Baxter sits forward, his nose inches from Michael's. "You're out."

"How much is he paying you to suppress the truth?" Michael taps the newspaper.

"Because while you were protecting Hawthorne, the *Post* printed what really matters. Every day you kill this story, more people get hurt."

Baxter's eyes widen beneath raised brows. "You can't prove anything."

Michael recognizes it as a question, not a statement. "I don't need to prove corruption. I've got something better—a real newspaper." He straightens. "The Post is unbiased, fair, and ethical. Everything this place used to be."

"If I publish that letter, Hawthorne will have my job."

"He already owns it. I'm just wondering what it cost you."

Michael picks up his box of belongings. "I thought you were better than this, Baxter."

Baxter falls back into his chair, defeated.

Michael walks to Effie's desk. Loud enough for the newsroom to hear: "Effie, I've been fired. I'm going to the Post. If you want to work for a paper that reports real news, I'll put in a good word."

"You mean this isn't a real paper?" Effie smiles. "I'll be in touch."

Michael turns toward the exit, his box of belongings tucked under one arm, hat tilted low over his brow.

A drawl cuts through the uneasy hum of the newsroom.

"You're a fool, Schumann. You think Hawthorne's gonna let you get away with this?" Pritchett holds a copy of the Post aloft, his smirk wide enough to choke on.

Michael saunters over to Pritchett's desk where a coffee mug with a cracked handle sits beside him.

He leans down, gives it an exaggerated sniff, and wrinkles his nose.

"Still starting your day with Irish courage, I see," he says, voice bone dry.

The newsroom goes dead still. Someone coughs into their hand to hide a chuckle.

Michael straightens, gives Pritchett a long, cold once-over, sizing up a corpse that just doesn't know it's dead yet.

"This isn't over, Pritchett. I'm digging graves. Men like Hawthorne, Pitts and toadies like you, will get yours in the end."

Pritchett's smirk curdles. His arms unfold in a clumsy defensive twitch, newspaper sagging like a defeated flag.

Michael doesn't wait for a reply.

He winks at Effie and strides out the door, leaving Pritchett staring down into his coffee like it held the last of his dignity.

On the sidewalk, the late morning sun hits his face.

His words mattered. Not just on the page—but in the newsroom.

And the days of fluff pieces? Gone.

He's done playing nice.

* * *

He finds a pay phone and calls Max.

"Got any openings for a junior reporter with a knack for getting in trouble?"

"My boss wants to interview you tomorrow. We've had several calls about Simpson's letter." His voice is jubilant. "Michael, you've uncorked the bottle."

Or unleashed Armageddon.

"I'm going to Nick's to celebrate. Meet me?"

"Can't. Got a deadline. And I promised Olivia I'd come over." There's a pause, then Max says, "Just so you know, I'm not trying to move in on your girl."

My girl. She wasn't. Not really.

Just a friend.

"She's not my girl. Do what you want."

A beat. Then another. A sigh crackles across the line before Max replies, "Sure, Mike."

The first whiskey washes away his paranoia about Max—his showing up at Nurse Franklin's place was genuine concern. Over the second, he examines his feelings for Olivia.

New. Raw. If he wanted to spend more time with her it had to wait. Wait until they had this investigation, or whatever it was behind them.

He wouldn't mind if Olivia was something more than a friend. But right now, she's chasing her father's ghost. And Victor Kendall was the kind of man who never wavered, never compromised. Michael's not sure he can live up to that.

Kellerman doesn't show. He heads home with a buzz in his head, and an ache in his heart.

Chapter Thirty-Eight

"Hawthorne's mad as a cornered rattlesnake. I hope this works Olivia." Uncle John's voice is fretful. "It's my reputation and my last shred of credibility on the line."

"After your letter ran in the *Post*, I'd think that's the last thing on your mind." She adds a chuckle to take the sting out.

"Yes, yes, of course," Uncle John says. "We've got to get your plan in place tonight."

"I'll contact Max and Michael. Is five-thirty good?"

Olivia calls Michael at the *Journal* but Effie says he's not in and isn't expected to return. Knowing Effie can't say much on her end, she asks a question that only requires a single word answer.

"Has he been fired?"

"Yes."

"Do you know where he is?"

"No."

Olivia searches for another question with a neutral answer, but Effie's whisper gives her what she needs. "Try Max."

A click and she's gone.

The *Post* operator connects her to Max. "Do you know where I can find Michael?"

"I hate when you don't greet me nicely, Miss Kendall. Says you don't love me like I hoped."

Olivia chuckles. "I'll be forever grateful if you tell me how to find Michael."

A shuffling and muted voices come through the receiver. She smiles when Michael picks up.

"You're on the hook now. He's already drawing hearts around your name on his blotter."

"What are you doing there?"

And unlike the whispers she's endured while working at the *Journal*, he's smart enough to tread carefully until he figures out who he can trust. "The *Post* hired me, but no pay until I deliver the story." He shifts gears. "You are calling me because..."

It's a lot to process, but she can get details later. "Hawthorne called John spitting mad, and they are meeting tomorrow morning. I need you guys to come to the office tonight. Five-thirty."

"We got him, Max!" Michael whispers. Then, into the receiver, he says, "We'll see you and John there with bells on."

Michael uses John instead of Simpson, suggesting a turning point in his regard for her uncle. The jury is still out on when she'll forgive him.

"You've lost your job for this, Michael."

"That paper doesn't deserve my respect. How can I work where I'm not trusted and certainly cannot trust them? It was meant to be."

Max's voice, distant, comes through the receiver. "See you tonight, darling."

"Michael, be careful. Hawthorne's cornered—and that's when people like him are most dangerous."

"Right," Michael replies, then adds. "Max will come get you."

She's grateful for the protection of these two men. "Tell Prince Charming to pick me up at five and I'll see you at the office."

She hangs up and despite the lighthearted banter, worries about what can go wrong, if their plan doesn't work. But as a glass-half-full kind of girl, she shoves the thought aside and heads for a bath.

* * *

They place the Dictograph sub-station on the floor under Uncle John's desk. They move the master from Adeline's desk into the filing room where it sits in the middle of a table, chairs pulled up beside it.

Max and Michael do the heavy lifting, while Olivia hides the wires under the carpet.

Their first test delivers muffled sound from the visitor's chair—the receiver under the desk is too far from the speaker. Michael drops to his hands and knees, inspecting the underside.

"If we tape it here, facing the chair, it should pick up better. Let's test it."

Olivia runs into the file room, Max stands in the doorway, while Uncle John occupies the chair and talks normally, using the time to practice his remarks to Hawthorne. "Tell me, Hawthorne, are you reviving the CPLE's stunts?"

Olivia shouts to Max. "Voice is coming through loud and clear. It's working."

"Max, go listen," Michael commands. "John, keep talking."

Max and Olivia switch places.

John says, "Your bully Howard Pitts has been caught red-handed instigating attacks on Ellington's citizens."

Olivia likes what Uncle John is saying. It's bold and just inflammatory enough to provoke Hawthorne. For the first time, they are setting the terms of engagement.

Max returns and checks his watch. "I think we're good. But I've got a dinner with colleagues tonight. Will you be all right without me?"

"We've got it covered," Michael says, already coiling the extra wire.

Max crosses his fingers on both hands and holds them up so Olivia can see. "I'll be waiting with bated breath for the results of this operation. Call me after."

As Olivia rearranges Adeline's desk, so the missing master station isn't obvious, someone appears behind the glass entry door. Her breath catches and her instinct is to hide. The only place is behind the desk. She crouches down. The latch clicks and the sharp click of a high heel strikes the floor. She desperately wants to see who it is and when the room falls silent, she tips her head back and peers over the edge.

Effie! Her relief is so profound, she drops onto her bottom, legs splayed in front of her.

Effie leans over the desk and chuckles. "Why in the world are you down there?"

Olivia's built-up adrenaline snaps in a snort of laughter that evolves into full-blown hysteria. A wave of relief washes over her, tangled with the absurdity of crouching behind a desk like a fugitive.

Michael rushes into the anteroom and halts at the scene—Effie frozen in confusion, Olivia on the floor, clutching her stomach, howling with laughter.

"What the heck?" He presses a hand to her forehead.

Olivia chokes out, "I'm not sick," each word wobbling between joy and disbelief. She points at Effie, her laughter dying, caught between fading fear and the hilarity of it all.

Michael sits beside her. "It's my fault. I forgot to tell you I asked Effie to come."

Olivia shifts her gaze from Michael to Effie. "I don't understand."

Effie removes her pocketbook from her arm and lays it on the desk. Her gloves come off and she says, "You need someone to capture what's said. I clock a hundred twenty words a minute, give or take. You two focus on tone—I'll catch every word. Takes secretarial school to a whole new level."

Olivia turns her head to Michael who is looking at her for approval. "Have I told you that you're brilliant?"

His lips, that she dearly wants to kiss, curl into a smile, a blush creeping across his cheeks. "Because of you, I feel brilliant."

In the filing room, the Dictograph sits silent and ready. Wires hidden. Microphone in place. When Hawthorne sits across from Uncle John, they'll be listening.

* * *

The file room is tight, stuffy, and hot. The dictograph hums like an electric nerve, as if the machine itself shares in the charged energy of the room's occupants. A steno pad on her knee, Effie scribbles curves and lines, a mysterious language Olivia never learned.

Men's voices alert them to William Hawthorne's arrival. Pleasantries are exchanged but Hawthorne's voice is tight, frustrated, walking a thin line between professionalism and disdain. The falter in Uncle John's voice is obvious to her, but the other man doesn't comment.

Michael, Olivia, and Effie huddle over the Dictograph, ears close as voices from the adjoining office crackle to life—muffled at first, then sharpening into focus as Michael adjusts the dials.

Olivia hopes Uncle John remembers her instructions to speak instead of nodding—they can't hear him shake his head.

"Your letter, John. Published in the *Post*," Hawthorne says, his voice gruff, demanding. "You're no innocent. Remember, you helped bury the Tinker Evans problem. You may think you're cleansing your conscience," he adds, his tone cold, calculating, "but you've opened yourself—and your office—to liability. False accusations. Slander. Incitement."

Hawthorne pauses long enough to let the implications settle. "That comes with consequences."

The threat hangs in the air. Then a chair squeaks.

John's voice comes through despite a slight tremor meaning Hawthorne's threat hits a nerve. "I'm not innocent. But I won't stay silent and let fear dictate what's right. My family has a right to live without that shadow hanging over us. And I have a right to hold my head up in this town."

Delia. Her heart aches for him. He was forced to choose when it shouldn't have been a choice at all.

"Your niece and a reporter have been snooping around. Dredging up old history. How does that benefit the community?"

"I have it on good authority that there have been attacks on four citizens. Three men with German heritage and a woman. One of the attackers bears a striking resemblance to Howard Pitts."

Hawthorne scoffs. "So? I don't have anything to do with Pitts."

"He was your flunky during the war."

"I don't control him."

"You used to. He carried out your orders, including threats made to me. The Goetz case clearly identified him, and you, I might add, for intimidating and harming members of this community."

"I did what needed to be done when I had the authority to do it. That campaign was when this town respected real leadership. I got results."

"William," a sharp rap startles the listeners, "we are not at war. What's happening is illegal. Anti-German sentiment will no longer be tolerated."

"Who are you to tell me what won't be tolerated? Hitler is on the rise. Soon Germany will be armed to fight again. I won't let Ellington be sympathetic to the Hun. Not now. Not ever."

Michael and Olivia's eyes connect, both with raised eyebrows. Is this an admission? She prays Uncle John will keep peeling back the layers of the onion.

"So, the CPLE is still active?" The simple question comes over the wire. Hawthorne's silence stretches uncomfortably.

The chair screeches again. One of them is standing.

Uncle John asks, "Are you behind these attacks?"

"I'm late for a meeting." A thud near the receiver rumbles through the speaker. Likely Hawthorne's shoe kicking the desk.

Uncle John's voice fades when he moves away from the microphone, but a moment later, his stern yet matter-of-fact tone comes through the wire almost as if he's standing in the room with them.

"Your actions are no longer protected. This town rationalized your actions when it seemed the Germans were taking over the world. I will encourage the good citizens of Ellington to speak out when something odd happens. If their trash bins are missing, it's on the CPLE. If anyone is robbed, the CPLE will be investigated." Uncle John's voice has escalated with each threat. "And if a man is run down by an automobile on a beautiful Sunday afternoon, you, personally, will pay."

Olivia's heart skips a beat.

"I had nothing to do with that," Hawthorne's voice drips with smug indifference. "But I will admit, the timing of Kendall's death was impeccable."

Olivia grips the edge of the table, blood pounding in her ears. That word—impeccable—lodges like a thorn behind her ribs. Her father, reduced to timing. To strategy.

She leaps from her chair, spins toward the door, and yanks it open.

At that very instant, Hawthorne strides out of Simpson's office. He sees her and stops cold.

Olivia stands in the doorway to the file room, eyes locked on his—unwavering, unafraid.

His gaze flicks past her to the Dictograph on the table with Michael leaning into the receiver. Hawthorne's sharp intake of breath hitches and all the color drains from his face.

Olivia faces him, hands on hips. "How does it feel, Mr. Hawthorne? To be the one on the other end of the Dictograph—watched, recorded, judged?"

Real fear flashes in his eyes.

He says nothing. Just stiffens, straightens his jacket, and strides out.

Olivia's mouth opens, another barb ready to hurl at the retreating figure, but Michael reaches out—his hand firm on her arm, pulling her back, into the safety of his embrace.

"He's a monster," she sobs into Michael's chest, tears choking her, clenched fists pounding his sternum.

In his protective arms, she waits until her heart slows, and her tears dry, until finally, a fierce clarity takes hold. Gripping his chin, she locks eyes with him. "You write that article, Michael. You write it to protect the Habers and Nurse Franklins of this town. And if that Dictograph didn't catch every word, embellish his statements—just like they did in 1918."

Michael nods with a grim smile.

Effie adjusts her glasses and smirks. "Oh, the irony."

The Dictograph hums on the table. Still listening.

Chapter Thirty-Nine

Max drops a stack of messages on Michael's desk. The pile teeters precariously.

"That letter got a lot of traction," Max says, pulling up a chair. "People are calling to talk about their own experiences—then and now."

Michael rifles through the stack. Each slip of paper carries a brief note summarizing the caller's claim: Missing dog. Watched. Store ransacked. Car stolen. The stories blur into a chaotic tapestry of Ellington's buried grievances.

"Are all these related to the CPLE?" he asks. "Or did we just open the flood gates for every unexplained problem in this town?"

Max shrugs. "Does it matter? You rattled the cage, and now everyone's screaming to be heard."

This is the response he wants. Proof that the town is waking up, ready to acknowledge wounds that haven't healed.

One note catches his eye: Henry Vogel. No phone number. Two words: Thank you. His grandfather's friend who paid the price with the others and has felt the cost of silence. He pockets this one.

Thumbing through the remaining messages, he says, "I need to talk to Kellerman, if we're going to stop this before someone else gets hurt."

"Will he cooperate?" Max asks.

"I don't know but there may be enough here to push the precinct commander off the dime to reopen the Haber and Doller investigations. With the public involved now, there's no shoving it under the rug."

Max sits at the desk opposite Michael. "You want me to do a quick outline for the exposé? My gut says this is a two or three-part story."

He's found an ally. With Effie, and now Max, he has people on his side.

He plucks his hat from the rack. "I'm going down to the station."

Max drops a blank legal pad in front of him, his notebook beside it.

As Michael heads out, Max calls after him, "Don't stick your neck out further than you can afford to lose it."

* * *

The day is hot and muggy. Removing his coat, he lets it dangle from a hooked finger over his shoulder as he heads to the precinct.

"Hey, McCabe," Michael says to the sergeant at the desk. "Kellerman around?"

McCabe is a husky man with a square head atop his shoulders, no neck in sight.

"Yeah, he's here," he says and drops his eyes to yesterday's edition of the *Post*.

"I see you've read that," Michael says.

"About time someone called them out."

McCabe flips the paper and Simpson's letter to the editor stares back at him. "You behind it?"

Telling him the truth can go sideways, so he replies with a shrug.

McCabe leans forward, sweeps a glance around the room behind him. "That letter raised the hackles around here. Chief is fit to be tied."

"Because?" Michael lets the word hang, hoping it'll reveal something about how they see him here.

McCabe lowers his voice. "Because we got reports of harassment coming out my wazoo. And, his highness, the City Solicitor's been here."

Michael's ears prick at the mention of Hawthorne in the station. He cocks his head as if he's just an interested party, keeping his anxiety in check.

"Chief threw him out," McCabe says, chest puffed like a man who just dropped a bomb. "Quite a row."

Biting his lip to quench the thrill that courses through him, he says, "I'm sure it was."

McCabe jerks a thumb behind him. "Kellerman's in with the chief now."

"Should I wait?"

McCabe glances around again. "Look, the mood around here's unstable. You might want to keep your head down."

"Can you let Kellerman know I'm at Dixie's? I need to eat."

"You got it." McCabe's voice carries a note of begrudging respect.

Michael steps into the humid afternoon and scans the street—a habit he's taken up, though he's yet to sense anything or anyone out of place.

The cracks in the CPLE's armor are showing.

* * *

The lunch counter is full. Michael spies an empty booth and slides in. Mabel shouts at him for his order.

"The special. And iced tea."

Michael fishes his notebook from his pocket. The simple thank-you message from Vogel comes out with it. He's done something good. Something right. He replaces the slip of paper, saving it to show Olivia and Clara. And as an afterthought, his mother.

At half past twelve, no Kellerman in sight, Michael drops his napkin on his empty plate and opens his notebook. On impulse he jots down the Habers' address and a note. "Meet me here if you want another ID on Pitts."

He hands it to the waitress with a dollar. "You know Abe Kellerman? The cop?"

"Short, fat, bad breath?" The woman teases.

"Give this to him if he shows up."

"He'll be here. Never misses the Salisbury steak special."

On the street again, he shuffles to the shady side where awnings provide a brief respite from the heat. His decision to visit the Habers is impulsive, but Vogel's note reminds him of the recent victims of the CPLE's evil actions. They deserve an update. And a check on their well-being.

He heads across town on foot. A slow-moving train blocks his route on Tenth, so he detours to the underpass on Eleventh.

The realization that he's retracing the steps that Wilhelm and Fredrick took that fateful night in May sets his heart racing. They went to get cigarettes and came home bloody, bruised, and broken.

He swallows at the tunnel entrance. Concrete pillars on both sides of the road. The walkway isn't exactly dark, but it's thick with shadows and mystery.

Chiding himself for being jumpy, he quickens his pace and slips deeper into the gloom, keeping his eyes on the rectangle of daylight, ignoring the shuddering noises from the train above, and the prickling sense of being followed.

As he approaches the exit, he considers closing the gap by sprinting to the end of the tunnel, but instead, quickens his pace.

Lifting his hat, he wipes his brow and settles it back on his head.

Then he's struck from behind.

The shove propels him forward, sending him sprawling on the ground. He throws his hands out to brace the impact of the fall, gravel stinging as they slide across the walkway. His knees strike the pavement hard, spikes of pain shoot up his thighs, then his nose slams into the ground. Stars shoot across a black background.

A voice. Rough and close. Michael forces one eye open.

He recognizes him. The one who hurt Charlotte Franklin, The one in the sketch. Howard Pitts.

A brown leather shoe enters his line of sight close enough to take out an eye and a hand holding the note he gave the waitress is dangled in front of his face.

Michael groans. At his stupidity or his injuries. It's unclear.

"Thought you could save those *dirty Huns*?" Pitts growls. "Your little project is about to come to an end."

Should he reply? Get up? Play dead?

There's no chance Kellerman can save him. All he can hope is muster enough strength to get up and defend himself.

Pushing himself onto all fours, his knees and hands screaming in protest, he's just about to get a foot under him, when the leather shoe flies past his head and slams into his stomach, flattening him. Instinctively, he curls into a ball to protect his midsection from another blow.

Another kick like that would finish him. He can't lie here. Can't let this jerk win.

Pain pulses through his ribs, but his thoughts reach past it to something deeper—the reason he's here on the ground. All he'd tried to do was protect his friends, family, the town of Ellington. A town just as helpless as he is, when powerful men decide who deserves punishment, leaving their victims with no choice but to lie down and take it.

But that ends now.

He licks his lips. Opens his eyes. Turns his head toward Pitts who looms over him like a fisherman waiting for his catch to stop flopping.

"You beat up old men. Scare women. It's not 1918 anymore."

Pitts laughs. "But Germans are still threats. As are you."

"I thrive on threatening you, Pitts!" Michael spits a punctuation mark.

The big man squats on his haunches, beefy hands dangling between his knees, near enough to rearrange his face.

"Thanks to your crusade, I got a visit from Kellerman. That newspaper picture, and you, seem to be the only things tying me to your witnesses. Hawthorne's not happy."

The casual mention of his boss makes Michael's skin crawl. It's one thing to know they're connected—it's another to have Pitts throw it in his face while he's flat on the ground.

His bug-eyes remind him of Peter Lorre, sinister, yet somehow ridiculous. "Thought you'd look scarier."

He won't beg. He won't back down. It's too late for that. But what he can do is...

"Hey!" A voice shouts sending echoes bouncing off the concrete. "What are you doing?"

Pitts pops up and assesses the interruption. "You're getting off lucky this time. Last warning, Schumann."

His fine leather shoes scrape the gravel before disappearing.

Footsteps echo, pounding through the tunnel toward him.

Michael catches a glimpse of Pitts as he bolts from the underpass and disappears around the corner.

The footsteps stop. Next to him. A face blurs above him.

"Are you all right?"

That voice. Or is his mind playing tricks on him?

"I think so."

"Michael?"

The fog starts to lift. He squints his eyes at the form, backlit by the sun. "Who?"

"It's me. Fredrick Haber."

Tears prick his eyes as Fredrick's hand clasps his. "I was on my way. To see you. To make sure."

"Make sure?" Fredrick helps Michael to a sitting position, his back against the underpass wall.

"That your family is safe." Michael still clutches his stomach, but the pain has dulled to a persistent ache, like a mallet strike reverberating through his core.

"That was him, wasn't it?"

He means Pitts.

Moving his head sends shooting pains ricocheting around in his skull. Talking is easier. "The shoes. I saw his shoes, just like you said."

He puts a hand on Fredrick's cheek—a thank you for not letting him die.

"Are shoes useful in courtrooms these days?" Fredrick asks.

Michael's half-laugh fractures mid-breath, crumpling into a raw groan that scrapes across his throat. "If not, they should be."

Chapter Forty

"The parade starts in an hour," Clara announces to the crowd gathered at Warner's Shoe Shop.

Cold dishes line the shop counter, ready for guests to serve themselves—a pseudo-picnic to celebrate the Fourth of July.

Olivia slaps Max's hand after he plucks a strawberry from the cake and pops it into his mouth. "Now you've ruined the stripes."

Max shifts two strawberries to close the gap, while Minnie Schumann stacks freshly baked rolls in a wicker basket. "For a little man, you eat a lot."

Grinning up at Michael's mother, he says, "The way to a man's heart is through his stomach. Can Clara cook as well as you?"

"Taught her everything I know."

Max twirls on his heel and stands next to Clara, who is talking to Charlotte Franklin.

"Hello, Miss Franklin. I'm thrilled to see your beauty wasn't marred by that hideous man." Then he pivots. "Can you cook?"

Charlotte stares at him, stunned into silence.

Clara closes her eyes and shakes her head. "Don't mind him. He's harmless."

Mouth agape, Max's hand flies to his chest. "I'm just looking for a girl who will let me eat my way into her heart. Either of you game?"

Clara plants a kiss on his cheek and says, "I'll cook till you explode if you'll stop flirting with every female this side of the Mississippi."

Hand in hand, the couple goes outdoors leaving Charlotte Franklin standing alone.

Olivia walks over. "Hello."

"Hi! Michael here yet?"

"He's on his way." Olivia examines Charlotte's face. "Looks like you won't be scarred."

"No, the outside is fine. But I still get nightmares."

"I would, too. Pitts is behind bars. You can at least rest easy on that front."

"I hope so. Effie's been kind, but I'm going home tomorrow."

"The Habers will be here. I'm sure they'd love to see you."

"Oh, me too! They're nice people. Well..." She pauses and leans in, "Except for Mrs. Haber."

Olivia laughs. "I hope her fears have been settled with Pitts in jail."

"Would you like something to eat?" Olivia guides her to the counter and hands her a plate. "Help yourself."

A distant trumpet blares, off key, signaling the high school band is assembling on the next street over.

She and Clara decorated the exterior with bunting and flags. Written across the window in white shoe polish is "Happy Birthday America."

Watching for Michael, Olivia realizes she's standing in the exact spot where the grandfather clock quietly orchestrated the demise of his grandfather.

Minnie moves next to her and wraps an arm around her waist. "Nineteen years ago, I was making potato salad, the same recipe as today. Mama was frying chicken and Papa was reading the *Journal* in the front room."

Olivia imagines the scene, positioning everyone as described. "Where were Michael and Clara?"

"Clara ran to a neighbor for mustard seed—Mama wouldn't let me make the salad without it. Michael was upstairs. We were laughing one minute, then the knock came."

A tear slips down Minnie's cheek, but she ignores it. "That day is a blur. But oddly, I remember the potatoes turned to mush, and the chicken burned up. Clara came in to find Mama screaming, me screaming for Michael to come back from chasing the wagon with Papa in it."

Olivia slips her arm around Minnie as the festivities go on around them, cocooned in the memory of a bygone holiday flipped on its head.

"What about you? Did you get answers about your father?"

"I may never know what happened," Olivia says quietly. "But because of Mother's letter, I know Father's story. And it's one I'm proud to tell."

Minnie doesn't speak, just watches her with quiet encouragement.

"But my mother. I think when she realized she'd never know if his death was an accident or something else, it broke her. Everyone thought she was crazy with grief when all along her bravery is what sent her down that cistern. That will take a while to settle with me."

"Hello, Olivia."

Olivia spins toward the voice.

"Uncle John!" She hadn't been sure he'd come, but here he is, and though she's still raw from his betrayal, she moves into his arms. Only days ago, she'd lost all trust in him, thinking him her enemy instead of her lifelong friend. His letter and the meeting with Hawthorne allow her a guarded forgiveness.

"So, this is the notorious shoe store," he releases her and looks around. "Much smaller than I imagined."

Olivia gasps. "You mean you've never been here? Why not?"

A hangdog look crosses his face. "I meant to. But Victor handled all that as lead defense counsel."

Olivia shakes off her remorse at his negligence and directs him to Minnie. "Mrs. Schumann, this is John Simpson. I'm not sure if you ever met."

John takes Minnie's hand as if it's made of glass and holds it like she's a queen. "We've met. I hope you're well."

"Mr. Simpson," Minnie lets her hand linger, though her shifting feet indicate her discomfort. "I'm glad you could come today. Thank you for blowing away the smoke that hid the CPLE."

"My pleasure. I'm sorry it took so long. And my part in it."

Minnie offers to fill a plate. "So, it's true—Pitts has been arrested?"

"Yesterday. Cops hauled him out of his law office in plain sight of the entire town."

"Did he confess?"

"Didn't need to. He was identified as the gang leader and spilled the beans on the two who did his dirty work. His attack on your boy tipped the scales and he's up on several charges of attempted murder. Judge denied bail, saying he's a flight risk and a threat to the community."

Minnie scowls. "Did Hawthorne have anything to say?"

"Police questioned him, but he denied any involvement. Called Pitts misguided and unstable." John shakes his head. "Hawthorne's always been quick to disown the monsters he helps create."

Olivia wanders outside, where Max is waving at someone. She prances down the steps to the sidewalk, her skirt fluttering under her knees, and follows Max's pointed finger toward Schmitty's Corner.

It's Michael. Her heart leaps. His arm is around Effie's shoulder for support; the pair approach the shop with measured strides to avoid jolting two broken ribs, courtesy of Pitts.

Olivia grabs Max's hand, who is holding Clara's, and she tugs the pair down the block. Michael lets go of Effie, and folds Olivia into his arms. She buries her face in his collar, his aftershave sharp and grounding.

"How are you holding up?" Pulling away, she assesses him. He's got circles under his eyes, but his weary smile gives her hope he's healing.

His forehead touches hers. "Did you see today's headline?"

"Not yet. We've been waiting for you."

Michael plucks the folded paper from Effie and snaps it to attention. A two-column headline dominates the right side of the page.

Pitts Arrested. Hawthorne Questioned

By: Michael Schumann.

A shout from behind alerts them to the Haber's arrival. Olivia and Michael pause to wait for them as Hans bounds up to her like a puppy dog, eager to tell her about his job and pitching for the Ellington Blue Jays Junior baseball team. His eyes no longer carry a wary view of the world. He's safe—like a fourteen-year-old boy should be.

Mrs. Haber picks at Michael's shirt sleeve. "Please. I talk with you."

Michael reverses direction and tells Olivia, "I'll be there in a minute."

Olivia guides everyone toward the front of the shop. Max climbs a chair, positioned just inside the door, preparing to address the crowd that flows onto the sidewalk and into the street.

Olivia glances around and marvels at the number of people in her life. Other than Uncle John and Hans, she hadn't known any of them six weeks ago.

Max shouts, "Pitts Arrested."

Applause and hurrahs thunder through the crowd.

An arm slips around her waist, and Michael whispers in her ear. "Mrs. Haber is human after all."

"Will wonders never cease?" She teases and moves in closer, offering support should he need it.

Max reads the article, one he and Michael co-wrote, though they'd agreed Michael's name would be on the byline.

Nineteen years ago, Ellington's citizens experienced prejudice born of an irrational fear of anything German. German was erased from schools, street names were changed, newspapers were shuttered, and families adopted non-German names to escape scrutiny. In this, our town was not unique—similar efforts swept across America. But what set Ellington apart was the unchecked power granted to the

Citizens Patriotic League of Ellington to enforce their vision of total national loyalty.

Under the Sedition Act, the CPLE had free rein. They harassed men into buying liberty bonds, twisted words into pro-German propaganda, and assaulted anyone deemed 'unpatriotic.' Even a priest was a victim.

Fear was their weapon and silence their goal.

Today, history is repeating itself. A spate of assaults has hospitalized three men and left a woman in fear for her life. These attacks, once again targeting German Americans, are not random. They are calculated acts of intimidation meant to suppress and divide us—just as they did in 1918. But this time, the people of Ellington are speaking out—not because they feel they must, but because they choose to do what's right.

Thanks to the diligence of this reporter and the Ellington Police, the ringleader, Howard Pitts, and two associates have been arrested and charged. Pitts, a former high-ranking member of the CPLE, has implicated William Hawthorne in orchestrating the recent attacks. Hawthorne denies his involvement, but his own words cast doubt on that denial. In a conversation overheard by me and other respected witnesses, including the honorable John Simpson, Hawthorne chillingly declared, 'The CPLE will do what needs to be done to protect Ellington's American values.'

While history books tell us the war ended in 1918, in Ellington, the battle lines of prejudice were redrawn, and fear never truly left. Now, we face a choice. Will we allow fear and hate to dictate our future as it once did, or will we reckon with our past and ensure such darkness never takes hold again? Ellington's future is in our hands. Let us choose justice, empathy, and unity over division and fear.

The listeners are still, absorbing the significance, as a drumbeat's cadence announces the start of the parade.

Max lowers the paper, folding it neatly as if sealing a chapter of their collective history. The group remains hushed, the weight of the words settling over them like the humid summer air.

Finally, Wilhelm Haber approaches Michael, his voice steady with an edge of emotion. "You did it, Michael. You gave us a voice—and a reason to believe things can change."

Clara nods, her eyes glistening. "Grandfather would be proud of you."

Michael shifts uncomfortably. Olivia's not certain if it's humility or his fractured ribs.

"It's not just me," he says. "It took all of us—Olivia, Clara, Max, Effie, Mama, John—everyone who had the courage to speak up, to take risks."

"Still," Fredrick Haber says, stepping forward. His voice, usually quiet, carries the gravity of a man who has endured too much. "You put it all together. You shined a light into the darkness and kept it burning until the truth was told." He pauses, placing a firm hand on Michael's shoulder. "For my family, for all of us—you're a hero."

"And if not for you, Fredrick, this little party would be short one journalist!"

The crowd titters uneasily. Michael's joke falls flat.

But Max saves the moment by shouting "Hip, hip, hooray!"

The group echoes his cheer.

Olivia catches Michael's eye and smiles, her expression a mix of pride and something deeper, more personal between them and no one else.

A figure weaves his way through the crowd, pausing at the steps. Heads turn and the chatter dies.

Michael straightens. He recognizes him from the sketch. The one with Pitts, Hawthorne and other CPLE members he sued.

Herman Goetz.

The elderly man removes his hat revealing a shock of white hair. Thick gray eyebrows furrow over rheumy eyes, his lined face unreadable. His gaze sweeps left and right before speaking.

"I'm looking for Michael Schumann," Goetz glances at a folded newspaper in his hand.

Michael steps forward, extending his hand.

"I read your articles," the older man says, his voice gravelly but steady. "I had my day in court, but all I got for it was a penny." His jaw tightens, his grip on Michael's hand unwavering. "But you—you gave me something worth much more."

Michael swallows. "What's that?"

Goetz releases his hand and surveys the bystanders—Olivia, Minnie, Clara standing near the door—before returning to Michael.

"The men who did this." His voice is thick with emotion. "You named them. You wrote it down, plain for the world to see. You made them answer for it." He exhales, shaking his head.

The words settle in Michael's chest, heavier than he expected.

For years, Goetz had been dismissed, his suffering reduced to a footnote in the city's history. Today, for the first time, he stands vindicated—not because of a judge's ruling, but because the truth had finally been laid bare.

"Thank you," Goetz says simply.

Michael nods, his throat tight.

The group stands silent as Goetz tips his hat to the women surrounding Michael and moves away, disappearing into the crowd.

A long beat passes before Max stubs a toe on the concrete. "Well, hell," he mutters, wiping his eyes. "Now we really have to celebrate."

A round of chuckles breaks the tension, and Olivia squeezes Michael's arm.

A drum beats, then another, until it has rhythm. The parade is starting. A horn blares, children cheer, and the sound of marching feet fills the air.

Effie breaks the moment with a wry grin. "Well, aren't you the conquering knight, Schumann?"

Michael laughs, shaking his head. "Not a knight. Just a reporter trying to do what's right."

Olivia whispers to him as the drums grow louder. "You're my knight."

"And you're the bravest woman I know." His smile lights up his eyes, crinkling the corners of a face that's both handsome and serious—a man who's crept into her heart and, she hopes, her future.

As they join the parade watchers, the midday sun breaks through the clouds as if in step with Olivia's buoyant spirits.

Michael stands beside her, his hand searching for, then entwining her fingers with his. Her gentle squeeze lets him know she approves.

Hans darts into the street, scooping up a peppermint stick. A man in uniform hands out flags. The parade rolls past.

And as Olivia watches it all unfold—the cheers, the sunlit banners, the boy with wide, fearless eyes—she understands.

What her father stood for.

What her mother needed to know.

What she will ensure lives on.

Epilogue

Michael stares at the front page of the competing newspapers.

One headline screams, "City Reacts to Exposé—Hawthorne Fired"

The other shouts, "Hawthorne Resigns. Says City Needs New Blood"

Michael leans over The *Post*. "Listen to this."

Setting her red pencil down, Olivia pauses grading homework.

> William Hawthorne, long the stormy petrel of Ellington politics and known for being "anti-everything," has "retired" to private law practice. City Manager Elmer Zink requested his resignation. When Hawthorne refused, Zink issued his walking papers. The office stands vacant effective today.

"Well done, Max," Olivia says. She gestures to the other paper. "What's the *Journal* say?"

Michael reads aloud.

> After years of service to the county and city, William Hawthorne has decided to take up private practice again. His years of public devotion have fractured relationships that no longer ensure the city runs smoothly and within budget. Hawthorne gave this reporter his point of view. "It's time for a city solicitor who is not constantly opposed by the city manager."

He folds the papers and puts them aside.

Michael shakes his head. "It's already happening."

Olivia studies him. "What is?"

He taps the folded newspapers. "The blurring of the truth." His voice tightens. "The city just wants to move on. No mention of 1918. No mention of the attacks. No mention of how many lives were ruined."

She reaches for The *Post*, smoothing out the creases, fingers trailing over the print.

"This truth will last."

Michael snorts. "You think?"

"We chased the truth all summer. And the consequences are there in black and white. But you're right—the *Journal* softened the controversy, made it easier to live with."

She taps the paper lightly. "That's what I try to get my students to understand. History isn't neutral. Someone decides what goes in the history books—and what doesn't."

She leans back, crossing her arms. "I might take these two versions into class and ask which one will be remembered." A folder labeled "Civics – 11/12" is filled with Dictograph case files, courtesy of Uncle John who is working to regain her trust.

He studies her, struck again by how she's slipped her way into his life—not with fanfare, but with clarity.

He hadn't known he needed someone whose compass pointed due north.

His won't always.

But it pointed here.

To her.

His job at the *Post* is everything he ever wanted. Real investigations. Stories with weight. A paper that answers only to the public.

Back when he was stuck churning out fluff pieces, he believed the only thing missing was the right assignment. The big story. The one that would prove he was more than filler copy.

But now, sitting here, while Olivia's red pencil checks and slashes, he thinks about it differently. It isn't about getting the story. It's about choice.

Let it go, pretend it wasn't happening—or expose the crime, the evildoer, and hope no one gets hurt.

The risk. The fallout. The way truth can drag the past, kicking and screaming, into the present—and the way some people will do anything to shove it back down.

He wanted this. He fought for it. And now he understands. Finding the truth has consequences.

For a moment, silence stretches between them. Outside, a car rumbles past, the sound fading into the distance. A breeze stirs the lace curtains, carrying the faint smell of jasmine from the trellises. A vase of wildflowers sits on the table. Something simmers on the stove—simple, warm, inviting. Michael takes it all in. Olivia's turning Aunt Becky's house into a home again.

"You're really staying," he says, not quite a question.

"I am." She nods but doesn't look at him. "Feels right."

Michael runs a hand over his jaw. There's something settling about her calling this house her home.

His eyes drift back to the newspapers. "Think it mattered?"

Olivia tilts her head. "The article?"

"The whole damn thing." He gestures vaguely. "The investigation. The exposé. Everything we put on the line."

She considers this for a moment. "Yes."

Michael huffs a quiet laugh. "You sound sure."

"I am. Aren't you?"

"I don't know what people think," he says. "But I know I'd regret it if we hadn't tried."

She meets his gaze, steady, unwavering. A moment passes, then two. Her eyes flutter and close, as she sighs, "Sometimes the truth is difficult to believe."

Michael wonders how she bears not knowing what really happened to her father. How she lives with her mother's unanswered questions—silence slowly wearing away her will to live.

He rises to get his hat. "See you tomorrow?"

A smile flickers at the corner of her mouth as she rises and rounds the table. Reaching up, she entwines her fingers in his thick brown hair and draws him in. "Stay for supper," she murmurs, her lips reaching up to find his.

THE END

Thank you for reading The Dictograph Case. If you enjoyed this historical mystery, please consider leaving a review on Amazon, Goodreads, BookBub, or wherever you share book recommendations. Reviews help independent authors like me reach new readers who love historical fiction and mysteries.

Your honest feedback—even just a few words about what you liked—whether it's three stars or five, makes a real difference in helping other readers discover books they might enjoy.

Author's Note

This is a work of fiction. But the fear that inspired it—and the silence that followed—were very real.

In 1918, German Americans across the United States were asked to abandon their language, their culture, their names—even their sense of belonging. It was as if America had forgotten that these families had once been welcomed, woven into every fiber of their communities. In my hometown, nearly 45 percent of the population was of German descent. They weren't outsiders.

Until suddenly, they were.

I am fifteen-sixteenths German. In all my conversations with relatives, no one ever spoke about this period in our history. Maybe it didn't seem important in the context of our family tree. Maybe they were too young—or had simply learned not to ask. But one thing was always clear: not a single member of my family ever denied that our people came from Germany.

This story is my way of honoring what they lived through—a story forgotten, buried, or quietly subverted. One I needed to tell.

While inspired by real events, this novel is a work of fiction. Names, places, and details have been changed or imagined in service of the story.

Acknowledgements

This book began with a single moment of curiosity and grew through the generosity of many people who believed in its importance.

To my cousin, whose family tree research led us both to the Schoborg name and opened the door to a story that had been waiting forty years to be told—thank you for that serendipitous connection that changed everything.

To my beta readers, who saw the potential in early drafts and helped me find the heart of this story. Your insights and encouragement kept me going when plot holes kept appearing and historical accuracy felt challenging.

To my editor Rhoda Douglas, who understood what I was trying to accomplish and helped me get there with precision and grace. And to my proofreaders, Dave and Mary, who caught the details that matter.

To the librarians and archivists who preserve these forgotten pieces of American history—particularly those at Kenton County Public Library, Covington, Kentucky. Without your dedication to maintaining these collections and helping researchers navigate them, stories like this would remain truly buried.

To Emma, a brilliant young artist whose work helped bring the cover to life.

To my husband, who listened to me talk about dictographs and German American persecution for years, never once suggesting I move on to a different obsession. Your patience and support made this book possible.

And finally, to the German American families who lived through this period of fear and forced silence—including my own ancestors who never spoke of what they endured. This story is my attempt to honor what you lived through and to ensure it isn't forgotten again.

The mistakes that remain are mine alone.

Further Reading

The following sources helped inform the historical backdrop of The Dictograph Case. They offer insight into the German American experience during World War I, as well as the cultural, legal, and emotional forces that shaped this story.

Gillham, Lisa, with Bethany Richter Pollitt. **J.H. Kruse, War & the Terrible Threateners: Anti-German Hysteria in World War I Covington.** A detailed and compelling account of how Covington, Kentucky—a city with deep German roots—became a site of cultural fear, forced assimilation, and legal overreach during the First World War.

Merriman, Scott A. "An Intensive School of Disloyalty: The C. B. Schoberg Case under the Espionage and Sedition Acts in Kentucky during World War I." A deep dive into a little-known Kentucky case that illustrates how wartime laws were used to criminalize dissent and punish perceived un-American behavior in everyday communities.

Horrocks, Kathryn. Where Was the First Amendment? Trials Under the Espionage and Sedition Acts During WWI. An essential exploration of how civil liberties were challenged—and often ignored—under the guise of national security, with case studies that echo many of the themes in this novel.

Reis, Jim. "'Americanism' Triumphed in Espionage Trials of 1918," Pieces of the Past column, The Kentucky Post (1917–1925). A journalist's retrospective look at how loyalty, fear, and patriotic rhetoric shaped courtroom outcomes and community memory during and after World War I.

Register, Woody. The Dictograph Era: Eavesdropping Technologies and the Quest for Social Knowledge in Progressive Era American Culture. A fascinating examination of early surveillance tools and how technologies like the dictograph fed broader cultural anxieties about privacy, authority, and morality.

Library of Congress. German-American Discrimination During World War I. A digital archive of government records, propaganda posters, and firsthand accounts documenting the shift from neighbor to suspect.

Kentucky Historical Society. When German Meant Enemy: Kentucky's German Americans During World War I. A state-focused examination of public policy, education bans, and cultural suppression across German communities in Kentucky.

Book Club Discussion Guide

Welcome to your book club discussion of *The Dictograph Case*

Set against the backdrop of 1937 America, this historical mystery unearths a dark chapter many have forgotten: the systematic persecution of German Americans during and after World War I. Through the intertwined investigations of journalist Michael Schumann and teacher Olivia Kendall, the novel explores how fear and nationalism can transform neighbors into enemies—and how the silences we inherit often hide both shame and injustice.

What makes this story particularly resonant is its exploration of themes that echo through time: the weaponization of patriotism, the courage required to confront uncomfortable truths, and the long shadow that institutional injustice casts over communities. The novel asks difficult questions about complicity, memory, and the price of speaking up when others choose to look away.

As you discuss *The Dictograph Case*, consider how the characters navigate the tension between safety and truth, how historical trauma shapes present choices, and what it means to seek justice when the law itself has been corrupted. The story offers no easy answers—but it provides a powerful framework for examining how ordinary people can become both perpetrators and victims of systemic persecution.

The questions that follow are designed to spark thoughtful conversation about the novel's characters, themes, and historical context—as well as their relevance to our contemporary world. Whether you're drawn to the mystery, the history, or the emotional journey of the protagonists, we hope these discussions will deepen your appreciation for this important and timely story.

Happy reading and discussing!

Opening Reflections

1. What scene stayed with you the most after you closed the book?
2. Who surprised you the most by the end of the book—and why?

Character Motivations

3. Michael begins the story wanting to prove himself as a journalist. How does his sense of purpose evolve? What role does his family history play in that transformation?

4. What drives Olivia to keep digging into her father's past, even when it puts her at risk? Do you think she's seeking justice—or something more personal?

5. Hawthorne believes he's protecting his community. How do people justify harmful actions by convincing themselves they're doing good?

Core Themes

6. How do characters like Olivia, Michael, Clara, Minnie, and Uncle John grapple with their own roles in maintaining or breaking silence?

7. "This wasn't a failure of justice. It was a design flaw. And that flaw was patriotism weaponized by law." What does this quote mean? Can you think of modern parallels?

8. The Dictograph device becomes a symbol in the story. What does it represent about surveillance, power, and ultimately justice?

Historical Resonance

9. What do you think motivated citizens in Ellington to support the CPLE? What parallels do you see in how fear and nationalism are used today?

10. The novel shows how ordinary people can become complicit in injustice. What factors make someone more likely to stand up versus stay silent?

11. The novel is set in 1937 but deals with events from 1918–1921. What does this suggest about how long injustice can echo through a community?

Ambiguity and Aftermath

12. Why do you think the author chose to keep the truth about Olivia's father ambiguous? Did that make the story more powerful or frustrating?

13. Do you think the story offers hope? If so, where do you find it?

Personal Reflection

14. If this story were set today, how might it be different? What would stay the same?

15. What did you learn about this period of American history that you didn't know before?

About the Author

Diane tells stories about ordinary people navigating extraordinary choices—strong women, complicated families, and the quiet heroism that history too often overlooks. Her work explores the grit and love of everyday sacrifice, the weight of generational legacy, and the emotional cost of injustice.

She's drawn to the small, domestic histories that rarely make headlines but shape lives in lasting ways. If you've ever wondered how personal stories intersect with larger historical forces—or longed to find yourself in the quiet strength of those who endured—these stories are for you.

Her debut novel, *Motty's Vow*, follows a young girl's courageous stand to hold her family together during the Civil War. Her latest work, *The Dictograph Case*, is a historical mystery about buried truths, dangerous propaganda, and the price of silence in a small American town.

Born in Covington, Kentucky—just across the Ohio River from Cincinnati, she finds her stories rooted in the places and circumstances that shaped her family. Diane lives in Cave Creek, Arizona surrounded by her family.

You can connect with Diane at:
Website: dianewahnshotton.com
Substack: dianewahnshotton.substack.com
Facebook dianewahnshotton
Instagram: @dianewahnshotton